HARD to LOSE

NEW YORK TIMES BESTSELLING AUTHOR

K. BROMBERG

PRAISE FOR K. BROMBERG

"K. Bromberg always delivers intelligently written, emotionally intense, sensual romance . . ."

—*USA Today*

"K. Bromberg makes you believe in the power of true love."

—#1 *New York Times* bestselling author Audrey Carlan

"A poignant and hauntingly beautiful story of survival, second chances, and the healing power of love. An absolute must-read."

—*New York Times* bestselling author Helena Hunting

"An irresistibly hot romance that stays with you long after you finish the book."

—#1 *New York Times* bestselling author Jennifer L. Armentrout

"Bromberg is a master at turning up the heat!"

—*New York Times* bestselling author Katy Evans

"Supercharged heat and full of heart. Bromberg aces it from the first page to the last."

—*New York Times* bestselling author Kylie Scott

ALSO BY K. BROMBERG

Driven
Fueled
Crashed
Raced
Aced
Slow Burn
Sweet Ache
Hard Beat
Down Shift
UnRaveled
Sweet Cheeks
Sweet Rivalry
The Player
The Catch
Cuffed
Combust
Cockpit
Control
Faking It
Resist
Reveal
Then You Happened
Flirting with 40
Hard to Handle
Hard to Hold
Hard to Score

Published by JKB Publishing, LLC

Editing by Marion Making Manuscripts
Formatting by Champagne Book Design
Printed in the United States of America

HARD *to* LOSE

Prologue

Ryan

"When we're done and out of here, man, I think we should all open a bar together," Shotgun says with a disbelieving laugh, pointing to the desert-brown plywood around us. Beyond that are concrete barriers with razor wire on top, more fencing, and security watch to keep out our enemies, who are probably sitting in the hills surrounding us, watching our every move.

Dickman holds out the bottle of whiskey to me. Or at least I *think* it's whiskey. We're not one hundred percent sure, but he got it from someone who knows someone who knows someone who knows our translator, and despite alcohol being illegal for us, we have it anyway.

Maybe that's why I'm hesitating taking it. The last thing I want is to get caught by our commanding officer and put on burning-the-shitter detail as punishment.

However, I reach over, take the bottle, and tilt it to my lips for one long, deep swallow. I wince as the burn fires down my throat but Jesus, it's welcome if only to help me forget for a few goddamn minutes where I am and what we're doing.

"A bar?" Richard asks.

"Yep. The four of us will buy a bar together and call it FUBAR as a silent ode to this once-in-a-lifetime experience we're enjoying right here." Shotgun's sarcasm rings loud and clear, and we all laugh.

"I can get on board with that," I say with a nod, the alcohol hitting faster than I expected. "Jesus, that's some strong shit."

Dickman laughs like a crazed loon, and we all shush him so we don't get in trouble. "It definitely has a higher alcohol content than the shit we have back home."

"Home," Shotgun murmurs. We all fall silent, because we know his girl just dumped him and he's taking it hard. Hell, we've only been here a month, so she didn't even let his sheets grow cold before doing it either.

He may have lost his girl, but I lost my dream.

Fuck. That definitely hurts.

"What is it you guys can't wait to get back to?" Richard asks as he hands the bottle back to me.

"Pussy," Dickman deadpans, and we all burst out laughing.

"No shit," Richard says, punching him in the arm. "I'm serious. Like we're here and shit, but what are you hoping for when you get back?"

"We should just kiss our old lives goodbye," Dickman says, "because nothing will ever be the same again."

"C'mon," I mutter. "That's not true."

"Like hell it isn't," Dickman says, and of course, we all pay more attention when he speaks because this is his second tour.

"No, I'm dead serious." He points to me. "Don't you get it? You're no longer PFC Ryan Camden. You're a faceless number among many. When the brass looks at you, they see a guy who mans the gun. Now to them, you're simply Gunner."

"Whatever." I wave a hand at him and dismiss his I-know-more-than-you bullshit.

"You think I'm joking?" He lifts his eyebrows. "Richard over there has been dubbed Nixon, because he's a tricky motherfucker who gets himself out of situations no one else can. Shotgun is . . . he's always sitting shotgun beside me, so yeah, that's what his name is."

"*And you?* Why are you Dickman?"

He snorts, his eyes glassy when they meet mine. "Because I'm a *dick*, man," he says in a total stoner voice. It draws a chuckle from us, but we all meet each other's eyes through the darkness. That nickname is like hitting a nail on the head. He's great, but thank fuck he's on our side.

"I'll drink to that," Shotgun says.

We fall silent as we hear a noise in the distance. It sounds like a gunshot, but we're so used to the sound in our short time here, none of us even flinch.

"Look, we all gave up something—a lot of things to be here—but the question is: what did you give up that you'll never get back?" Dickman continues on his depressing roll.

His words have me thinking, wondering, cringing at the decisions I made and how I ended up here.

"Isn't hope a good thing?" I finally ask. "Why give it up when it's something we can look forward to?"

"You're not getting it, *Gunner*," Dickman says and takes the bottle from my hand. "Everything has changed. No one *there* cares about you anymore like you thought they did. Or if they did, it's now different." Concern flickers through Shotgun's eyes. "The easiest thing to do, for your own sanity, is to pick the one thing you loved the most and say goodbye to it. Make it official and let it go. Hell, you might as well write your *last letter* to *whatever* or *whoever it* is, and say goodbye as if you'll die."

"I'm not buying it," I mutter, then get up and leave the pow-wow, a little less steady on my feet.

Regardless of how much I know his comment is, in fact, complete crap, it runs on repeat in my head.

Over and over.

I lie in my bunk, thinking of everything I gave up. *The doubts, the what-ifs,* the *maybe I should've fought a little harders*, eat away at me.

And then to think of what my mom found after I left for deployment. The voicemails from agents. The interest and belief in my talent.

All wasted now.

"Let it go, Ryan," I mutter to the darkened ceiling. Tears burn in the back of my throat and I squeeze my eyes shut to force them away.

Maybe Dickman is right. Maybe holding on to hope is only going to cause me more pain. It's not like the MLB will want me after my four years are up anyway.

Let it go, Ry.

Maybe holding on to a dream that's already dead and gone is pathetic.

Let it go, Camden.

I sit up in my bunk, turn on the light, and grab a pen and paper. *The easiest thing to do, for your own sanity, is to pick the one thing you loved the most and say goodbye to it.*

Let it go, Gunner.

Chapter ONE

Chase

I toy with the corners of the envelope in my hand, half-listening to the conversation going on around me, half making up a history to the name and contents inside of it.

Who was he?

What's his story?

Its edges are worn and tattered, the stamp all but falling off, and the ink so faded it's barely legible.

But it's the date on the postmark that catches my eye.

"And you're not paying attention to a word I'm saying, are you, Chase?"

I glance up to find four sets of eyes staring at me. All curious. All expectant.

"What?" I ask with a quick shake of my head.

"Langley?" Dekker, my older sister, asks—or rather my eldest sister since all three of them sitting around the conference room table are older than me.

"What about Langley?" I ask.

My dad, Kenyon Kincade's, chuckle fills the room. "Should I be worried about whatever new goal you're so focused on, that you can't concentrate on our meeting at hand?"

"Oh, Jesus," Brexton mutters and earns a roll of my eyes. "Can you stop being the overachiever for once? I mean, the rest of us are sick of looking like slackers around you."

"Oh, please," I mutter. "Maybe if you stopped being so gaga over Drew you, too, could accomplish more like I do."

"Little brat," Brexton says with a grin, which *should* convince me that love just might be all it's supposedly cracked up to be, and then tosses a paper clip at me. "I'm holding my own just fine."

"In between lunchtime sex dates," Dekker says, causing our father to bark out a cough in shock.

"Christ Almighty," he mutters before clearing his throat to try and gain control again.

"Lunchtime sex dates, says the pregnant one," Brexton replies, as Dekker rubs her hand over her abdomen where she's just starting to show.

I snort. It's all I can do, because what the hell do I know or care about this kind of shit—love and babies? I have way too much to accomplish to allow either of those two things to cross my mind. In the future? Perhaps. My mind isn't made up on that yet.

But for now? My plate is too full, my goals too varied, and my future too wide open in front of me to be distracted with the things my three sisters are now all experiencing.

Am I happy for them? Of course.

Is it for me? That remains to be seen.

"Ladies, can we get back on task?" our father asks drolly, fighting a smile. "Your sex lives are the last thing this old man wants to know anything about."

"This is one of those times I'm more than happy that I get to Zoom in," our sister Lennox says via the monitor and speaker on the wall in front of us. Her smile is sharp and her eyes are full of humor as she looks at the four of us from her home in England.

Dekker raises a middle finger to her in response, and we all laugh.

"Six-month progress reports. Can we finish the last one so we can get on with our work? I know we're all rather busy," he redirects and gets varied responses of yes from the four of us.

All eyes turn back to me.

"So I've checked off everything on my list. I have a fifteen percent increase in client growth. I've upped my pursuit of endorsement deals and am more than pleased with the return. A quarter of my clients are getting first-time deals, which is huge. I've added depth to my roster by adding one of just about every sport we represent and—"

"And I'm so perfect that I make my sisters sick," Lennox says in a singsong voice to mock me that has Dekker and Brexton bursting out in laughter.

I stick my tongue out to the camera so she can see it. "I know you all wish you could be as perfect as me." My grin is pure cheese and I do it for the sole purpose of annoying them.

"No thanks." Lennox makes a show of rolling her eyes and pushing away from her desk as if she's not having any of it.

"Please tell us there's something you didn't accomplish. *Please?* That way we can all feel a little better."

I fight my grin. When you're a little sister who is the last to get to do everything, you take a lot of pride in doing something they didn't—like smashing all of the goals the team set for you.

"I thought the point of goals was to hit them," I say in my primmest voice. "I'm not going to apologize that I didn't hit them because I got sidetracked by a man."

There's a rumble of disagreement despite the smiles on their faces.

"Maybe that's exactly what you need," Lennox says. "If there's one thing I've learned in the past year, it's that having a work-life balance is important."

"Okay, Oprah," I mutter.

"No, she's right," Dekker chimes.

"She is," Brexton adds.

"I think we need to add a goal to your list," Dekker says.

"Maybe she needs a cause to fight for," Lennox chimes in. "Something to put her Type-A personality behind because then she knows shit gets done."

There's something about Lennox's words that strike me. Maybe she's right. Maybe I need to find something—*a cause*. Is that what I'm missing? Knowing I'm making a difference somehow?

"Or instead of a cause, we could always get her a man," Dekker says.

"And that's where this conversation can end," I mutter.

"No, seriously. How long has it been since you last dated?" she persists.

All eyes wait for an answer as I give a panicked glance to my dad, who's no help to me when he holds his hands up in surrender. His accompanying chuckle is just as bad.

"It's been at least two years, hasn't it?" Lennox asks. "Finn was the last guy you were serious about and—"

"And let's not talk about him or have this discussion at all. Shall we move on?" I ask, my smile tight and insincere.

"No, we shall not," Dekker persists. "You don't date."

"I date."

"Dating a guy and going out compared to a booty call to heat up your sheets are two completely different things." When our father groans and shakes his head, Dekker waves her hand at him and continues. "Are you going to argue that?"

"I'm going to argue that what I do outside of work is none of my nosy sisters' business and leave it at that," I say.

"I'm not knocking booty calls," Lennox says. "God knows I've been down a time or two—before Rush, of course—but I used to think like you . . . and there's so much more, Chase."

If they didn't know that tugging on the collar of my shirt was my "tell" that I was uncomfortable, I'd be tugging on it right now. But I will not let them see me sweat. Cannot let them. I know that will just egg them on.

"Can the *let's scrutinize Chase's life* portion of the program be done now? Please?" I implore this time with a more convincing smile.

"We're adding a goal to your list," Dekker says with a decisive nod.

"You're not the boss," I say with a shrug that just earns laughter from everyone.

"We're adding a goal because we all know you well enough to know that you're competitive, and if we lay it out there like this, you're too Type A not to prove to us that you can do it."

"Wow. Really, Dekk? You think I'm that easy to manipulate?" I ask, while secretly cringing at *not* accomplishing a goal assigned to me.

"Yes," all three of them respond without hesitation.

"I'm feeling a little set up here." I laugh to ease my own nerves. "I don't adhere to peer pressure, let alone the Chase-needs-to-have-a-boyfriend plan."

"That's not the plan," Brexton says.

"Then what is?" I ask, fully aware that if the three of them are answering questions for each other, then this has been a topic of discussion behind my back.

"The goal is to get you to go on dates. At least two dates with two different men within the next two months," Dekker says, giving me the mother look. You know, the stare that says she's *not* budging.

"That's total bullshit." I shove my pad of paper away from me. "What will that prove? That I'm not a spinster?"

"You don't have to get angry," Brexton grumbles.

"I'm not angry. I'm pissed," I state, knowing they're one and the same. "I love that we're all a close part of each other's lives, but you don't get to tell me what to do in my love life. I'm not built like you . . . and while I respect you and your personal decisions, I'd like to think you'd do the same for me and mine."

We all stare at each other until our father sighs. "On that note . . ."

"We weren't ganging up on her, Dad. We just want to make sure she's happy."

"Happiness is subjective." I glare.

"This meeting went way off the rails," he says with an uncomfortable chuckle. "The last thing this father needs to hear about is the sex lives and booty calls of his daughters . . . so let's call this meeting over and get back to work."

"You've heard worse," Brexton says with a laugh.

"Why are we talking about me and not Finn Sanderson?" I ask, pulling attention back to work, off me, and on to our rival agent—*and my ex-boyfriend.*

"You actually want to talk about him? That's a first." Lennox snorts.

"Not him per se, but did any of you see the coverage of him fulfilling the Make A Wish kid's dream to be signed with an agent and an NBA team?" I ask.

"How could we not?" Lennox says. "It's been on every damn news station, sports channel, and newspaper. It's maddening."

"Whoa. Have a heart," Dekker says, which prompts a sigh from Brexton.

"That came out wrong." Lennox gives a quick shake of her head. "The story is awesome and heartbreaking all at the same time. It's just more maddening that Finn is getting all this feel-good PR when we all know the only reason the man took on fulfilling the kid's wish was for the press it would bring him."

"Typical Finn," I say, not really wanting to think about my ex in any capacity.

Brexton's cell phone rings and she jumps up. "I've got to take this," she says. She presses a kiss to the top of our dad's head as she walks past him on the way out.

"Twenty bucks that's Drew calling for a lunchtime quickie," Lennox says of Brexton's fiancé.

"I could have lived without knowing that," our dad mumbles.

"On that note," Lennox says, "I might just go do the same." Her laughter is all we hear as she waves to the camera and signs off.

"I'll be leaving too," Dekker says and raps the corners of her papers on the desk, "but not for a quickie." She rises from her seat and points her cell phone at me. "I'm serious about that goal, Chase. I want to see proof of dates with two different men," she says in her best imitation of our father.

My only response is a lift of my middle finger as she heads out of the conference room door.

"Well, that was fun. *Not,*" I joke, then chuckle, as I lean back in my chair and close my eyes. "How did we get so sidetracked when I had ideas and things to talk about and . . . *Christ.*"

"Ideas?" He looks like a gopher sticking his head up out of a hole, begging for a change in topic. "What ideas?"

I laugh and ask, "How is business going?"

"Meaning?" He sets his pen down to show I have his full attention.

"Meaning we started this operation *Screw Finn Sanderson,*" I say referring to the undercutting and stealing of clients from my ex, "to save Kincade Sports Management. Have we been successful? Have we made a dent in recovering more clients? How is our bottom line and future looking?"

He nods slowly. "This is a fickle business, Chase. What one client hates in the form of management, another might prefer. Every contract is a gamble. Every new client a chance to hang on a star."

"You're talking in your fatherly metaphors." I laugh. "Can you just say what you mean?"

"KSM is doing better." He lifts his eyebrows to make sure I hear him. "We've taken on more clients, more contracts . . . but I don't know, kiddo, I feel like I'm stuck in the dark ages, and maybe I'm dragging down the agency with it."

"That's the most ridiculous thing I've ever heard."

How can he think that when he built this incredible business? This place, which has anchored our family since our mom died, is past its prime.

"Finn's the king of public stunts. He gets people talking. Maybe I'm old because I think they're all stupid, but they do seem to reel in athletes fresh from college. They like flashy and he's definitely flashy."

"Umm, I'm younger than Finn, Dad. Are you telling me I'm not doing my job?"

"No. Not at all . . . but I've been thinking a lot about the Make A Wish thing he did too. It was great publicity for him. It put him in a great light, and he was all over social media getting praise from athletes. It's like they all know his name now, so guess who they're going to call when they need a new agent?"

"Our name is still known, Dad. KSM is still a desirable agency."

"I know, but it doesn't *feel* like it anymore to me. I don't know. Maybe instead of the ridiculous goal your sisters gave you to date someone, what about guiding KSM toward using more current trends and strategies? Consider new branding with a business strategist. Have someone analyze our use of social media and tell us how we can target more efficiently. Maybe look into if we could benefit from using a PR firm. On paper, our portfolio is strong, but I don't feel we have a presence. I want you to figure out how to make our presence stronger." His sigh is heavy, and I hate that he suddenly feels irrelevant. Yet at the same time, my heart is full that he'd look to me to take something like this on.

I love knowing he can depend on me.

"I'm flattered you'd ask me, and I'd love to take that on. You know I'm always up for a challenge. What if I—" And just as the words pass over my lips, the thought hits me. "Oh," I murmur, as I try to wrap my head around my unexpected idea.

"I know what that sound means." He chuckles and lifts his eyebrows. "You have my attention."

"What if we generate some positive press ourselves? What if we're part of—or perhaps *manufacture*—a feel-good story that would give us some attention not only with potential clients, but with the sports world and public in general? As Finn's demonstrated, a little love goes a long way these days."

"Go on." He nods, his lips twisted in thought as he does when he's pondering the validity of something.

I motion to the letter. "What if I found *him*?"

"Who?"

"This Ryan Camden guy."

"I'm listening," he says and steeples his hands in front of him.

"This letter has been lost in the mail vortex for five years, Dad. Aren't you the least bit curious about what happened to him? I mean, it could be a great PR story for us. The ace baseball pitcher who had all the talent in the world including a one-hundred-mile-per-hour fastball, but who decided to serve his country instead. A letter he sent you, thanking you, on his way to war, which has been MIA until now. What has happened to him since then? What if he still has a killer arm? He'd be in his late twenties, but I think with our connections we could get him an audience with a major league team."

"We both know a team would never pick him up and sign him after all this time—"

"But think of the spin we could put on it. Helping a selfless veteran realize his dream he thought was dead and gone. It's something heartwarming—a dream come true even after all these years type of thing. We could even set up a veterans' All-Star game—a *thank you for your service* PR opportunity with press and the whole nine yards. The sports world needs some good in it. Something beyond its overinflated egos and ridiculous salaries, and this could be it."

"Salaries, I might add, that you profit handsomely from."

"I never said I didn't, but . . . don't you just need to feel like you're doing something good? Don't you ever get burned out from it all and crave the humanity in this business?"

"Yes, but let's be clear. A manufactured PR stunt is not humanity."

His words feel like a scold when they're merely being honest. "I know." The words come out as a sigh and sound like defeat.

His nod is slow and deliberate, his eyes serious as they hold mine. "What's going on with you, honey?"

I purse my lips and shrug. "I don't know. I need a new challenge? I guess you just gave me one, but maybe it's more than that. Maybe I'm curious about this man who's close to me in age and who felt so strongly about his duty, that he gave up his dream to fulfill it. That kind of selflessness is rare. Maybe . . ." *Maybe I feel a connection to a man I've never met—someone who, like me, didn't conform to predictable expectations—and have to figure out why.* "There has to be a reason this letter was delivered now."

"I never thought you were one who adhered to the notion or romanticism of fate."

"I don't. I do." I throw my hands up. "I don't know what I think anymore."

"Look. I get it. It's okay to feel a little lost sometimes. Dekker's about to start a family with Hunter. Lennox just got married to Rush. Brexton is deliriously happy with Drew. You're feeling lost."

"No. That's not it." I raise my voice to him. "I'm feeling frustrated. Trapped. Like that is what's expected of me next when I don't want it to be me. That's the last thing on my radar, and today's stunt by my sisters just proves my point."

He chews over my comment as his eyes hold mine. "No one wants you to feel trapped, Chase. I certainly don't. All I want for you is to find your own path, find what makes you happy, and run with it."

I hear his words, know he means them, but have a hard time accepting them.

"Thank you." My voice is soft as I look back down at the letter and the unknown story behind it. "Do you remember anything about him?"

"Vaguely. He was a wild child with one hell of an arm."

"Was he nice?"

He gives me a half-smile. "You're testing my memory here. Can I say he was cocky? Will you accept that as an answer?" He laughs. We both know most twenty-year-olds good enough to be recruited by any professional sports team are cocky. It's part of their MO.

"You're no help," I joke. "What else do you remember about him, if anything?"

"Believe it or not, when we received the letter in the mail, I pulled up my old recruiting logs. I only had a few notes on him. It was his junior college coach who reached out to us, trying to drum up interest for a player who wouldn't naturally be on our radar."

"The kid had a one-hundred-mile-per-hour arm. How was he not on everyone's radar?"

My father gets a far-off look in his eyes and then gives a quick shake of his head. "I guess that's the question, isn't it?"

I nod, understanding what he means as I pull the letter from the envelope and unfold the worn, lined paper.

Dear KSM,

I just recently learned of your interest in me as an athlete and wanted to thank you. However, my dream to play in the major league is over. I've been advised to let old dreams go. To accept that life has changed forever.

-Ryan Camden

"This letter makes no sense. Why would his dream to play be over if he had genuine interest from clubs and agents?" I ask, hating that every time I read the letter, I'm overcome with a sadness I can't shake.

Giving up a dream is like saying you've run out of hope.

"I don't know, honey. The only other comment I had in my notes was about Ryan's father. I wrote 'gatekeeper' beside his name. In fact, I don't have any records of ever talking to Ryan himself. Something was weird with the whole setup from my vague memory. The dad said Ryan wasn't good enough, said he was a troublemaker. Just shit you don't say about your kid who's trying to win over an agent."

"Ugh." I reread the letter again. *I just recently learned of your interest in me*... "You think his dad never told him, don't you?" I ask, knowing my father's expressions well enough to read his thoughts.

"At the time I couldn't put my finger on it, but now? Now that I've read that letter . . . I don't think he did."

"Who would do that to a kid? Steal their dream?" I ask, my heart hurting for Ryan.

"People do a lot of shitty things that make no sense," he muses.

"See? That's why I need to track him down and tell him the truth. Tell him that you were interested."

"In the name of good PR?" He lifts his brows, and I hate that I feel like I'm flatfooted in answering.

Because yes, it's in the name of good press for KSM . . . but it's also because I'm inexplicably drawn to this letter, and I feel more than ridiculous admitting that. "Anything for the company, Dad," I finally say and know he can see right through me.

"There are a million things that could go wrong with this scenario, Chase," my dad warns, ever the cautious one.

"Like?"

"Like he was injured or God forbid, he died in combat." He grimaces at the thought. "Like he's angry at you for hunting him down over a dream that came and went that he's no longer interested in. Like he resents you for using him for your own benefit."

"He wouldn't know I was using him for our benefit."

"Of course, he wouldn't, but you know what they say about best-laid plans . . ."

"Dad." The word is a frustrated sigh.

"I'm just trying to cover all the angles."

"Clearly." I snort and try a different one. "If you walked away from something you truly loved, wouldn't at some point you want to know that others thought you were good too? Sure, it might be too late to fulfill the dream, but wouldn't you still want to know?"

He nods, his lips pursed. "I suppose. It would sting at first, but then there would be pride."

"Exactly," I say with a resolute nod. "By finding him, I'll be helping *him* and *us*." I clap my hands together. "Problem solved."

We stare at each other for a beat. "So you're going to go traipsing off to find this Camden guy in the name of publicity for KSM? Is that what you're telling me?" His smile is soft, knowing, before I say a word about my intentions.

He knows me too well.

"I need a break, some space from all the love and baby talk going on around here." It doesn't help that we're nearing the anniversary of my mother's death. I always get antsy this time of year, but for some reason, the letter has just added to it.

"Okay." He draws the word out.

"I know you probably don't agree with me, and I can take my vacation time if need be, but I want to pursue this. I want to find Ryan Camden and see for myself what became of him. See how maybe I can use the opportunity for KSM." And I pray that I don't find a headstone in a cemetery instead of a living, breathing man.

He simply stares at me when he could say so many things—all of which would be some form of *you're crazy* and *this is so not like you*, but he doesn't. He must see that I need this somehow.

Some freedom from the everyday role I fulfill in this office. The i-dotter, t-crosser, and stickler on rules.

"I'll continue to do my work, of course, as well as finding the right people to help give KSM a stronger visual presence. I won't drop any balls, nor will I—"

"You don't have to ask for permission, Chase. I know your work ethic. I trust you and hope that you'll get what you need out of this."

"Who said I needed anything?" I ask, but know that I do.

The big question though is: what exactly is it that I need?

Chapter TWO

Chase

THE DOWDY WOMAN ON THE OTHER SIDE OF THE RECEPTION DESK peers at me above the bifocals perched atop her nose. Her blue eyes are sharp and critical as they take me in. "Ryan Camden?" she asks.

"Yes. I was hoping to talk to someone who might know where to find him," I say with a warm smile, attempting to butter her up.

"And you are?"

"He sent a letter some time ago while he was in the military. Strangely, it just got to me, and I wanted to speak to him about it. I'm a sports agent interested in seeing if he still plays baseball. Still pitches."

She studies me for a moment. "He doesn't go here." Her voice is flat, the corners of her lips so stiff it would require a crane to lift them up as she clicks away on her keyboard.

"I'm aware he doesn't go here—"

"Hasn't been here for a good six or seven years if I recall." Another tight smile. "And the records here on my screen say the same."

"Like I said, I'm aware he no longer goes here. I've asked around and no one in town has a beat on him so I thought maybe if I could talk to Coach Bassett, he might know where I could find him."

There's another prolonged stare from the apparent keeper of Downship Junior College followed by a huff. "Please, wait here." It's all she says before she strides away, her nylons swishing and her shoes squeaking on the linoleum floor.

Only a few moments pass before she can be heard swishing and squeaking her way back down the hallway toward me.

"Exit out of this door," she says, motioning with her hand, "and then take a right down to the locker rooms. Coach Bassett will be waiting for you outside. He'll be the one wearing all the muscles and the baseball hat."

"Okay." Odd way to put it, but she's kooky in her own right so I let it go and follow her directions toward the locker room. The school is on the outskirts of Charleston. It's small but it sprawls across lush green grass, and a grove of trees supplies its picturesque backdrop. The school's colors of blue and gold adorn the walls in murals and posters . . . and even the coach as he stands waiting for me with his arms crossed over his chest.

"Coach Bassett?" I ask and receive a curt nod in response.

"Yes, how can I help you?"

"Chase Kincade with Kincade Sports Management." I reach my hand out to him and he shakes it.

"I currently don't have any players even close to the caliber needed to play in the major leagues so I'm quite curious what this is all about."

"Ryan Camden." I smile and shift on my feet as his expression grows guarded.

"What about him?"

"I was wondering if you happened to know his whereabouts or how I can get in contact with him?"

He eyes me beneath the bill of his cap, his arms still crossed over his chest. "Why?"

Why? A part of me sags in relief at the simple word, because doesn't that mean Ryan is still alive?

I didn't realize until right now how much I feared I'd find out otherwise. And I'm not certain why it's so damn important to me that he is alive.

I draw in a shaky breath and clear the thoughts from my head. "It's going to sound weird, but long story short, we tried to recruit him off an email you sent us almost six years ago. He never responded to us and then two weeks ago, we received a letter in the mail from him. A letter he mailed more than five years ago from a Forward Operating Base in the Helmand province of Afghanistan. Apparently, it's been lost in the mail all this time and . . ."

"You expect me to believe that you're coming to recruit a player from five, six years ago when he's older now and there are new crops of athletes in your face every day?" He lifts his eyebrows. "C'mon now."

"I never said I was going to recruit him. All I said was I was looking for him—"

"For what?" He raises his voice, and I shake my head to deny the accusation in his voice.

"To tell him we got it. To see where he is and what he's doing and maybe highlight his plight somehow—"

"Come to think of it, I didn't see you present anything proving you are who you say you are."

"Oh. Yes." I'm flustered—when I'm never flustered—as I reach into my purse and produce a business card. He takes it and stares at it for a beat. "You can call the number to verify I am who I say I am."

He turns the card over and over in his hand. It appears he's grappling with something unbeknownst to me. "Why do you want to find Ryan?"

"I don't have a direct answer for you on that," I fib. "But something is telling me I need to follow up with him."

When Coach Bassett looks up to meet my eyes, his lips are pursed and his stare's relentless. "So let me guess, you're looking to recruit a 'war hero' and gain media attention for yourself in the meantime? The spotlight's that irresistible? You agents are all the same. Every time I think it'd be different, one of you go and prove me wrong."

"Excuse me?"

He emits a short laugh. "I know I'm not a big-shot agent or anything, but I'm astute enough to know you're not telling me the whole story. Five, six years ago everyone wanted something from him but damn, it's amazing how quick they forgot about him once they got what they wanted."

My head spins with the information he's providing but isn't clarifying. He's adding pieces to a puzzle I don't even know the picture of to solve.

"I'm sorry, but again, I don't know what you're talking about."

"And yet, you're still looking for him?" Sarcasm laces his tone and I shake my head ever so slightly as I try to understand.

"I'm not sure how I've offended you, Coach, but I'm simply looking for Mr. Camden. His letter came five years too late. For some reason, it arrived on my desk, and I can't let go of the feeling that I need to find him, even if he's in his mid- to late twenties now. My father was interested, and I guess, I want Mr. Camden to know that. That he was . . . noticed."

"So you're going through all this trouble to throw it in his face and let him know he had his chance and oops, now he doesn't? Sounds kind of cruel to me."

He has a point, and I hate that I'm suddenly doubting why I'm here.

"What's it to you?" I ask, getting frustrated. "Are you his keeper? Isn't it up to him if he talks to me or doesn't?"

Coach Bassett nods slowly. "It is."

"And who's to say that he still doesn't have a chance? Stranger things have happened—unless, of course, you know something different about him."

"Can't say that I do," he says.

"If you respect him as much as it sounds like you do, then isn't it up to him who he talks to? Besides, why are you so protective of him if he no longer even lives in this town?" My question is a fishing expedition, and I'm hoping Coach Bassett won't shut me down.

"Because the kid was given the shit end of a stick most of his life. The most he had going for him was baseball. He may have been rebellious, had a bit of an attitude, but when it came to pitching, that was the one thing he could focus on. The kid was gifted—so much so that I've yet to see another one like him in the past six years."

"That's why you reached out to recruiters," I say, more than surprised that he's giving me so much information when he was so guarded moments before.

But I'll take it. I'll take anything I can get to help me find Ryan.

He nods. "I wanted to help the kid but was in no position to interfere in his family dynamic. Regardless, I was surprised there weren't teams lined up looking at him. Then again, this is a small town and rumors go far—especially when you're a scout who prefers to steer clear from what you perceive to be trouble."

"And yet you still tried."

"Ryan had good in him. He just needed to know someone saw it." Coach looks out to the empty baseball field for a moment before looking back at me. "He left here and never came back."

"Do you know where he is?"

"I haven't talked to him in a few years at best. Rumor is he's in Destiny Falls."

"Where's that?" I ask.

"Some Podunk town outside of Virginia Beach."

"Is he still enlisted?" I ask.

"Not that I know of."

"Thank you, Coach. I assure you I have the best intentions when it comes to Mr. Camden."

He chuckles. "When you meet him, then you best not tell him you're an agent upfront or he sure as hell won't talk to you."

"What's that supposed to mean?"

"Destiny Falls," he repeats, effectively ending the conversation. And I don't push. I know it was hard enough for him to give me this much, and I'm more than grateful that he did. "Thanks. I'll check there. Thank you for your time."

I'm about ten steps away when he says, "Miss Kincade?"

"Hmm?" I turn back to face him.

"I'm trusting that you'll do right by him." Our eyes meet. Hold.

And with a nod, I walk away with more curiosity than when I showed up here. Strangely, I'm also glad that Ryan Camden did have someone in his corner. *That he wasn't completely alone.*

Chapter THREE

Chase

"Destiny Falls?" Brexton asks through the speaker of my car. "It sounds like a cutesy town name from one of those cheesy, Netflix, made-for-romance series."

I look around at my surroundings. Clapboard houses with well-manicured lawns. Mature trees with yellow ribbons tied around their trunks. Rocking chairs on stoops with an American flag waving from the rooftop.

"Pretty much." I laugh as I drive through the town. "The question is now that I'm here, what am I supposed to do? Where do I go?"

I twist my lips in thought as I make a split-second decision to ignore my GPS directions and turn left onto a street that looks like it leads toward the heart of the small town.

"You didn't think to ask yourself this before you drove all that way to get there?"

I roll my eyes. "Not everyone plans every little thing out."

"You do."

Touché.

"That's beside the point."

"How big is this town?" my sister asks.

"Bigger than a dot on a map but not huge by any means." I pass a man taking trash out to the garbage can on the curb and marvel at how different this life is from my Manhattan skyrise. Neighbors waving to neighbors down the street versus my life where we all tuck our heads down, keep to our own business, and don't make eye contact, because

God forbid that means we might have to talk to one another. "From what I gather, it's a military town through and through."

"So is this guy still enlisted?"

"Not according to the coach."

"What did his social media tell you?" She asks the question like I'm a dumbass.

"I can't find him on it."

"Everyone's on social media." She laughs.

"I know but I've looked and he's not on there."

"Maybe he's on there but uses a different name. An old safety precaution from his military days."

"Perhaps." I shrug and slow down when I come upon a group of kids riding their bikes. "All I've found upon searching are a few grainy images of him pitching from his junior college and high school newspapers. The photo from his military award showed a stern, clean-cut soldier, mostly hidden by the bill shadowing his face. He could be any guy from anywhere."

"You sure he's still alive? I mean—"

"No obituaries. Not that I could find."

"And your purpose again in doing this is what exactly? I mean, I see you trying to one-up Finn in the public display arena, but it sounds like you're on a wild goose chase."

"Where exactly should I go?" I ask, nipping in the bud this same damn line of questioning that I got from both Dekker and Lennox. I guess they're doing tag team little-sister therapy, and I'm not here for it.

"Jeesh. Testy. Testy. You're obviously still pissed at us for the meeting last week."

"Not at all." I feign indifference.

"Oh." She sounds surprised. "In that case—"

"That conversation is over. No need to rehash it." My hands clench the steering wheel. "Where do you think I should look?"

"A bar."

"What do you mean *a bar?*" I ask, breathing a sigh of relief when I see a decent-looking hotel. So far it has been slim pickings and not that I'm high-maintenance or anything, but—

"You're silently freaking out about finding a place to stay, aren't you?"

"No," I answer too quickly.

"Because you're distracted and I can all but feel your panic attack through the phone," she teases.

"I am not having a panic attack. In fact, I just pulled into the parking lot of what looks to be a respectable one."

"You are such a freak." *That* has my spine straightening.

"I am not. Once you find a bed bug crawling on the pillow next to you in a hotel room, you'll never look at them the same."

"Jesus. Chill. I'm just teasing you."

I exhale an audible breath and put the car in park. "Can we stay on track, please? Why do you say *a bar?*"

"It's a small town. The bar is where the locals hang out. Where they'll gossip. My bet is you mention his name and you'll find someone who knows him or knows of him and so on."

"I guess you're right."

"I know I'm right," she says, and I can see her gloating smile through the phone. "But here's the thing, you can't go in there asking everyone about this guy."

"Um, why not?"

"Because you're in a small, military town. They like to protect their own. If you go in there with guns blazing—pun intended—I guarantee they'll clam up and not give you any information whatsoever. Besides—"

"So what am I supposed to do?"

"Make friends." I don't respond, because the thought is annoying. Why do I need to make friends here? It's not like I'll ever be back in this town again. "Look, I know you're used to blowing into town, making your pitch, winning a client over, and flying back out, but this is going to take finesse. This is going to take earning their trust. The coach said this Ryan guy's not a fan of agents, so this slow approach might help win you what you want—whatever that may be."

"That's annoying."

"What, the small-town vibe or the fact that New York Chase has to adjust how she does things?"

"Both." I laugh. "Thanks for the advice. I don't know if I'll heed it—"

"You will if you want to find this guy and then you'll be thanking me," she says in a singsong voice.

"I've got to go." I reach for my purse on the seat next to me.

"Don't think we didn't notice you chose to go rogue in this month of all months."

Her words stop me mid-motion. *And the therapy session has commenced.* I pretend I don't know what she's talking about. "What do you mean?"

"You're twenty-six, Chase. You running off to find Lost Letter Boy isn't going to make the anniversary of her passing any easier." Brexton's words are soft, compassionate, and I hate hearing the empathy edging them.

Of course, she's talking about the death of our mom, but in true Chase Kincade fashion, I deflect from the topic and pretend everything is perfectly okay.

"Seriously? Did it ever cross your mind that I needed a break from you guys and your prying eyes? That maybe I needed to get laid without my three sisters sticking their noses in my business?"

"No, but it crossed my mind that you make sure you're nowhere to be found around this time every year. You have a habit of making sure you're on a recruiting trip or a vacation or somewhere other than here so we don't know if you're okay."

"Your point is?"

"My point is that it's okay to need someone. *To need us.*"

"Noted," I say in a clipped tone, wanting to click the padlock on Pandora's box before she tries to pry it open.

"You're our little sister. It's okay to be worried about you."

"I'm a big girl," I add. A big girl who shoves her feelings away so she doesn't have to live in the painful reminder that her mother missed out on so much of her life.

"Just promise me you won't be alone on the anniversary."

"Yep. Will do." I huff out a sigh.

"Chase . . ."

"That's my name," I taunt, like the little sister I am and have no shame in doing so. "Besides, maybe I needed a change of venue for a bit. After all, you guys did challenge me with dating someone new."

"So you fled one of the most populated cities in the country?" She sighs. "Classic Chase deflection."

Nothing will ever bring Mom back.

Nothing will ever fill the hole her death created.

Nothing.

"Now if you don't mind, I'm going to check in to this hotel, pray there are no bed bugs, and then find a nice, friendly bar to butter up the bartender for info."

"I didn't mean to upset you," she murmurs.

"You didn't." My smile is tight even though she can't see it. "You know me, I have my sights set on something—"

"And therefore, nothing else matters."

"Exactly."

But when I hang up, I sit back in the driver's seat and close my eyes.

Is this why I'm so hung up on finding Ryan Camden, who by all accounts could be a complete jerk and undeserving of my time?

Am I desperate to fix his misfortune because I know I can't fix mine?

Chapter FOUR

Gunner

She owns my attention the minute she walks into the bar. A new face in this bar gets noticed pretty damn quick to say the least. The town is small. The bar patrons are regulars.

She's not one of them.

I wipe my hands on the towel hanging from my waist, lean my hips back against the counter behind me, and study her across the distance.

Her dark hair falls a little past her shoulders in long waves as she swings her head from side to side to survey the lay of the land. Her lips purse, and I can assume she's contemplating where to sit. She has an athletic body with curves in all the right places, and yes, I'm noticing. Especially how her red V-neck sweater is snug, her deep-blue jeans hug said curves, and the heels on her feet are more than sexy.

Most women don't walk into a bar without a gaggle of other women around them. If they do, then they're meeting someone, and I know almost everyone in here right now. Either that, or they're looking for *one* thing.

Maybe I just might want to be of service for her and that *one* thing.

A pair of fingers snap in front of my face and pull me back to the task at hand, running FU-Bar. "Earth to Gunner," Nixon says and holds up his empty glass. "Care to refill this so I can keep my buzz or do I need to go hit on her just to get your attention?"

I glare at him as I snag the glass from his hand and pull down the tap. "A man can look."

"Mentally you were already in bed with her."

"Fuck off."

I might forget to slant the glass so his beer has a huge foam head as payback. But he's right. I was thinking that. I still am. And it would be a great goddamn place to be.

Besides, when was the last time someone caught my eye as much as she has?

"Here." I slide the foamy beer back toward his usual seat to the right of me at the bar, my grin a solid *fuck you* back at him when he notices my pour.

"Bastard."

"I think you meant to say *thank you*," I joke.

"It's okay to have impure thoughts," he says in his holier-than-thou voice.

"Impure is an understate—" The words die on my lips when I turn back to look for Snug Sweater and find her taking a seat right in front of me. She looks up, and I'm met with a pair of the biggest, bluest eyes framed by thick lashes that I've ever seen.

She's even prettier up close.

What's worse? When she smiles, her entire face lights up, and the emotion in her eyes dances unlike anything I've ever seen before.

She's stunning. Her eyes are too big for her face and her lips are fuller than average to offset a button nose . . . but Jesus, it works somehow in the best of ways.

"Hi." She offers me a confident smile that both unnerves, and sends a thrill shooting down my spine.

"*Heels?*"

"Excuse me?"

"It's a Wednesday night. Most women don't wear heels in these parts unless it's Friday or Saturday, so either you're looking for a man for the night or you're here for business," I say, flirting and offering a warm smile.

"And what business is it of yours if I am, in fact, looking for a man?" She lifts her brows.

"Maybe I'm applying for the job."

Her smile cracks, and Jesus fucking Christ, I'm stunned. Something about her smile brings so much warmth to her eyes and an approachability that . . .

"Maybe I'm turning you down." Her eyes flutter up to meet mine, and they don't match a thing her words are saying.

I thump a fist to my chest. "I'm wounded."

"You should be. I'm a good catch."

I bark out a laugh and shake my head, my eyes never leaving the dark blue of hers. I'm rarely taken with a woman. Looks are a plus—and she's definitely got them—but I reserve my attraction until I know if a woman can make me laugh. A bad sense of humor is a deal-breaker for me.

And a good comeback like that only adds to her allure.

Nixon snickers to my right but I ignore him. I'm sure he's taking too much pleasure in seeing me get schooled at the moment.

"I guess I'll have to take your word for it," I murmur. She licks her lips and if she didn't already have my attention, she sure has it now. "And yet, here you are."

"And yet, here I am," she says and rests her hands on the bar top. No ring on her finger. I can definitely appreciate that.

I nod, her statement telling me she's most definitely not from around these parts. "Yes, ma'am."

"You call me ma'am, and I'm going to turn around and look to see if my grandma's here."

"Well, if you're staying in these parts long, you'll need to get used to being called ma'am every now and again," I say. "Now, how may I help you?"

"Thirsty and waiting for my friendly bartender to ask me what it is I'll have."

I angle my head to the side and smirk. Her words are quick, but her eyes are slow as they run over my biceps while I wipe down the counter in front of her before looking back at me. "Well, Miss . . ."

"Chase. Chase Kincade," she says as she extends a hand across the bar top, while I repeat her name in my head.

"People in these parts call me Gunner or Gunny or anything of the sort." I take her hand in mine and shake it. Of course, I hold on to it a little longer than normal—but it's not like she pulls her hand away either. "Let me guess. You're a rum and Coke girl." Her eyes narrow. "A martini then? Extra dry?"

"Too pretentious."

"Gin and tonic. Bombay Sapphire."

She purses her lips and nods. "I'll take option number three with a twist, please."

I nod and get to work making her drink for her, but my eyes keep flickering over to her as she casually looks around and offers a smile to Nix, who's no doubt staring at her.

Then I snap my fingers when it hits me who she is.

"Kincade?" She nods, but I swear to God there's a small startle in her eyes too. "Are you Duncan Kincade's little sister? I heard he was having a big blowout to celebrate his retirement. Word around base is that—"

"You're making me wish the answer was yes, but no, I'm not related."

"So if you're not Duncan's sister, are you just passing through or staying a while or . . ."

"Considering you already had me pegged as a Camo Chaser here looking for a soldier for the night, why don't you tell me what you think I'm here for?" She laughs.

I slide her drink in front of her, cross my arms over my chest as she takes her first sip, and narrow my eyes. "The possibilities are endless."

"That's not an answer," she says coyly.

"Let me see. You're in Destiny Falls for a temporary stay because you're determined to find the man that you were madly in love with. He fell in love with the lion tamer, when you're more of a tiger kind of girl, and now you want revenge."

She laughs at my lame attempt at humor and shakes her head. "That would imply that I care about a man who cheated on me. Hate to break it to you, but I wouldn't. Chasing after a man isn't my style."

"No?" I ask, loving how straightforward she is.

"No. My time is too valuable to chase after a man who's not smart enough to see me for what I'm worth in the first place."

I emit a long, low whistle and follow it with a smile. "Your confidence is quite becoming."

And it is. A woman who knows what she wants is fucking hot.

Her cheeks flush, and I like that a compliment does that to her. That means she's not so used to them she's immune to them.

"My confidence is off-putting to a lot of men."

"Not this man," I say and walk over to take care of some other customers. The whole time I'm making their drinks, I'm thinking about the woman at the other end of the bar. Of her incredible smile, warm eyes, and sexy confidence.

And I know without a doubt I'll be asking her out before the night is over.

I hand over the drink order to Aubrey, my waitress, and then walk back toward where Chase is sitting, laughing at something Nixon's said.

"You're back," she says. "Nix was just telling me here—"

"Let's hope Nix wasn't telling you anything about me because he has a hell of a lot of dirt he can dish."

"Nothing bad at all. He's a good wingman." She winks at Nix and now, of course, I want to know what they were saying.

"I figured out why you're here and who you are," I say to get her attention back to where I want it—*on me*.

"I told you my name so you know who I am," she says and laughs. "But please, I'm curious."

"Chase Kincade is an alias. You're really a huge pop star who needs a break from the crazy crowds and stalkerish press, so you've decided to come to Destiny Falls during festival season for a little reprieve."

"Festival season?" she asks.

"There's at least one every weekend this time of year. There's the Strawberry Festival, the Wine Festival, the Destiny Falls Town Fair. Then there's the Beer Festival, Summer Fest . . . I could go on and on."

"Good to know I stopped in a town where I can get lost in the crowd."

"You have good instincts."

"Apparently," she murmurs moments before her lips wrap around the tiny straw in her drink and steal my attention again.

"So, Gunner, if I'm a ridiculously famous pop star, what's my hit song?"

And that's a flirt, ladies and gentlemen. A definite flirt. Teeth biting on her straw. Eyes looking up at me beneath fluttered lashes. A soft smile and a continuation of a conversation that she could have let die.

That was definitely a flirt.

I assume my position opposite her, a playful smile on my lips and my hands braced on the counter between us. "You have many popular songs. Gunning for You. Heartbreak Warfare. Battle for Love. But the big one—the one that put you over the top of all the other pop sensations was I Did A Vet and I Liked It," I say, making a play on a Katy Perry song.

Chase bursts out laughing and even snorts in the process, which is the cutest damn thing. The best part, she isn't even fazed by it when most women would die of embarrassment.

"I've got to hand it to you, Gunner. That was a good one. Creative. Witty. I love a man who can think on his feet . . . but no dice."

"No dice?"

"Nope."

I begin to pour a draft beer for another order Aubrey places—the bar is picking up—and slide a glance over to Chase again. She's sitting there comfortable as can be in a bar where a lot of men are staring at her.

I like that about her.

Hell, I like a lot about her.

"So, Chase," I say when I head back her way, "if you're not in love with a tiger tamer, not a ridiculously famous pop star trying to escape the limelight, why are you here?"

"It's a bar and I wanted a drink." She's coy as she plays with that straw of hers. "That's it."

"I was referring to Destiny Falls."

"I'm doing research," she says.

"For?"

It's the first time I've seen her hesitate to respond. Shit. Maybe I shouldn't have asked.

"My thesis. I'm writing one."

"On?" I prompt.

"It's nonfiction," she states.

"About?" I laugh.

"Deployment and children."

Chapter FIVE

Chase

GUNNER STARES AT ME LONG AND HARD WITH THOSE DARK BROWN eyes in a way that makes me feel like he can see straight through the lie I just pulled out of my ass.

Not really my ass.

More like straight from the article I thumbed through in the hotel magazine that was in my room. It talked about the mental and emotional toll deployments took on children of military families.

Gunner kept pushing for an answer. I panicked, giving him the first thing that came to mind.

The upside? I'll probably never see him again.

The downside? Maybe . . . I want to.

"If that's what you're researching, you definitely came to the right town for that," he says with a strained smile before heading to the other end of the bar where the redheaded server waits with more drink orders for him.

I glance around FU-Bar. It's dim where it needs to be dim so that people can slink in the shadows if they prefer, and light where it needs to be light, like over by the pool table where a few women are showing off their assets to their dates.

Military mementos are everywhere with each one of the bar's walls dedicated to a different branch of it. There are flags, pictures, plaques, memorabilia, and more representing someone's history down the line somewhere.

I have a feeling that within these walls, soldiers, vets, and their families have celebrated as many victories as they have defeats or losses of lives.

The music is low but present, the laughter is loud and frequent, and it seems the man who currently holds my attention is the maestro of all of it with his kind smile and friendly words.

"He really is that good of a guy, you know."

"What was that?" I ask, turning to my left to face Nix. He's tall and burly with a dark skin tone that does a good job of camouflaging an array of burn scars I can make out just beneath its surface. His eyes are dark and his smile warm as I meet his eyes.

"Gunny. He really is that good of a guy. We're talking a true decorated war hero."

"Is that so?" I murmur and glance over to where Gunner is chatting up his patrons at the other end of the bar.

"Yep. He's a total badass. Like the kind they hand medals out to during fancy ceremonies with lots of high-ranking people." His grin is wide and gloating. "So when he asks you out later, you're going to want to remember that."

"He's going to ask me out, is he?" I ask, drinking in Gunner once again. His dark hair, which is a little long over his collar. The cuffs of his black V-neck that are a little tight on his biceps.

I shake my head. He's so different than most men I find attractive. He's the furthest thing from sharp-suited-yuppy-looking guys who are always on their iPhone and in between business meetings.

I stare at him a beat longer and wonder what it is about him that won't let go of me.

It's more than just his good looks—not that any woman would balk at that chiseled jawline and his broad shoulders—but there's a magnetic appeal to him. A definite sex appeal. An ease with which he carries himself that says he knows women are noticing but that he doesn't take it too seriously. That, of course, is part of his charm.

Not to mention his sense of humor. Oh, and his smile too. Jesus, when he smiles it absolutely lights up the room.

You'll say yes.

You'll say yes, because you're smitten with him and your libido is in some desperate need of attention. Attention he can most definitely give.

So I'll say yes if he asks. I'll say yes without any shame because there's something about this unexpected find—*him*—in this pretty cool bar that makes me want to explore things a bit more.

Besides, how better to find out more about this town—possibly about where Ryan Camden is—than to befriend a local?

And maybe have a bit of fun.

"He is, indeed." Nix takes a sip of his beer. "Hell, if any more sparks fly between the two of you, this whole bar is going to catch on fire and burn to the ground."

"I doubt that."

"Women come in and out of here all the time. Pretty ones. Funny ones. Downright forward ones. He's rarely fazed by them, but this time around—mmm, mmm, mmm—he's definitely fazed by you."

"I—*thank you*—I guess?" I laugh the last words out as my cheeks heat and my smile widens.

"No need to thank me," he says and winks. "Just remember that we never had this conversation."

And the last words clear his lips when Gunner steps up to the counter between us and looks from me to Nix and then back again. "Is he being my wingman again or should I worry he's telling my deep, dark, sordid secrets?"

"You worried?" I tease.

"Not in the least," he says, that brilliant smile of his now a bit crooked. "Another?"

I glance down at my empty glass and contemplate whether or not another one will be me overstaying my welcome. "Nah. I think I should head on out. I had a long day and it's catching up to me."

I swear Gunner's expression falls some, and my ego appreciates the sight of it. "So soon?"

I slide some cash across the bar top with a more than generous tip. "Maybe I'll stop in tomorrow night."

"Sorry. I won't be here."

"Oh?" I hate that I'm disappointed by the mere thought. "Okay."

"I'll be taking you out on a date instead."

"What?" I cough out the word through a laugh.

"Is that going to be a problem?" he asks, his voice low, his smile soft, and his eyes hopeful.

God, he is charming. And good-looking. And . . . "Not at all."

He nods, his smile turning to a grin. "Good to know. I had to make sure and ask before you're asked ten more times as you walk out that door."

"Ten more times?" I ask.

"Maybe five." He scrunches up his nose. "It's a slow night so I'm thinking . . . five."

"And if you're right?" I lift my eyebrows.

"That's up for you to decide what my reward is."

"You like rewards, do you?" I ask coyly.

"Doesn't everyone?" Our eyes hold, despite someone calling his name. "Meet me at six o'clock tomorrow outside Grandy's."

"Grandy's?"

"You'll figure it out. See you then." Gunner winks and emits a chuckle as he heads toward his next customer.

I stare after him as I shake my head.

But he was spot-on. *Five times.* That's the number of times I was stopped on my way out of FU-Bar by men giving me half-hearted proposals. They were all in jest but funny nonetheless.

And just as I walked out the door, I looked back to see Gunner smiling at me.

This was not how tonight was supposed to go.

The thought is on repeat as I drive back to my hotel, flop back on my bed, and stare at the ceiling.

"So much for going in there with guns blazing," I note and then chuckle.

Hell, I didn't even think of Ryan Camden more than once, let alone ask about him. Isn't that why I'm here?

And to complicate matters more in my little charade? A thesis on deployment and how it affects kids? I told the man I'm going on a date with tomorrow that that was why I was here in Destiny Falls. Now what am I supposed to do when he asks me about said work?

I could be a no-show. That would solve the problem.

But the ridiculously stupid grin on my lips tells me that's not going to happen.

There's no way I'm standing him up.

Not a chance.

It's not just the incredible sex I've already predetermined that we'll have, but more so the fact that he's going to be my in to finding Ryan Camden.

Then again, maybe it is the sex. Five months is a long time for a dry spell.

Maybe parts of me are already fantasizing about that.

Chapter SIX

Chase

"Kelly, it's so nice to talk to you. It feels like it's been forever," I say and lean back against the pillows and headboard at my back, trying not to disturb the stacks of papers all around me on my makeshift desk—*the hotel bed*.

"It has. I think the last time we all saw each other was when your dad invited me to hang out at the Super Bowl two years back," he says, the warmth in his voice flooding through the phone.

"Has it been that long?"

"I believe so," our longtime family friend says. "What can I do for you, kiddo?"

"I need you to find someone for me."

He chuckles. "Poor bastard."

"What's that supposed to mean?" I laugh.

"If you're looking to find someone, that means he's wronged you and"—he whistles—"I wouldn't want to be him when you do."

"I am not that bad." I'm met with silence and then a chuckle. "Then again . . ."

He joins in with the laugh. "I'm a little backed up at the moment so I won't get to it for a few days. If you're okay with that, then—"

"Private detective business that busy at the moment?"

"Yes, and none of it juicy or scandalous, sadly," he says.

"I can wait. I'm just looking for a guy who sent my dad a letter . . ." and I proceed to tell him the story about the letter, Ryan Camden, and why I'm in Destiny Falls.

"Destiny Falls, huh?"

"You know this place?" I ask.

"I've been there a time or two. Mostly passing through. Cool town though."

"I don't know, I've yet to really leave the hotel room."

"Chase," he warns like an older brother. "You need to stop and smell the roses occasionally. You're all business, all the time, and someone your age should have a little fun. Let loose."

"Yeah, yeah," I say and roll my eyes even though he can't see it.

"I can hear you tuning me out." He chuckles. "But you're having no luck finding him so far?"

I open my mouth and then close it, because I really haven't looked yet. "I only got here yesterday. Brex told me that I needed to be low-key about it. That—"

"That they protect their own. She's right. Besides, it shouldn't be too hard to find him. I can call a few buddies of mine who deal in military personnel if need be, but I should be able to knock this out by next week."

"Really?" I ask, more than grateful for his help.

"Really. Or maybe I'll take my sweet time finding this Ryan guy so it forces you to figure out how to take some R&R and mosey around town for a while."

"Mosey?" I snort and then start laughing.

"Yes, I said mosey," he sighs, to cover what sounds like his own laugh. "Send over what you have on this Camden guy, and I'll get back in touch with you when I have something."

"Thanks, Kelly. You're the best."

I end the call and toss my cell down on top of the notepad directly in front of me. It's a list. The list I made this morning when I woke up to keep me on task. It's lengthy and detailed and so incredibly essential to my everyday life, so I made one. It's a list of things I plan—no, *need*—to accomplish while I'm down here for however long I end up being here.

I was thinking two weeks, but I'm beginning to think that it might be a bit longer.

So I made a list. At the top of it and underlined twice is: "Find Ryan Camden." Then research public relations companies. Do a deep dive into our competition to see what their social media presence looks like compared to ours. Then look into hiring a company to possibly analyze our social media to tell us where we are lacking or can improve. Research veteran sports and events of the past. And then I added all the stuff for my day-to-day job—review contracts, follow-up on endorsement deals, recruitment calls.

It's a long list but lists make me happy. They make me feel organized seeing everything I have to do laid out and then accomplished when I get to draw a line through each task I complete. The next step is to map out an achievable daily planner to keep on track and meet my goals.

I even added "Sex with Gunner" to it, because even if it's a ridiculous thing to add to a list, if my probable interlude isn't on it, then that means it would be haphazard and unexpected. It would be on a romantic (bleh) whim. By it being there, it—Gunner—sex with him—will stay as it needs to be, compartmentalized so it doesn't distract me from the task at hand.

Because let's face it, I let last night get away from me. I was tired and easily flattered by a more-than-attractive man. A man I'm excited to meet up with later . . . but I cannot allow that momentary blip on my radar to distract me from what I came here to do.

As it is, I complicated things enough with my *I'm a grad student writing her thesis* bullshit.

The positive? I've made some headway on my list. It's superficial at best, but at least I've gotten a start on it. Calls have been made, a plan set in action, and now that I'm organized, I feel like I can move forward.

That, and I know what and where Grandy's is.

I get lost in my work after Kelly's call. Contracts and researching what exactly social media analytics entails and tips on unhappy athletes I might be able to snag from another agent. It's only when the alarm on my phone goes off the second time that I pay attention to the time.

From there, I'm a scrambled mess of what to wear and how to do my hair. Of shaving legs and putting on makeup. Of driving to where I've been directed to Grandy's is, only to find that every available inch of parking space in Destiny Falls seems to be taken for one reason or another.

So I park where I can, and then walk the rest of the way to the old school ice cream shop a block from the town's main boulevard. I'm surprised how many people are milling about on a Thursday evening. I assume there's a high school sports game of some sort and, since sports are my life, am obviously interested in what sport.

Ryan Camden could be anywhere in this town. Hell, he could be the guy who just walked past me or he could have moved on and now lives elsewhere.

I turn around to give one more look at the crowd who just passed me, as if I even know what Ryan looks like beyond the grainy photos I found on the Internet.

Focus, Chase.

The irony in that thought is not lost on me. I'm here to find Ryan Camden but I'm telling myself to focus on my date with the bartender from last night.

And so I forget the notion that Ryan was in that crowd somewhere, and I head to Grandy's.

I don't get nervous before dates. I never have. I know that's arrogant of me but doesn't that simply say more about me than the guy I'm meeting? That dating is simply a source of fun and definitely not something I look at as using to find my match or mate or whatever ridiculous colloquial term people use. Soulmate is the one my sisters prefer, and that term just makes me nauseous.

Soulmate. Meh. No thanks.

But turning the corner to where Grandy's is located, I swear my breath hitches when I see Gunner standing there. He's got a pair of faded jeans on, brown boots, and a dark-blue T-shirt hangs loosely against his broad chest. His smile is wide and his free hand is gesticulating wildly as he takes the hand of an elderly woman and helps her down the curb. She's about half his height and definitely more than triple his age, but he jokes with her as he opens her car door for her.

The sight makes me smile. He's not at a bar paying attention to customers. He's not trying to pick me up. He's being kind when he doesn't know he has an audience. That's a good measure of a man, and one that makes me glad I said yes to meeting with him.

Gunner waves goodbye to the woman who can barely see over the steering wheel and then notices me standing there. He looks startled, but his smile widens to epic proportions when he sees me.

"You showed," he says and pulls me in for a warm and unexpected hug. He smells nice, his chest is firm, and his arms make me feel safe.

Safe?

That's the oddest thought, and I push away as soon as I realize it, but now it's at the forefront in my mind.

"You say that like you're surprised I did," I murmur when he steps back, and I angle my head up to meet his eyes.

"I am." He says it just like that. No games. No dancing around the truth. New York City men could take a cue from the man in front of me.

"Really? You could have asked for my phone number last night, and then you would have known for sure that I was."

"I didn't figure you for the type who'd hand it out."

"Is that so?"

"Mm-hmm." He fights a smile.

"What did you figure me for, then?"

His gaze devours me deliciously, as it runs down the length of my body before coming back up to meet my amused eyes.

"You're definitely independent—"

"What makes you think that?"

"It takes guts for a woman to walk into a bar on her own that she most likely knows is going to be full of horny servicemen."

"I trusted they'd be able to control themselves," I say, noticing that the brown in his eyes have the coolest flecks of gold in them.

"I was ready to jump in and protect you should they not have—but then again, you would have been insulted, as that would have implied that I didn't think you could take care of yourself."

"I wouldn't have been insulted." He stares at me as if he's questioning that comment, and I laugh. "Maybe. *Perhaps.*"

"Definitely."

"I'll give you that," I say. We stand with goofy grins on our faces outside Grandy's, where people are coming and going constantly in and out of the ice cream parlor.

"Thank you for coming," he murmurs, breaking the silence.

"Thank you for asking me."

"Shall we get going?" he asks and holds his hand out to me.

I stare at his hand for the slightest of seconds, not used to this simple gesture, and loving it all the more because of it.

Men back home don't do this.

Correction, the men that I've dated back home don't do that. Almost as if the old-school gesture isn't hip enough.

"Sure." I link my fingers with his as we start walking toward the main drag. "Is there a high school game tonight or is this town always this busy?"

"You'll see for yourself in just a second," he says cryptically.

It takes everything I have not to pepper him with a million questions about where we're headed and what we're doing. The upside to that is my silence forces me to observe, to notice: the excitement of the kids running past us; how almost everyone who passes us on the sidewalk says hi; the warmth of Gunner's hand against mine; the blue of the horizon.

And when we turn the corner to where it seems everyone is heading, my feet stop.

The main drag has been closed to all traffic, because one of the longest tables I've ever seen spans for at least a few blocks down the middle of it. There are chairs set up on either side, what looks like a two-foot divider that runs the length of the table, and matching boxes are at each seat. Hanging in a zigzag line from one side of the street to the other and back are strings of lights providing a soft yellow glow. There are vendors on the sidewalks—food and wares and what appears to be kegs of all things.

"What in the world . . ." I ask but then look to where Gunner is pointing. The sign above our head reads "Lager and LEGO."

"You ready to play?"

"Play?" I laugh the word out, equally confused and intrigued. "What are you talking about?"

He looks at me with a twinkle in his eyes. "I warned you Destiny Falls was a town of festivals so be ready to experience your first one." He steps in front of me and holds his hands out to his sides. "This is Lager and LEGO, where the gist of the game is this: we all start out with the same pieces. Along with that box of LEGO bricks, we each get a cup of lager—aka beer. After drawing random numbers, we sit down in those assigned seats, and face off in a timed round against the person sitting opposite us."

"So it's a competition?" This is absolutely crazy.

"It is."

"You just build anything?"

"No." He shakes his head and waves at someone who calls his name. "Each round has a topic to guide you, but you can use that topic and be as creative as you want."

"And at the end of your time when the bell or dinger or whatever rings, do you have to have both your beer drunk and your structure built?"

"Structure only, but the cups are tiny for those who want to finish it with each round."

Gunner stands in the pale-yellow light, as the night darkens around us, with the softest of smiles on his handsome face and makes me want . . . so many things, but none of which I can put my finger on.

"Who thinks up this shit?" I laugh.

"Us bartenders at FU-Bar might have had a hand in helping devise this one."

"You're serious?"

"I am," he says with a definitive nod.

"But if it's bricks and beer—"

"Haha. I see what you did there." He points his finger at me and grins.

"—why are there so many kids here, since they won't be chugging beer?"

"Because they are the judges." He lifts his brows as I startle.

"The judges?" I look around at all the kids standing on the curbs. Some have treats in hand, others clipboards, but all have excited smiles on their faces.

"Yep. After each lightning round, the builders—*us*—step back from our tables, and they step forward to judge the best structure out of the two at that particular table. Whoever they pick moves on to the next round."

"And to the next beer?" I tease.

"Exactly."

"Oh my God." I stare at the length of the table again. "There must be a million rounds. The people at the end must be—"

"I told you they're tiny cups of beer."

"This is insane." I look around and take it all in. "And so awesome."

"So you'll play?" he asks, holding his hand out to me, which I promptly take.

"Was there any doubt?" I ask as he pulls me closer to him.

"Should we make a wager who will get the farthest?"

"That's probably not a smart thing to say to me," I warn and push playfully against his chest. "I'm uber competitive and it is our first date, after all. You probably don't want my ugly to come out."

"Ugly?" He laughs. "I doubt it, but rest assured, I'm man enough. I can handle a defeat, Chase. I won't pout or throw a tantrum."

"All men pout and throw tantrums when they lose."

"Then maybe you're hanging around the wrong men."

Our eyes hold as his smile dares me.

"Fine. Sure. We can make a bet," I say, "but rest assured I'll win."

"Nothing like being sure of yourself."

"Exactly," I say as he tugs on my hand to head toward what I now see is a registration booth. "So what are we wagering?"

He stops walking and gives me a shy smile that makes every part of me stop and stand still.

"A second date," he says, confusing me.

"But . . . that doesn't make sense. How does that benefit—"

"If you win, I get a second date with you . . . and if I win, you get a second date with me. See? Easy."

"You're smooth, Gunner."

"I know."

Chapter SEVEN

Gunner

"You literally tried to bribe that judge. How old was he? Twelve?" I laugh as Chase takes a few steps in front of me and spins around.

"Yes. But he really wanted that ice cream, and I was more than willing to deliver on a triple scoop cone if he happened to decide my design was better."

I shake my head and laugh, knowing she still delivered, even though the boy didn't vote for her very odd-looking Tyrannosaurus Rex she built—if you could even call it that.

"I told you," she says and shrugs. "I have absolutely no shame when it comes to winning."

"I'll have to remember that next time," I say, taking my last sip of beer and throwing it into the trash can beside me.

"Next time?" Chase asks, her smile making the sapphire in her eyes come alive more—if that's even possible.

"If you stick around long enough, I'm sure there'll be something else we can compete at sooner than later."

A little tipsy and a lot adorable, she throws her head back and laughs.

There's something about her that owns my attention. Was she uber competitive at LEGO building? Yes, but she laughed and joked and charmed everyone she sat next to.

I know, because I couldn't take my eyes off her. Hell, I probably lost my round against her because I was so busy looking up and laughing at how serious she was and the expressions on her face.

"Gunner?"

"Hmm?" I ask as her eyes find mine, and a sheepish smile plays on her lips.

"I think I made a tactical error."

"A tactical error?" I ask, taking a step toward her. "How many days have you been in Destiny Falls, because it seems you're already picking up the lingo?"

"Funny." She sways.

"You okay?"

"Tactical error," she repeats. "I worked all day and was so busy that I kind of forgot to eat anything."

I chuckle. "And now you have a good buzz going on an empty stomach."

She takes my hand without hesitation, when previously she's been more tentative. Her guard is lowered, and I love that I get to see both sides of her in such a short span of time.

This woman. Jesus. She does funny things to my insides.

I could have taken the easy route—hit on her and taken her back to my place—but there was something about her that made me pause. Maybe I wanted this instead. Time. Getting to know her. Winning her over.

While I'm not one who hops from bed to bed, I'm not immune to some unadulterated, no-strings-attached fun here and there.

But dating someone? That's typically not my thing. The oversharing. The letting each other in. The vulnerability.

I've been hurt enough in my life, the last thing I want to do is to step into that shit willingly.

And yet oddly with Chase . . . with Chase, I want to share. Want to make her smile. Want to talk.

"I do. I am. Buzzed. I'm buzzed."

"And you're worried I'm trying to get you drunk to take advantage of you, huh?" I tease.

"There's no need to get me drunk to take advantage of me, Gunner. It's not taking advantage when we both want it."

I open my mouth and then close it, stunned by her forwardness, and so damn enamored with her confidence. And before I can recover from surprise over her words, she laughs, then takes a few steps into the street before us. With the lights in her hair and a smile on her lips, she spins in the middle of the empty street.

Fucking hell, how is it possible that such a simple act can make me lose my breath?

She's gorgeous with her short shorts, red Converse, and her hair pulled up into a messy ponytail. Gorgeous in that carefree, she doesn't give a shit about what anyone else thinks about her as she twirls like a loon in the street.

I'd give anything to kiss her right now. *Fucking anything.*

But I need to get her food first.

Then I'll kiss her.

The funny thing is I thought I was starving, but when we sit down at Lou's café and order, I lose my appetite. Or maybe not lost my appetite but rather found something way more interesting to pay attention to: *Chase Kincade.*

"So New England, right?"

She stops mid-chew and smiles. "How'd you know?"

"I figured it was either NY or LA—a big city anyway. Which one?"

"New York." She pauses a beat before asking. "Why?"

I chuckle and take a sip of my milkshake. "Because you're mesmerized by the slow pace here. You stop and stare as if people being nice to you *just because* is abnormal."

"Like how you were helping the lady in her car earlier," she murmurs, and I think of ninety-five-year-old Delores, her beloved weekly trip to Grandy's, and her all-knowing smile.

"Doesn't everyone do that?" I ask.

"No. Actually, they don't." She gets a look in her eye across the dimly lit patio, but when she shakes her head it clears from her eyes.

"What?" I ask.

"You're just nothing like I expected is all," she murmurs and leans back.

"What did you expect?"

"I don't know, but not you." She laughs. "You're nice and considerate and you took me to build LEGO. I mean, who does that?" Her tone is playful but there's genuine sincerity that tells me she's utterly surprised by tonight.

"Don't all your dates take you in their power suits to build LEGO?"

She narrows her eyes at me. "What do you mean?"

"I mean, I think you're used to guys who are so self-absorbed with looking the part that they forget the point of a date is to have fun and get to know each other."

"That's quite a presumption," Chase murmurs.

"Perhaps. Maybe not, but I think you were expecting me to be more like them and are a little surprised that I'm not."

"You use a broad stroke when you paint a picture, don't you?"

I shrug and lean back, arm on the top of the chair beside me. "Am I wrong?"

"You can't say something like that and not explain yourself. Why do you think I only date self-absorbed guys?" she asks.

"Because you're big city. All the big-city guys I've met before are self-absorbed and more worried with looking the part, with being on an Instagram date so they can post photos and get likes. They're all about the show and less about doing something *real* and getting to know the woman they're with." I shrug unapologetically. "Standing behind a bar night after night allows you to learn a lot about people."

"And that's something you've learned, is it?"

"Among other things."

She laughs. "And what, may I ask, do you post on Instagram?"

"Nothing. I don't do social media. If I need to talk to someone that matters, I'll pick up the phone."

"Humph." She studies me and for the briefest of seconds, I wonder what she sees. "So you think I date Instagram-fixated men who only care about themselves, do you?"

"Am I wrong?" I repeat.

"No." She shrugs shamelessly. "*You're unexpected.*" And the way she says it, as if it's the most normal thing in the world, takes me by surprise. "And I love that."

"I could say the same of you. I expected to be at LEGO and Lager tonight, but I most definitely didn't expect to have my ass handed to me by a city girl who can hold her liquor."

"I think that's my most favorite compliment to date," she says playfully. "What about you? What's your type? Where are you from? Give me the good stuff."

I chuckle and prefer to avoid the topic altogether. "What do you want to know?"

"FU-Bar? Why there? Is it yours? What's up with the name?"

"FU-Bar is named aptly after FUBAR, another term you'll hear if you stick around here long enough."

"And it means?"

"Fucked up beyond all recognition."

She laughs and it's such a great sound. "I've heard that before. I just didn't put two and two together. Isn't it used for a mission gone wrong or something?"

"A mission. A training exercise. A disastrous date. Anything."

"I sure hope you don't think this date has been FUBAR," she teases, and I'm quick to shake my head.

"Furthest thing from it."

"Whew. Good for me."

"And me." I smile.

"Speaking of FU-Bar, the bar feels very *you*."

"And what exactly do *I* feel like?" I ask, curious how she sees me. *Fucked up beyond all recognition?*

"Warm and welcoming but with the edges steeped in your service." She eyes me with a smile toying at the edges of her mouth.

I purse my lips, liking her assessment. "That's fair."

"Is it yours?"

"In a sense." I nod and think about all the nights the four of us spent beneath a darkened desert sky. We either sat and wished for home or talked endlessly about the bar we were going to open. The pipe dream was our solace as a means to combat the nerves we had while out driving our Humvee through IED country. "We made a pact to open a bar together. Whoever made it back anyway and . . . well, I was one of the lucky ones who did so"—I shrug away the guilt—"I followed through with my promise."

"One of the *lucky* ones?" she asks. "I'll be the first to admit that I don't know much about the military—or even the veteran—culture, but I have a feeling that those who come home, don't always feel so lucky. Is it right to assume there's a lot of guilt there too?"

If only she knew just how accurate that statement is. I've never felt *lucky* just . . . confused.

Why me?

Why was I spared?

But I won't delve in to that depressing topic right now. Nothing like sucking the life out of a fun date with survivor's guilt.

"I'm lucky because I get to live in a town where people look out for each other. I work in a place I love. And I have friends who I trust my life with. So lucky, yes." I sigh, the sound so very contrary to the words I say. But I ignore her question about guilt, hoping she'll take the hint that this area of my life is currently off limits.

She studies me for a moment, those intelligent eyes noticing what I'm not saying perhaps.

"You're kind of incredible." Her smile is sincere, inviting, and the need to kiss her grows. "Can you please tell me you have some horrible habit that makes you not so perfect? It would make me feel a little less inadequate sitting across from you."

"I drink milk from the carton sometimes. Every once in a while, I don't rinse my dishes before I put them in the dishwasher," I confess then take the bill from our server and set it beside me. "Does that help tarnish my image?"

"You are quite the rebel." And there's a moment where the two of us just stare at each other as people walk by on the sidewalk and waitstaff swerve between tables. The silence between us sparks with what feels like anticipation for what might come next, while sexual tension also reverberates between us. For the life of me, I can't remember the last time I wanted a woman so badly.

"So, Chase, what other information were you fishing for?" I narrow my eyes, pretending to be annoyed, and smile at her.

"I wanted to know your type," she says. She wraps her lips around her straw and sucks on her shake. *All I can do is stare.*

"My type?" I ask, forcing myself to avert my eyes, because that sight is not boding well for me walking out of here and not having a hard-on. She nods, her lips curling up at the corners. She knows exactly what she's doing. "Preferably she wears red Converse, has a killer competitive streak, and likes chocolate milkshakes."

"That's all you've got for me?" She angles her head to the side as I wonder how to explain.

"I don't do this often."

"No?"

I shake my head. "It's rare that I find a woman I'm interested in enough to want to."

"I'm flattered."

And I'm smitten.

Shit. Where did that come from, Gun?

"Where are you from then?" she asks.

"A little bit of everywhere. Once you've been in the military—grown up in it and served in it—you're kind of from every place you've been."

"So your mom or dad was in the military?"

"My father was before he died in combat."

"I'm so sorry."

I nod, never wanting to dwell on that aspect too much. "Then my stepdad was in the service. And the stepdad after that." I give a self-deprecating laugh. "We don't have enough time in the day to delve into that chaos. What about you? Mom? Dad? Only child?"

She does a double take. "Only child? Why would you say that?"

"Because only children are typically more independent and know what they want," I say. "That's you."

Chase smirks. "I am the last of four girls."

"Your poor parents," I groan.

"You don't know the half of it." She smiles as if she's thinking of them, and I notice a softness to her expression that tells me they're close. You spend enough time around other soldiers and behind a bar, you to learn how to read people. "But it's just my dad. Our mom died when we were little."

"I'm sorry," I murmur.

She shrugs. "As you unfortunately know, it's more shocking to others when they hear it than it is to you since it's been your reality for more of your life than not."

"Very true."

"So on to happier things." She nods and twists her lips for a moment as she studies me unabashedly. "Nix told me you were a badass. Care to elaborate?"

Fucking Nix. I shake my head and emit a half-sigh, half-laugh.

Nothing makes you a badass in combat. Fear. Worry. The unknown. The what-ifs. Horror. That's what combat is about. I shiver from the memories that still haunt me and my dreams.

"Some days just living to see another day in combat makes you a badass," I finally say.

"Your humility is becoming."

"Thank you, but I assure you I'm not all sunshine and roses all the time."

"No one ever is," she murmurs.

If she looks at me like that one more time—those big blue eyes a mixture of amusement and desire—I'm going to have trouble standing up.

"You ready to go?" I slide cash under the salt shaker and hold my hand out to her. She takes it and we head out of the outdoor café back to the street that's still bustling with people.

Music is playing now, a local live band at the end of the long table. Kids have sat down and are building their own creations while their parents are dancing or chatting with friends.

This is Destiny Falls. Take it or leave it. In my early days here as an enlisted soldier, I wasn't sure which one I wanted of the two. Now as a civilian, I couldn't imagine myself anywhere else.

"Thank you for this," Chase says as we skirt around the edge of the dance area. "Like I said, it was unexpected and perfect."

"Is that so?" I tug on her hand so that she turns and our bodies meet. Desire surges through me in all the most torturously delicious ways as we stare at each other, our lips inches apart, and I finally give in to what I've wanted to do all night. Hell, since she first walked into FU-Bar last night.

Her breath hitches. I can feel it against my chest, and I know she feels this too. The sexual tension. The desire. The pure need.

And just as I lean in to kiss her—

"*Gunner?* Is that you?" comes from behind me in that high-pitch drawl I would recognize anywhere. *Fuck.*

I debate kissing Chase anyway, but it'd be rushed and interrupted, when I most definitely want it to be neither of those. *I want more. Much more.*

"I'm sorry in advance."

Chapter EIGHT

Chase

I stare at Gunner, not understanding what he means. When his name is called again, his shoulders sag in defeat and he chuckles sardonically.

He turns, and I'm met with an assault on all senses by a woman old enough to be either of our mothers. The voice owner's hair is blonde and teased to epic heights. Her clothes are tight, her heels are high, and her makeup dramatic.

But not as dramatic as her voice and her expression when she finally meets Gunner's eyes.

"Oh. My. Gosh. *Full stop*. I thought that was you over here all by your lonesome," she says and Gunner's hand tenses against my back.

"Not by my lonesome at all," Gunner says, offering a polite smile to her.

"Well then." She reaches out and rests a hand on Gunner's bicep, and I swear to God I get jealous, even though his arm is wrapped around me. "I am so glad that I saw you standing over here because I wanted to let you know that I made a pie today, and I know how very much you like *my* pie. I made sure to use the tartest, juiciest apples," she all but moans. "And the sauce is gooey and warm just like every man I know likes it."

I cough out a laugh as my eyes all but bug out of my head. She hasn't looked my way once—she only has eyes for Gunner. And hands apparently. He's tried to shrug his shoulder away and she just keeps her hand planted firmly around his bicep.

Gunner clears his throat when she finally stops talking about her ooey, gooey mess and how it will absolutely melt in your mouth. "Thank you, Heloisa. I appreciate the offer, but—"

"Oh come now, sugar. You know I love treating the men around here to my pie, but I know you especially love my apple," she practically purrs. If I wasn't seeing this with my own eyes, I would never believe a woman could be this . . . whatever she is. "I even have some apples set aside, marinating in sugar and cinnamon, so if you tell me a time you'd like to stop by, whether it be a day or in an hour or two, I can cook another pie up real quick so that when you dive into it, it's warm and juicy and oozing with everything good and mouthwatering that you like."

I stare, blinking at Heloisa as she flirts herself right out of her skin-tight pants and into Gunner's.

Meanwhile, Gunner shifts on his feet and stutters, "Thank you for the offer—I'm more than appreciative, but—"

"But you'll be by later, right?" She winks and licks her lips. "I'll be waiting for you."

"No. I won't. I . . ." But just as quickly as Heloisa and her warm, moist pie came into the picture, she stalks right out with her hips swinging so noticeably I'm surprised she doesn't throw her back out.

We both stand there staring at her and shaking our heads. "What—or rather *who*—was that?"

"Don't ask."

"Oh, I'm gonna ask," I say playfully.

"She's harmless. Just a lonely, old widow who comes into the bar sometimes and—"

"And you entertain her so as not to be mean to her?"

"Something like that," he grumbles with a roll of his eyes.

"Dare I ask if her warm, apple pie is as moist and delicious as she swears it to be?" I tease, imitating her voice, and I love that Gunner turns ten shades of red. "I mean, she was just offering to have sex with you." I'm still astounded. And aghast in the oddest of ways.

"She was not," he says but starts laughing.

"It's the warmest, juiciest, hottest thing you'll ever sink into," I mimic until I burst into laughter. The kind of laughter that doesn't stop, especially when you want it to. And every time I meet Gunner's eyes, I start laughing even harder, to the point where the humor renews itself all over again.

"Oh. My. God," I say in between laughter.

"Full stop," Gunner pipes in.

I double over again, my sides hurting and my cheeks aching. I hold on to him to steady myself. But when I look up, I find his mouth inches from mine—right back to where we were before Heloisa interrupted us.

Except this time, there's no Heloisa. There is just Gunner, his big brown eyes, tempting lips, and his fingers reaching up to tuck a piece of hair behind my ear.

He leans forward and brushes his lips against mine. The kiss is soft and tender and makes my insides feel like I've just grabbed a live wire.

I want more . . . so much more that it's almost embarrassing.

And with his hand on the side of my neck and his thumb brushing over the line of my jaw, Gunner delivers a little bit more.

He kisses me again, but this time his tongue slips between my lips and meets mine briefly in a kiss that hints at things to come, but doesn't make a gross public display of affection to the people still present in the middle-of-town event.

"I've wanted to do that all night," he murmurs, the heat of his breath against my lips. My body hums with the desire that has been building since I first saw him tonight.

"Well, I know a place you can go if you want pie," I offer, to which we both erupt into laughter again.

Sex with Gunner is definitely on my list of items to cross off while in Destiny Falls, and while I have no problem having a one-night stand occasionally, this is a small town. People talk in small towns, and the last thing I need is a bad reputation when I might need some of the locals' help to find Ryan.

Yes, the same Ryan I haven't even mentioned to Gunner yet when he's a bartender and knows more people than most in town.

However, my resolve to *not* have sex with him tonight on our first date was tested the moment I saw him standing in front of Grandy's. And I know it was thrown out altogether when he kissed me on that grassy hill under a dark sky.

And now that I'm standing under his front porch light as he unlocks his front door, I know I'm going to dive in and appreciate the decadent temptation that is Gunner.

In fact, it wasn't even like it was a discussion—but more like a known fact that this was where we were going to end up after that first kiss.

There wasn't a "*your place or mine?*" Just more stolen kisses here and there as we laughed and laughed while he gave me insight into small-town facts.

There was simply a tug on my hand as we walked down a few side streets in the warm evening with lightning dancing in the distant sky and a baited anticipation bouncing around us.

"It's not much," Gunner murmurs as he leads me inside his home. There's a toss of his keys on the table. The shutting of the door behind me. The whisper of my name in the dark.

And when I turn to face the sound of Gunner's voice, his lips are on mine. The kiss starts out slow and sweet, like a symphony's first strings to capture your attention.

But there's no need to draw me in. No need to seduce me with a soft melody when I'm already there, already gone.

We kiss in his entryway with moonlight streaming through the windows and slanting over us. His hands frame my face as our tongues flutter over one another's and our hands map the lines of each other's bodies. My hands run up the plane of his back, so I can feel the corded muscles beneath constrict and flex. His run from my hips to beneath my breasts.

We are slow and deliberate with our actions, almost as if we're on the same page. The one that says once we unleash this need—*this exquisite desire*—there will be no going back. Need will turn to greed. Desire will shift into lust. And climax will be the only goal.

We take our time getting to know each other's bodies. I gasp when his lips find the spot just beneath my jawline, the stubble of his five o'clock shadow teasing my sensations right along with his mouth. He moans when the chill of my hands hits his bare skin beneath his shirt, and I pull it up and over his head.

And then he freezes and sucks in a breath when I run my hands up the front of his torso and then chest and feel what I can only describe as indentations marring its surface.

Scars.

Like the kind they hand medals out for during fancy ceremonies with lots of high-ranking people.

Nix's words hit my ears again, and I'm at a loss for what to do or if I just upset him. So I stare at Gunner in the moonlit dark, searching for an answer I don't have any right to ask.

"It feels worse than it looks," Gunner says quietly, and offers a half-hearted smile as he runs the backs of his knuckles down my cheek.

I lean in and press a kiss to his lips before stepping back, pulling my shirt over my head, and unclasping my bra. When I let it drop, I love and simultaneously hate the sudden rush of vulnerability *I* feel as he stares at me. As he takes me in.

"They feel better than they look," I offer with a soft smile, hoping to ease the moment and the vulnerability I can only imagine he feels.

"They look more than beautiful to me." He reaches for my hand and tugs me against him. Our lips find each other's again. This time a little more desperate, definitely a lot hungrier.

We proceed to slowly make it down his hallway, my back seemingly visiting every wall as we go. The one beside the kitchen for a deep kiss. The one nearing the bathroom for a slide of his mouth down to nip my collarbone as his hands find and cup my breasts. Just outside the bedroom so my teeth can gently tug on his bottom lip while I unbutton his jeans.

Then his room. He leads me in by the hand and then stares at me through the dim light. "Are you sure? I don't want you to feel—"

"I wouldn't be here if I wasn't." I keep my eyes on his as I shimmy my jean shorts down over my hips and stand there naked before him. "The question is, what are you going to do with me now?"

His cocky grin reappears and his eyes fire as he takes a few steps toward me. A soft chuckle falls from his lips as he copies my actions and shoves his jeans to the floor.

Well, hello there.

He's gorgeous. And not just because he pulls a condom out and jackets up without questioning. But because as he does, I'm allowed a glorious moment to study him. The broad shoulders. The strong forearms. The trim waist that leads down to a very healthy, very hard dick. The firm thighs below it.

As a woman who unabashedly enjoys sex—the buildup to it and the act of it—I'm far from disappointed in what greets me when Gunner stands there naked before me. Sure, it's dark in the room, but this is going to be exceptional.

So damn exceptional.

"What am I going to do with you?" he murmurs and narrows his brow, as he closes the distance between us. He reaches out to my waist and pulls me against him. Our bodies touch without anything between us for the first time.

My skin hums from the feel of him.

My body aches in the most deliciously sweet ways.

And when his lips slant back over mine and his fingers find their way between my thighs, every part of me wants to beg him to touch me everywhere. His kiss captures my moan when his fingers slip between my slick heat and tuck into me.

"Christ, Chase," he says against my neck, the heat of his breath sending chills over my skin. His fingers slide over nerves inside and deliver their own sensual assault.

My hands grip his shoulders, fingernails digging into already scarred flesh. I want to reach down and stroke him, feel him, return the favor, and yet I'm held captive by his touch in the best way possible.

His mouth moves to my breasts, the roughness of his stubble, and the warm heat of his mouth against my sensitive nipples, is like adding kerosene to the fire he's stoking between my thighs.

"Gunner," I moan as he continues to slide his fingers in and out at the same time his lips and tongue tempt and tease me into a riotous bliss.

My core aches and burns and begs for more and when it hits—when the crescendo of the symphony he's built hits—my body doesn't know if it wants to tense or collapse in a heap as my muscles pulse and tighten around him.

"That's it. Come on," he encourages as his teeth nip my shoulder. "Come for me, baby." He groans, his hand now soaked and his dick pulsing against my abdomen, begging to get in on the action.

My breath is shallow as his chuckle heats my ear. "That was good to start with, but I can't wait to feel you wrapped around my cock like that." His tongue pushes between my lips and demands more from me. "Taking me all in." A line of open-mouthed kisses down my jawline. "Fucking me."

I already ache for him to fill me. I just climaxed, but where his touch is akin to a match, his words are incendiary, taunting me to want more.

And I definitely want more.

"Gunner," I whisper, as I slide my own hand between my thighs. I coat my fingers with my arousal and then wrap my hand around his cock and slide up and down.

It's his turn to freeze. His turn to groan. His turn to have his fuse ignited.

And that's all it takes to ignite the flame we've been toying with. Within seconds, Gunner pushes me onto the bed at my back. I scoot back on my elbows and revel in the sight of watching him crawl onto the bed.

He stops to kiss one of my calves.

Then another kiss to the opposite knee.

A playful bite on the side of my hip.

Then a soft suck on one of my nipples before his lips meet mine again.

My body writhes in desperation to have him. To feel him. To give him the same type of pleasure he just gave me.

Gunner kisses slowly at first. Softly. Each time our lips meet, the hunger intensifies. A tinge of desperation morphs into an all-out onslaught of need and greed until I'm spreading my legs and lifting my hips, practically begging him.

"Please."

Thankfully he obliges when he leans up on his knees and places his hands on the backs of my legs as he settles between my thighs.

His first push in is indescribable. Equal parts burn and bliss as my body stretches to accommodate him in all his engorged glory. We both groan in pleasure. I arch my back and close my eyes to revel in the sensations he just created.

From there it only gets better. His hands find my hips. My fingers grip the sheets. The delicious stretch as he thrusts in, running the crest of his cock over every sensitized nerve within before pulling back out and doing it all over again.

We move in sync. Two bodies pushing for the same release. Two people reveling in the chemistry that has led to this.

He leans over to pull my nipple into his mouth, which makes him bottom out completely within me. We both still at the sensation, and he grinds his hips against mine a few times. The breathtaking sensations of him being in me, and his mouth being on me, push me toward the edge.

"Yes. Again," I demand in the most sex-drugged voice as the sensations try to pull me back under the haze of lust and desire.

"You like that?" he says as he grinds again, hitting and re-hitting the spot within that makes me go mad.

My mewl fills the room. It's all I can use to describe the sound I make as my orgasm bears down on me with a freight train-intensity I've never felt before. My body's electrified. From my core to my toes to my head.

My breath is shallow and my head dizzy as my muscles pulse uncontrollably around Gunner.

"Fuck, that feels incredible," he groans. His fingers dig into my hips as he tries to maintain control.

But I don't want him in control anymore. I want him to lose his tight grasp on restraint, so I push him by purposely tightening myself around him.

"Chase. Good God." And those are the last coherent words he utters.

There's something to be said about watching a man work himself up to the point of no return. The taut neck. The tension of his abs as he thrusts into you. The way his eyes glaze over when he looks down to see where he enters you. His bruising grip on your flesh. His Adam's apple when he throws his head back and loses himself in you.

And Gunner is all of that and then so much more when he comes.

He's freaking perfection, and I have no clue how we climbed so high so quickly . . . so effortlessly. *So immediately.*

Chapter NINE

Chase

I WAKE WITH A START.

It takes me a second to remember where I am since I've been discombobulated anyway now that I'm staying in a hotel.

But I definitely remember my whereabouts when I shift to find Gunner lying on his stomach in the bed beside me, sheets covering one of his thighs and basically nothing else.

I do what any normal woman would do—I thoroughly study him. But it's not like I didn't get intimate knowledge of him last night and the few times we decided to see if we could in fact, come one more time.

The answer was yes. Yes, we could.

I shift, a delicious soreness between my thighs, as I study the intricate tattoo just below his left shoulder blade. It's some kind of Celtic cross with initials carved in its hilt but it's too hard to see in its entirety because of the angle he's lying at. Instead I take another peek at his very fine ass before moving back up to his face.

Thick lashes fan over suntanned cheeks. A lock of hair hangs down and covers one of his eyes to rest on his strong nose.

Not classically handsome as some would define handsome, but the man is drop-dead sexy, an attraction all in itself.

I look around his bedroom. It's basic. Beige walls with hints of grays and blues. A pair of jeans are hung over a chair in the corner and one boot rests on its side beneath it. There's art hung on the wall and a few framed photographs on his dresser that look like they're of a grandfather in uniform, but I couldn't be sure.

Definitely all signs of normalcy, which is important when you're a woman who took the plunge and decided to go to the house of the man she doesn't exactly know all that well.

The problem was I never had any intention of staying here, but he was so cute and the sex was *so* good, that it would have been a shame to leave.

But I need to leave. I need to head out, get to work, and cross this off my list: *great sex with Gunner.*

The best part about being busy all the time is that sex is just that. A physical need to satisfy. I don't have time to get tangled in relationships. Hell, I don't even want to.

So this is perfect for me. Some physicality on a quick trip to Destiny Falls. Some satisfaction and a mind-blowing release—or *five*—to revel in.

Can't complain in the least.

And the moment that thought crosses through my mind, Gunner shifts beside me and the memories from last night come back vividly.

I smile. How can I not after I had one of the most memorable and unique evenings I've had in some time?

Shifting on my side, I study Gunner again.

There's something to be said about a man by his touch. A woman knows it from the moment he lays a hand on her. Greed is easy to identify. Selfishness too. But when a man knows how to touch a woman well—there's enough pressure but not too much. Friction applied intermittently. A well-timed kiss with alternating intensity. The reverence in how he runs a hand over your body in foreplay juxtaposed with how he grips your hips when he's driving you both to bliss.

There is definitely something to be said about a man's touch when he's tuned in to the woman he's with. And Gunner no doubt knows how to touch a woman.

It's a rarity for sure.

Gunner sucks in a breath of air and jolts up in the bed, startling the hell out of me. "Oh my God, I'm going to be late." Then he looks to his side and the sexiest, sleep-drugged smile slides onto his lips. "Good morning. I should start with that." He reaches out, takes my hand, and presses a kiss to the center of my palm. "I should most definitely start with that," he says and runs a hand over my ass and up my back.

Ache sparks to life from his fingers. Need that I thought was sated isn't far behind.

"Morning," I murmur. My smile is automatic.

He leans forward and presses a kiss to my bare shoulder before climbing out of bed. "I'm sorry to do this to you," he says as he walks toward his closet, "but I've got to get going, or else I'm going to be late for work."

"Work?" I ask, sitting up in bed cross-legged, comfortable in my own nudity and not caring that the sheet is solely covering my bottom half. "The bar is open already?"

"No." He looks over his shoulder and catches me checking him out. He grins. "My other job. Or rather I should say where I volunteer. I mean—I mentor boys who have lost a parent in combat. It's nothing really. Just . . ."

I don't hear the rest of his words. The ones that explain how his volunteering isn't a big deal because I'm too busy realizing that he's genuinely real. That good guys, *unicorns like him,* really do exist.

And I don't even know how to react or what to say as he pulls out clothes to wear. He was right last night. I am used to selfish assholes. To pricks. Ones worried about if they're going to get enough time in at the gym after work, let alone make life better for a kid.

Hell. What is Gunner doing with me when I'm probably just as self-absorbed as the men I typically date?

From now on when someone says good guys don't exist anymore, I'm pointing them in the direction of Destiny Falls.

"That's incredible," I murmur as he looks back over his shoulder and smiles again.

"Not really. It's just . . . it recharges my tank in a sense. I get as much out of it as they do. Or at least I hope they do."

"Still, it's . . ." My words fade when he turns to face me and for the first time, I'm met with the tapestry of scars that crisscross over his chest. They reflect a horror story all on their own that leaves the utter devastation to one's imagination.

My eyes lift up to meet his and he offers me a shy smile. "I know they're hard to look at."

"No. You are definitely not hard to look at," I say. "Seeing them just makes me think of probably a million things you had to go through to first get them, and then heal, from whatever caused those scars." His expression softens as emotion swims in his eyes. "It means you were stronger than whatever it was that tried to hurt you."

"Not stronger," he says with a slight chuckle. "Just lucky."

His humbleness is on display again and it brings me back to last night. The vulnerability I felt standing there naked in front of him, and I can imagine he feels ten times more than that every time someone sees his scars.

"Well, I'm the lucky one," I murmur as I sit up on my knees and pull him against me for a long, slow kiss. A kiss that restokes the embers left burning from last night.

"This is a cruel joke," he says against my lips as I feel his dick hardening against me. "Leaving a beautiful, naked woman alone in my bed is definitely a cruel joke."

His lips meet mine again as his hands cup my ass and pull me against him. Christ Almighty, how are either of us even physically able to consider another round?

His groan reverberates around the entire room. "I need to take a shower." Another kiss. Another scrape of his teeth against the underside of my jawline. "They're counting on me."

"I'll just lie here then while you're in the shower and finish myself off," I tease—only partially. Because the man already has that ache burning so bright from the feel of his body and the taste of his kiss alone.

"You're cruel."

"And you're gorgeous," I say against his lips.

He leans back and looks at me, his fingers tucking the hair that's fallen in my face behind my ear. There's amusement in his eyes, but also something more that I can't put my finger on. His smile is soft. "I'll be in the shower. And if you lie right here, you can get a good angle in the mirror to see me in there." He pats my ass. "You know, should you need any visual stimulation to help get you off."

"You're a bastard," I tease.

"That's not what you said about"—he looks at his watch—"three hours ago. I believe then you were praising me profusely."

The grin he flashes me is mesmerizing. *God, he's gorgeous.*

All I can do is shake my head and flop back on the bed, wondering how the hell this happened, and be grateful that it did.

Because Gunner is most definitely something else.

I look through the open doorway and into the mirror. It's fogging with the moisture of the shower, but I can see him soaping up and washing his hair.

Thoughts of sliding my hand between my thighs and finishing off the desire he flamed moments ago crosses my mind, but I know I'll be left with a half-hearted orgasm and not completely satisfied.

Who is this man? Funny. Great in bed. Lighthearted. Sexy. Selfless. I mean, what in the heck is he doing with me?

Groaning, I hoist myself off the bed and gather my clothing. I can't remember the last time I was so unmotivated about getting to work.

By the time I'm dressed, the shower has stopped and Gunner is hurriedly walking into the bedroom, pulling one pant leg on.

"No?" he asks me when he meets my eyes, a devilish grin playing on his lips.

"No?" I ask. He looks at the bed and then at my hand and I shake my head. "It's not the same."

He throws his head back and laughs. "Am I allowed to take that as a compliment?"

"Definitely." I bite my bottom lip and take him in again, careful to only allow my eyes to skim above his chest.

He shoves a shirt over his head and runs his hand through his hair. "I've gotta run. I can either give you a ride or you can see yourself out whenever you're ready."

"Wait, you're just going to leave me alone in your house?" I ask, flabbergasted.

"Are you going to rob me blind?"

"Er, no."

"Then, yes, I'm going to leave you here alone. This isn't the big city, Chase." He pulls a baseball cap off a shelf in his closet and puts it on, adjusting the bill. "Besides, I tend to trust the people I sleep with so I'm not too worried."

"Oh."

"So, ride? No ride?" He grabs his car keys off his dresser.

"No ride. My car isn't too far away."

"Okay. Just lock the door on the way out. *Shit,* I'm late. I have your number now. I'll call you later." He heads out of the bedroom leaving me standing there, staring at the empty doorway.

"Bye," I say and then startle when he walks back in the room on a definite mission.

"I forgot something," he says seconds before he pulls me against him in a libido-stirring, panty-wetting, all-consuming kiss that leaves me absolutely breathless when he steps back. "Now, I can go."

And without another word, I hear his footsteps on the floor and then the door shuts with a slam.

My fingers touch my lips and my head spins. I'm here in the house of a man I've known less than forty-eight hours . . . *and yet I feel like I've known him my whole life.*

Chapter TEN

Gunner

I SAG AGAINST THE WALL ON THE GYMNASIUM FLOOR. *WHAT A FUCKING day.* It didn't help that I got very little sleep, but it was a fucking day nonetheless.

"So you going to tell me who put that pep in your step today?"

I look up to Ellie. "I don't know what you're talking about."

Oh, but I do, because all day long my mind kept drifting back to last night and this morning. To Chase and her laughter and the sex—Jesus Christ, the sex was *incredible*. But it was more than that. It was . . . just *her*. The ease I had in talking to her. The laughter. The conversation. This morning. The way she didn't look at me like I was crazy or even worse, with pity, because of my scars.

So yes, I've been distracted today. Distracted by thoughts of a woman that shouldn't give me pause because she was supposed to be just that—*a distraction* from my troubled sleep and craving a little fun.

Distracted, because I want to see her again, taste her again, when it's been less than eight hours since I left her in my house with those bee-stung lips and huge blue eyes.

"You don't know what I'm talking about?" Ellie snorts. "I hear your words, Gunny, but that grin tells me otherwise."

"That noticeable, huh?"

"Kind of." She laughs as she sinks to the floor beside me. "And *she* is?"

"No one. Someone." *Everything.* "I don't know what the hell she is but she sure as shit knocked me on my ass."

"Typically, being knocked on your ass isn't a good thing."

"No, I mean it in all the best ways possible."

"Humph. That's a good thing, then?" she asks.

"It is."

"Are you going to see her again?"

I look over to my counterpart. Her dark hair is pulled back in a tight ponytail and her gold hoops are bigger than the ears she hangs them from. Her smile is knowing and her dark brown eyes searching as they study me and wait for an answer.

"I don't know." That's a lie. I know damn well I want to.

"Well, how did you leave it?"

I chuckle and thoughts of Chase, and that naked, warm body of hers, fill my mind. Close behind are her words about taking care of herself while I was in the shower, and her admission that I was better than her own hand. *What man doesn't want to hear that?*

"Do I even want to know the shit that you're thinking about right now?" she asks in her motherly tone she uses with the little girls she mentors here at The Center when they step out of line.

"Probably not."

"So?" She raises her eyebrows. "How did you part ways?"

"I left to come to work after one hell of a goodbye kiss."

"Okay, okay," she says and nods dramatically. "Now we're getting somewhere. So she spent the night. Your place or hers?"

"Does it really matter? There was a bed." I laugh.

"It matters."

"Mine."

"Humph. You really do like her, don't you?"

"What the hell is that supposed to mean?" I ask.

"Men don't take one-night stands back to their houses. They take them to hotels. They take them to the woman's place . . . but never their own. Unless of course, you want to see her again because if so, you just showed her where you live."

"Your logic is . . ." But I can't finish my train of thought because she's right. I honestly don't think I've ever taken a one-night stand home with me.

"You sure your girlfriend ain't crazy? Because if she is, you're going to have to move."

"She's not crazy, Ellie. She's . . ." Perfect. Sexy. Funny. Intelligent.

She cackles out a knowing laugh. "I'll repeat myself: you really do like her. So when are you going to call her?"

"I don't know."

Her sigh is heavy. "Gunner, Gunner, Gunner. Honey, this is not like you."

"It's not?"

"No. I've seen you come in here after a good night of sex and all, but this one—this woman—has you a little tied up."

"I wish she had me a lot tied up," I tease.

"The kids were as exhausting today as you're being right now," she mutters.

"Funny." I close my eyes and lean my head back against the wall.

"I know I am. But I also know if you like her this much, then don't be playing those stupid-ass games men like to play. Call her. See her. Enjoy her. You know better than most that life is too goddamn short to play games."

"Amen to that," I murmur and close my eyes again to block the flashbacks that come when I do.

The acrid smell.

The concussive blast.

The violent pain.

The world falling apart all around me.

And the carnage when it was all over.

I shake my head to rid it of the past. Of the memories that I'll never get over, never forget, but somehow need to move on from.

"Trey is struggling," I say, because it's easier to focus on one of the kids than it is to focus on me.

"I know and it's heartbreaking."

"It's always heartbreaking," I say, as I think of the little boy and his big gray eyes. How they looked up at me with huge alligator tears in them as he asked me why his daddy wasn't coming home.

"You remember that far back, yeah?" she asks. There's a reason we both do this. Two army brats who both lost our fathers and then became soldiers ourselves.

"Bits and pieces, but sometimes I wonder what's real versus what I've seen in pictures and then fabricated in my mind from there."

"I think we're all like that."

"But more than anything, I remember looking out the window and even though I'd been told he wasn't coming back, still looking for him to come up the walkway in his uniform with those black boots squeaking as he went."

She nods and places a hand on my thigh. "We do good here, Gunny. It's easy to lose sight of that sometimes, but we make a difference."

"Yeah, I know."

"I have to get going. I know one of my boys is probably already complaining and wondering what's for dinner." She chuckles, stands, takes a few steps, and then kicks the toe of my shoes. "Don't think I'm not noticing that you're not addressing Wendy's resignation today."

I squint when I look up at her. "I'm not ignoring it. I'll find someone. It's a temporary job, so it can't be that hard to fill."

"Yeah, but until you do, the two of us are stuck doing it, and this momma doesn't have any more time to give."

"I'll take care of it or will find someone who can fill in a few hours to help us out. Not a problem." But it is a problem because like Ellie, I don't have more time to give . . . but unlike her, I don't have a family.

A family to watch me coming up the walkway.

A family to go home to.

"You keep looking at that door like you're expecting someone to come walking on in," Nix says from his usual perch to the side of me.

"I don't know what you're talking about," I say and move toward the right to wipe down the counter.

It's been a busy night. Fridays always are here and there's no shortage of people wanting a reprieve from the workweek. The music is loud, the drinks are flowing, and I should be one happy bar owner.

The problem is Nix is right. I keep looking at the door. I keep wondering if Chase is going to walk through it with that fucking gorgeous confidence she wears like a sexy negligee. I keep remembering every goddamn minute of last night.

"You just looked again."

"Fuck off, Nix."

His chuckle is low and taunting. "So what gives? She that good in bed? She's fabulous at her conversation skills? She's—"

"I slept a whole fucking night without a nightmare. How's that?" I snap at him, but when I meet his eyes, there's understanding and compassion that most people would never comprehend.

"Shit, Gunny."

"Yeah. *Exactly*." I walk out from behind the bar and start collecting empties from tables. It's not my job to do, but I need a fucking minute to let the words that just fell out of my mouth sink in.

When was the last time that happened? When was the last time I wasn't finding every excuse not to sleep to keep the nightmares at bay?

Granted, I did exert myself fairly heavily, but still . . .

I glance over to Nix whose head is down, watching his thumbs play with the label on the beer bottle. He knows the gravity of what I just said. Of the unattainable night without nightmares.

He was there with me that day. He remembers too.

I let myself get lost in the small talk with customers to clear my head. Some are regulars, some are not, but most know who I am. Luckily, all are respectful and don't ask the questions they're wondering. The questions I would probably have if I were in their shoes as well.

That's enough for me.

I move back behind the bar, dropping the empties in the sink with a clatter. One of my servers narrows their eyes as they try and figure out why I'm helping them out. I just smile and give a shake of my head that it's no big deal.

And when the door swings open, I look again.

"You going to see her tonight when you get off?"

"No," I grunt.

"As per usual, you make absolutely perfect sense," he says into his beer and my response is a lifted middle finger. "Seriously, though. Why not?"

"Because . . ." I turn to face him, hands out in a shrug. "Do I have to have a reason?"

"If you're going to bullshit me then yes, yes, you do." He chuckles.

"I don't know why the fuck I'm not going to see her tonight, but it feels like I need to wait. Is that good enough for you?"

"Why wait? A booty call is a booty call."

"She's more than—" *Fuck.* I catch myself but it's too late, and Nix's imagination is running wild.

"I see." And his silence is deafening in this loud bar. But he doesn't tease me, and he sure as fuck doesn't dare question me. "Humph."

"Humph?" I ask.

A slow smile crawls over his typically stiff upper lip. "My guess is the lights will be glowing tonight then?"

I slide a glance over to him, sigh, and shake my head. It's a good thing to have someone know you as well as he does. *And a bad thing.* For both of us.

"Meaning?" I ask.

"Meaning, when you can't sleep or you can't figure shit out, that's where you go."

"And of course, your place has a bird's-eye view of the lights."

He brings his beer to his lips. "That it does." But when he takes a sip, his eyes stay locked on mine.

Fuck.

"I already put in a call."

And when Nix laughs, it drowns out everyone else in the whole fucking bar.

Chapter ELEVEN

Gunner

7 Years Ago

"Look at you," Boone says and then hisses when the shot of whiskey hits the back of his throat. "You're actually going to let him get away with that?"

I move my jaw from side to side and wince. By the way my cheek feels, the shiner that's coming is going to be a fucking doozy.

"I'm not letting him get away with shit."

"So you punched the fucker back?"

"Nah." I take a sip straight from the bottle. "I just don't fucking care anymore."

"Shit," he says drawing the word out, "you gotta show that bastard who's boss."

I lie back on the grass and stare up at the darkened sky overhead. If there were any stars to be seen, I'm certain they'd be spinning on me like the ground beneath feels like it's doing.

"No one's called, Boone."

"What the fuck are you talking about?"

"No one's called. Coach sent out all those letters and emails and, other than that one prick who came asking for money, it's been goddamn crickets."

I sit up long enough to take another swig.

"You think it's that bastard's doing?" he asks.

"Coach's?"

"Nah, your old man's."

"He's not my old man. Let's get that straight," I snap.

"That's right. I forgot your old man—"

"Died. Yes. Poor little orphan boy should be so fucking lucky his momma found another man to help support them."

"Shit, man. I wasn't going to say anything like that." He holds his hands up in front of him. "I was just asking if you think your step-pop is fucking with you?"

"Why would he? If I signed somewhere—even some Podunk single-A team, I'd be out of their hair. That's what he wants. Me gone so he can control my mom even more."

He blows out a heavy sigh that sounds like how I feel. "So what's the shiner for tonight?"

"For being disrespectful." I shake my head. "Supposedly I didn't say thank you enough times for the food he provided. So I told him to fuck off." *No surprise, that didn't end well.*

"All while your stepbrother, Perfect Marcus, had his ass kissed over how great he was, I bet."

I look over at him and roll my eyes. "Good guess."

You are nothing, boy. Will never be anything.

Marcus's the one going places in ball. Not you. No one would take a chance on a bonehead, snot-nosed punk like you.

Your useless ass is lucky you still have a roof over your head. If it weren't for your momma's begging, I'd have kicked your worthless ass out a long time ago.

His insults run laps through my head. The anger I felt then and still now, vibrates through me. His son is perfect . . . I'm just a reminder his wife used to be married to another man.

"If I were you, I'd show him he doesn't own you or this house," Boone continues.

"Whatever, man." I say the words, but his comment burrows its way under my skin.

"You know what would be the ultimate *fuck you* to your step-pop? Taking that prized possession of his for a spin. Making sure your ass sits in those pristine seats of his and blowing the doors off that engine he babies like a pussy."

Normally, I'd never give the suggestion a second thought. That 1965 Mustang is my stepdad's baby.

Normally, I'd tell Boone to fuck off and that he's crazy.

But there's something about tonight. About the words Sal said and the vengeance behind his punch that I can't let go of. That fucker wants me gone because I'm my father's son and not his. Because I'm better than his kid and he can't handle it.

I look at the closed garage door and know the keys for it are hanging on the rack inside the laundry room cupboard.

The more I think about what Boone said, the more I hear Sal's insults. His cruelty. And the more I want to say *fuck you* again to him.

"Hey, where you going, man?" Boone asks as I shove up off the grass and stumble for a second before the world rights itself again.

"Getting the keys." I scrunch up my nose. "I think it's a nice night for a drive."

Chapter TWELVE

Chase

"Ms. Kincade?"

"Yes?" I stop midway through the hotel lobby and turn to look at the desk clerk. She can't be more than twenty, standing there with her little pregnant belly, her college textbooks cracked open, and a small wallet-sized photo of her husband in uniform taped to the edge of her computer screen. From our conversation yesterday, I know he's currently deployed in the Middle East somewhere.

"That guy you were asking about? The baseball player? The one who pitches?"

"Ryan Camden? Yes. What about him?" She immediately has my interest. After a fruitless day yesterday asking around about him and getting nowhere, I'll take any news I can get about his whereabouts.

Yesterday was frustrating to say the least. First, no real leads on Ryan, and then fighting my own staunch determination last night not to head to the bar—or check my phone for the hundredth time to see if Gunner had called or texted.

The worst—or my sisters might call amusing—part was that my usual chant of *it's just sex* or *he's not that big of a deal,* fell on my own deaf ears.

I wanted to go to the bar.

I wanted to see him again.

Because I know whatever happened to us the other night was more than sex. There was chemistry there, and I don't have time for fucking chemistry. I have time to find Ryan, to see what happened to him and, in loose terms, take advantage of the situation for KSM's benefit . . . and then move on.

And yet, I was surly and grumpy and even annoyed myself with it because I wanted to see him. His smile, his—

And that's why I didn't go.

That's why I had to prove to myself that I didn't need to see him. That my hours spent trying to figure out what mentorship program he worked for was simply because I needed a break in the work monotony.

I glance at the clerk's name tag, Sara, and offer a huge smile as I wait for her to answer.

"I'm not sure what the guy's name was, but I was driving home late last night from my mom's house when I noticed there were lights on at the baseball field. The baby was kind of restless, kicking up a storm, and I knew if I went right home that I wouldn't get much sleep anyway, so I figured I'd go investigate for you."

"Wow. Okay," I say and smile. I'm grateful for her help, but know I'm not going to haphazardly find Ryan pitching somewhere.

"I tell you, it was hard to see from where I was parked in the lot, but there was a guy out there pitching. Over and over and from what it looked like, he was throwing real fast."

"Really?" I play along, not wanting to hurt her feelings and more than aware that *real fast* could mean a lot of things depending on a person's knowledge of the game and distance from the field. "What time was this?"

"Like one or two in the morning or something crazy like that."

"That late?" I ask. Definitely drunks out trying to relive their high school careers. And then I realize Sara's looking at me as if she just solved the mystery for me, so I ask a question to make her think she's helped me. "What field was this?"

"The one down off Hawley Road," she says and points to the right of her.

"I really appreciate you telling me. Maybe it's time I take a few late-night, early morning drives and see if I can find him for myself."

"Fingers crossed you find him."

"Me too." I hold my crossed fingers up to show her.

"After you told me that you're trying to find the man who wrote you a letter, I keep having all of these daydreams about how you're going to find him, and it'll be love at first sight. Like it was all meant to be. I hope it comes true, for your sake."

I smile and nod as I say goodbye and step away. She's a sweetheart no doubt, but I don't live in her reality. Not that hers is a bad one, but marriage and kids at her young age? I shudder thinking of myself that young and so shackled.

It's definitely not for me.

My no-strings-attached lifestyle suits me more than well. I can work however long I want without worrying about others. I can go wherever I want without answering to anyone.

Some may call me selfish.

I call it knowing what I want and being okay with it.

Maybe someday I'll want what my sisters want—the white picket fence and the family that goes with it—but not now.

Not at this stage in my life.

When I emerge from the hotel lobby, I contemplate where to spend my time today. Yesterday was spent taking a small nap—*great sex is tiring*—and low-key queries about Ryan Camden. I even left messages for the baseball coach of a local state college a few towns over to see if he knew of any Ryan Camden but have yet to hear back.

Today definitely has to be devoted more to contract review, social media planning, and client calls.

And that's what I do for the next four or five hours. I get lost in my work. In the anticipated, in the unexpected, and in the new and noteworthy. I win over a new client, review a proposal from a PR firm I contacted yesterday, and talk to a few social media analysts to see what each offers.

It's mid-afternoon when I emerge from the folksy tunes and dark walls of the Grind Me Coffeehouse. It's cozy and quaint and has served as my office for most of the day, but the need to stretch my legs and feel the sun on my face has won over my need to cross more things off both my daily and my monthly checklist goals.

I search in my bag for my sunglasses and just as I'm about to put them on, I look up and meet Gunner's eyes. He's across the street, and he freezes momentarily at the sight of me before jogging across to me.

"Hi," he says and I swear to God, if going all warm and fuzzy were a thing, I would vouch that it just happened to me.

But that isn't me and it's definitely not Sara's, the hotel desk clerk's, world.

He smiles—or rather he was already smiling and it just grew wider—and the sight of it and the warmth in his eyes already has my body singing.

"Hi," I say back to him in that awkward, *I want to kiss him, but maybe I shouldn't, because I don't know if we were just a one-night stand* type of awkward. "You didn't call."

And if we were a one-night stand, now he's going to think I'm *crazy*.

He angles his head and his expression softens. "I didn't want to seem too—"

"I get it. I didn't mean to say that." I give a quick shake of my head and busy my fingers with playing with the strap of my purse. "I just wanted to make sure the date wasn't *FUBAR* so to speak."

Gunner laughs. We stare at each other on the sidewalk, and then without preamble, he steps up, puts his hands on either side of my cheeks, and full on kisses me.

And it's not a brush on the lips, *I'm going to placate you,* kiss. This is the kind of kiss that makes me forget I'm holding my bag or that I'm on the sidewalk of downtown.

It's equal parts heart and heat. Like a drug I didn't know I was addicted to until I had it again.

"What was *that* for?" I ask, a little breathless, a lot enamored, when the kiss breaks. He leaves his hands framing my face so he can run his thumb over my lips.

"I figured that might clear up some of the awkwardness." His smile is shy as he shrugs. "There was never any before and there sure as hell shouldn't be any now."

"Well, okay then." I laugh.

"Second—"

"*Second?* I didn't even know there was a first," I say.

And again, I find his lips on mine *and* my body aching.

"That was the *first*," he says, the warmth of his breath feathering over my lips. "You forgot about it way too soon, so I needed to remind you of it."

"Remind away," I murmur and then snap myself out of sounding like an idiot. "But then again, maybe second was even better?"

He lifts his eyebrows. "Second, can we just agree that I wanted to see you again and that you wanted to see me again?"

"I think that kiss pretty much sealed that shit up."

We laugh. I hate admitting to myself that I love the feel of his hands on my face. The way his smile warms me. How much I didn't realize that I was looking forward to seeing him again.

"That's settled, then," he says with a definitive nod. "So when can I see you again?"

"Gunner." My smile is shy and my want is real. "I have to be completely honest with you."

"Why does that not sound good?" he jokes, his hands running down my arms and linking fingers with mine.

"It's not bad . . . it's just . . . my being here in Destiny Falls is a temporary thing. The last thing I want to do is give you a false sense that I plan on staying here. I mean—"

His lips close over mine again. Just a simple brush of lips but so very potent in how it makes me feel.

"What was that for?" I reach out and put a hand on his cheek.

"You're talking too much about shit that doesn't matter, Chase. I learned that living in the moment is so much better." He lifts our linked hands up to his lips and kisses the backs of mine. "So let's start living in the moment, shall we?"

It's the best idea I've heard in forever. "I quite like that idea."

"You do, huh?"

I nod, and my smile is constant as we start walking down the sidewalk aimlessly. "What exactly do you have in mind?"

"Well—"

"Coach Gunner?" a voice to the left of us calls, and I turn to see the cutest little boy waving at Gunner from where he stands in the open doorway to the Central Nail Stop.

"Trey? What are you doing out here?" Gunner says, his entire demeanor transforming at the sight of him. He reaches out and does some elaborate handshake with the tiny cutie. "Shouldn't you be in school flirting with all those cute girls?"

"Yuck," the boy says with a dramatic flair. "And it's after school already."

"Your momma getting her nails done?" Gunner asks.

"Yep," he says with a roll of his eyes before turning his attention to me.

"Hi there," I say. I'm guessing he's about seven or eight years old. His eyes are a light gray, his skin tone is a light brown, and he has the most gorgeous head of hair. He's definitely going to be a heartbreaker when he grows up.

"Trey, this is Chase," Gunner says.

"She your lady?" he deadpans with a lift of his chin that has both Gunner and me fighting back smiles.

"I'm working on it," Gunner says and winks as I stand there trying not to laugh.

Trey eyes me again and nods. "Try harder."

"Trey?" a woman's voice calls from inside the salon. "Who are you—oh, Gunner. Hi." A woman with the exact same coloring as Trey steps forward and presses a kiss to Gunner's cheek. "I was going to ask how you were doing, but it seems to me you're doing just fine," she says, eyeing me much like her son and then cackles at her own joke.

Gunner introduces the two of us moments before she's called back into the salon.

"You better be ready to win tomorrow," Gunner says to Trey.

"When have I ever lost?" he says with a devilish grin and a lift of his hands before he turns and heads back into the salon.

Gunner shakes his head and just laughs.

"He's adorable, funny, and going to cause his momma a lot of trouble someday when he realizes how good-looking he is," I say as we start walking again.

"He already knows it."

"He called you Coach?"

"Yeah. We call ourselves coaches at The Center instead of counselors or mentors. That way the kids don't really feel like we're trying to pick their brain apart. They have base psychologists that do that. To them, I'm just a goofy coach who makes them laugh, get some fresh air, and hopefully help them forget for a little bit."

I nod, reminded once again of his selflessness.

"That was Trey. Eight years old from Tennessee. Father died—killed by a roadside bomb in Kandahar. For the most part, he's doing okay now, but we had a rough patch last year that took a while to work through."

I simply stare at him.

"What?" he asks, embarrassed under my scrutiny.

"Why do you do it?" I ask. "I mean I know why . . . but still, *why?*"

He shrugs. "Short story? Because it makes me feel good. Long story?" He blows out a long exhale and shoves his hands in his pockets as he looks straight ahead instead of me. "Because I have a lot of guilt over those I couldn't save. The ones who left behind little boys who'll never see them again. Little boys who'll struggle to know what it means to be a man. So I help teach them a bit of that as an apology that I couldn't, in fact, save them."

I blink away the tears he can't see as he falls quiet. There's nothing I can say to give anywhere near enough praise for what he's doing.

"Gunner. I don't even know—"

"I have an idea," he says, knocking all words of praise from my lips when he faces me with a big grin and his huge brown eyes.

"What?"

"You said you're researching military life, right?"

Shit. "Yes. I am," I lie and don't feel good about doing it at all.

"Are you looking for work? Do you know anything about sports? We could use help if you want to give it." His questions come out rapid-fire.

"I'm nowhere near following you right now."

"Sorry." He shakes his head. "I don't mean to imply that you need work or a handout or—"

"What do you need help with?" I ask.

"It's not that. I mean sure, we need help—*we always need help* since we're strictly volunteer based—but if you're looking to write about military life—*real military life*—then you need to make sure to talk about the kids. The military brats and what they're struggling through and those organizations that try to help them."

I stare at Gunner with the oddest sense of resolution. The same sense I get when I want a client and know I'm going to win them over.

Maybe you need to find a cause.

Lennox's words ghost through my mind as I stare at a man, who's not only a hero—according to Nix—but who continues to be one even after he was discharged from service.

"Do you know anything about sports?" he asks, and I stare at him doe-eyed, trying to not laugh at the irony of the question.

"Sports?"

"Bats. Balls. Goals. Baskets. Mismatched uniforms. That kind of thing," he teases.

I swat at him. "Of course, I know sports. Who doesn't?"

"I know this sounds crazy, but . . . we need some help at The Center. It's the beginning of our rec league's baseball season and so we need help organizing teams and sign-ups. It's just for a couple of weeks. All simple. It's a way to earn some extra cash while you're researching your thesis. And, it would be a chance for you to get some great insight into military life. On the emotional toll these kids experience. The ups and downs of it."

I immediately feel like an ass. For him thinking I'm here for my thesis. For him assuming I'm a broke graduate student who needs to earn extra cash.

For all of it.

And I know I need to tell him the truth but . . .

"C'mon. Can I entice you by saying you'll get to see me more, too?" Those eyes of his are beguiling.

"You're so cute when you beg," I say and step up and give him a kiss to rival the kisses he's won me over with. "But there's no need to beg. I'd love to help out. To volunteer." And I'm serious. It's not until the words pass over my lips that I realize how much I do in fact want to do this. I've been a kid who lost a parent. I've been lost, grieving, and lashing out. Something about this is just too right for me. "Besides, you can repay me in other ways." I wink.

"I don't think I'll be too hard-pressed to figure out how to do that."

Chapter THIRTEEN

Chase

If someone were to ask me how this happened—how I, Chase Ava Kincade, ended up sitting at a front desk of a rec center telling seven-year-old Guillermo that a half-eaten chocolate chip cookie is not an acceptable form of bribery to get a girl, *me*, to go on a date with him—I'd tell them they were crazy.

That I'd never be in this situation.

I am the furthest thing from the nurturing, playful type when it comes to kids, and yet here I am.

The Center is an old YMCA property. It has a gymnasium in desperate need of some work along with some cracked asphalt courts outside and a baseball diamond on the far side.

The facility is worn and aged, but what it lacks in curb appeal, it definitely makes up for with the laughter echoing around and love emanating through its space.

"So the gist is this," Ellie, Gunner's counterpart, explains. "We run and facilitate sports programs for all kids on base to help us offer *more* to those kids who have lost their mom or dad."

"And what do you think—" My words halt as Gunner runs by the window. He has one little boy hitching a ride piggy-back style and another chasing after them while Trey shouts at them from farther away. But it's not the kids or the actions that catch my attention, it's the expression on Gunner's face. Pure freaking joy. And in all honesty, I'm not one hundred percent sure why it hits me so hard, but it does. *He's . . . beautiful. Selfless.*

"Yeah, he's kind of amazing," Ellie says, breaking through my fog. I startle and look at her.

"*What?*" I ask, flustered.

"You were mid-sentence when he ran by and then forgot to finish what you were saying." She shrugs and gives me a knowing smile. "So I figured I'd finish your thought for you."

I clear my throat and force myself not to look out the window again, where it seems there's an epic invisible battle of some sort taking place. "Yes. He is. Uh—where were we?"

"You mean before or after you were admiring him?"

I give her my best Dekker-glare but she just laughs. "Before."

"Oh, right." Another smirk. "I was explaining how we use managing the rec league to help pay for these kids." She points to the six boys currently pretend-attacking Gunner. "Any child who has lost a parent in combat receives any and all that we offer at no cost."

"*Why?*" It's a simple word but it can ask so many questions.

"To help their remaining parent out. To give the kids some of what they are now missing. A father or a mother figure. We try to help ease the grief associated with losing a parent in a way where the kids don't feel like they're making the parent they have sadder."

I nod over the lump forming in my throat. How many times did I bury my head in my pillow to cry at night so I wouldn't make my dad more upset after we lost my mom?

"That's amazing. So it's just sports or do you—"

"It's more than sports. We do community service events like park clean-up or facilitate them mentoring younger kids."

"Mentoring younger kids?" I laugh. "They're kids themselves."

"Yes, but for kids who feel like their lives are out of control, the notion that they are 'helping' other kids gives them confidence that they've got a handle on whatever it is they're struggling with. Kind of a reverse psychology type thing if you will." She shrugs. "We also do a Trust-Fall Retreat once a year where we take the kids and challenge them to do outdoorsy things. Little do they know, all staff are trained grief counselors who push the kids to make them feel alive again. Everything we do is to help them cope." Her smile softens as more laughter floats in from outside. "Why?"

she restates my question, her voice filling with pride. "Because we can and because we make a difference."

"What can I do to help?"

Ellie puts me through the rather simple paces. How to sign new kids up. What forms and waivers their parents or guardians need to fill out. The fees to collect. And once I have all that, how to categorize them so they can be put on teams according to their age group.

It's only when I'm sorting through the forms I've pulled in for the day, that I look up to find Gunner standing in the doorway, shoulder propped against it, and his hands in his pockets.

"Hi," he says after a beat.

"Hi. Everyone picked up?" I ask about the last of the kids who were waiting for their parents.

"Picked up? Yep."

"Was it a good day?"

"Let's see. I ran into you. I convinced you to work here. Joey laughed more than he cried today." He nods. "That means it was definitely a good day."

"Joey?"

"My human backpack today."

"He's a cutie." His big blue eyes and spikey blond hair come to mind.

"He lost his father last month. Suicide bomber took him out at a roadside check. His mom is a mess." He shakes his head as sadness owns his eyes. "I've been trying to do all I can to help him while she figures stuff out."

"This project is incredible." I rise from my seat. "*You* are incredible."

Gunner shrugs. "Ellie and I do our best with what we have."

"You're not good with compliments, are you?"

He chuckles and averts his eyes. "We just wish we could do more so we could help more."

"Is there any other way for you to get funding?" I ask, fully aware that he's dodging the compliment comment. A humble man. That's not something I'm used to finding much these days.

"Other than the sports leagues, we do a few fundraisers. We petition colleges for their used equipment. We get a few veteran-owned businesses to donate here and there. But it's not about the sports equipment or the donations. Sure, the kids think they're here for the sports, but our aim is to build a comradery or community with other kids who understand each phase of grief they're going through."

"And it doesn't hurt that you understand them," I add, and his eyes grow somber.

"Yes. We all understand them. Me. Ellie. *You*. It's a club none of us want to belong to but unfortunately do."

"What happens when they get too old?"

"It's the military. We do the best we can with the time we have. Most kids move in and out, staying only a few years. Some kids have both parents in the service, so they're stationed elsewhere. Most aren't here that long." He looks down and then back at me. "And some, like Joey . . . man, they hit you straight in the gut."

They *are* making a difference. The smile on Joey's face today and his laughter bubbling up showed that earlier.

I'm excited to do this. To be a part of this.

I smile and take another step closer to him. Gunner's smile turns shy, and his eyes darken as he reaches out to take my hand in his. Just that simple touch has my body aching for him.

"Is it against the rules for me to kiss you?" It's all I want to do right now. Kiss him. Touch him. *Connect with him.*

"It's allowed," Ellie teases as she walks in.

"Go away, Ellie." Gunner laughs and waves a hand at her. "I'm about to be kissed."

Her laugh can be heard with the squeak of her sneakers as she heads down the hallway. "Enjoy yourselves, children. I'm heading home. You'll lock up?"

"We're kissing here," Gunner says, before pulling me against him and brushing his lips against mine. It's gentle and tender. He leans back and looks at me for a moment before doing it again. This time his tongue slips between my lips and I welcome it. There's a softness to the kiss compared to those we shared the other night in the throes of passion. The kind of gentleness that warms me from the inside out and makes me want to melt into him.

And when the kiss ends, Gunner slips his hands around my waist, clasping his fingers at my lower back, and pulls me against him. It's an unexpected move, and one that takes me by surprise, but more so because I welcome it rather than want to push him away as would be my usual MO.

"The last thing I want to do right now is head into work."

I groan, and then question my reaction. I can't remember the last time I wanted to spend as much time with another human like I do Gunner. Typically, I feel smothered easily, needing breaks and space and all of the clichéd terms you hear. Normally I'm good with the between-the-sheets part, but the out-of-the-bed part becomes stifling.

And yet, here I stand with Gunner's heartbeat against my ear and my disappointment so very real.

"Can I be selfish and tell you that the last thing I want you to do is to head into work too?" I laugh and press a kiss to the underside of his jaw. "But alas, I must get some work done too."

He groans like I did and we both laugh until his lips find mine again. "Tomorrow? Do you want to do something then?"

I think my kiss is answer enough.

Chapter FOURTEEN

Chase

"So any updates on the mystery baseball man?" Dekker asks across the Zoom connection. Her hair is up in a messy bun like mine is, but there's also an empty container of Ding-Dongs next to her that she is completely shameless about.

"Not yet. I've been asking around but haven't had any luck. Kelly's working on it for me."

"Then you'll have an answer shortly," she says, knowing how efficient Kelly is. "So what else are you doing other than being way too productive for someone who's not in the office?"

"What's that supposed to mean?" I ask, sinking back against the headboard behind me.

"It means how many freaking emails did you send out yesterday?" I open my mouth and then close it because I did send quite a lot. "I mean, did we or did we not talk about you maybe finding something—"

"I am relaxing. I'm—"

"What have you seen?" she asks. "Where have you gone? I mean, if you're out there doing more than just working and living some, then you should have some stories for me."

"I do have stories. I have narrowed down the top three possible social media managers. I finally signed Micah Hanover, and we both know what a pain in the ass he's been. I am in contact with a social media analyst to tell us what we're doing right and wrong and how to appear more appealing to athletes. I have—"

"I'm talking about non-work stuff, Chase. Quit deflecting." She rolls her eyes, then her husband, Hunter, walks by in the background.

"Save me, Hunter," I say and put my own hands around my neck in jest.

"Ha. I'm out of this one," he says and holds his hands up.

"Thanks a lot," I mutter as he laughs.

"Quit changing the subject," Dekker says in her most motherly voice as she crosses her arms over her chest, having to adjust them to her pregnant belly. "Tell me the places and things you've seen."

"I've seen"—Gunner's face flashes through my mind. The way his teeth dug into his bottom lip when he pushed into me. And I fight the laugh that bubbles up out of nowhere—"*Things*."

"Things?" she says, her brow narrowing.

I lose the battle in fighting the smile. "Yes, *things*."

She stares at me across the connection and a mischievous yet knowing smile slowly spreads across her lips. "Things? Meaning a man. You've been there less than a week and you're already seeing someone?" she demands in a harsh whisper, as if I'm going to get in trouble for it. "Who is this unexpected piece of yumminess?"

"Yumminess?" I bark out in laughter. "You really are getting into Mom-Mode with words like that."

"What would you prefer I say? Beefstick?"

"Gross." We laugh and then when it fades, I'm left with my oldest sister staring at me expecting an answer. "He's the bartender at the bar I went into to ask around. His name is Gunner and he's a way better human than I've ever been."

"Meaning?"

"Meaning he's too good-looking for his own good on top of being a really good guy."

"That's a lot of 'goods' in one sentence."

"He volunteers his time with kids. Supposedly a decorated war hero."

"He said this or—"

"Another person said it. Gunner plays it down."

"Huh," Dekker says. "Oooh, I'm picturing nice muscles, a tattooed sleeve on one arm, and hair falling into his eyes as he broods at you across the bar."

"Or when he's hovering above me," I deadpan and then all but die at the transformation in her expression.

"What? *Wait.* You *have* slept with him? I was joking before." She moves at lightning speed and shuts the bedroom door just as Hunter comes walking in, eyebrows raised, wanting to hear the juicy stuff. "This is sister talk," Dekker says and puts a hand on his chest, pushing him out the door. When she sits back down, she has a huge grin on her face. "So tell me everything."

It's times like these that I *do* love having sisters. It's like having three best friends who love you unconditionally—good and bad.

Now to have some fun with her. "I've decided to volunteer while I'm here."

"Hold up. I didn't just kick Hunter out so that I could hear about you doing something decent. You don't do decent. You do calculated. You do things that elevate your status. So don't tell me about you being decent when I want to hear about you being dirty."

I burst out laughing. "That's cruel."

"And the truth." She waves her hand at me. "So, dish."

"It's connected. I promise," I explain and she levels me with a glare. "Gunner volunteers as a mentor at a sports program for kids who've lost their parents in combat. He asked me if I wanted to help with the registration for the sports league. I agreed. No big deal. It might be fun."

"Did you just say being with kids might be fun?" she teases, knowing damn well I've yet to decide if I actually want kids or not.

"No, what I said was I'm volunteering because *one,* it will make me feel good. *Two, Gunner.* Need I say more? And three, maybe it will get me closer to finding this Ryan guy."

"I always know when you count out your lists like that, that you're serious."

"You're being annoying," I groan.

"I know. It's fun." She grins. "I'm just . . . impressed is all."

"Aren't you the one who gave me the goal to find a cause—"

"That was Lennox who told you to find a cause. I told you to find some dates."

"See? I killed two birds with one stone and nailed both."

"Of course you did," she says with a shake of her head. "*Only you.*"

"I have to go now."

"Wait."

"*What?*"

"You never gave me the down and dirty details."

I bite my bottom lip as I contemplate what to say. For a woman who's never shy talking about sex, for some reason this time, I am. "Let's just say that I'm anxiously awaiting my first chance for more."

Dekker mock shivers and grins. "You go, girl . . . but uh, what happens when you find the letter guy and you have to leave Netflix town?"

"Netflix town?"

"Brex told me the name but we both agree it sounds like a town on a sappy Netflix romance show."

"You two are ridiculous."

"What happens, Chase?"

"Nothing happens. I've been upfront with him. He knows I'm only here temporarily. Besides, you know me, I'm never with a guy that long."

"Uh-huh."

"Stop it."

"*One,* you're volunteering with him," she mocks. "*Two,* he's a hot bartender and hero. *Three,* you just said you can't wait to have deliciously hot monkey sex with him again."

"Hot, monkey sex? *Jesus!*"

"You know exactly the kind I'm talking about." She mock shivers with a grin so wide I'm surprised her cheeks aren't cracking. "Sounds to me like little Chase-y might be getting an affinity for Hot Bartender Boy."

"An affinity. *Not love*. Stop implying shit that's asinine."

"So you say now. Check back with me in a few weeks when it's time for you to come home."

"I have too many things to tick off my list before love will ever be written down to achieve."

"That's proof you're looking at it all wrong. Love isn't something you set out to achieve. It's something that happens unexpectedly."

"For you, maybe. We're all built differently."

But even when we hang up, I hate that her words continue to hover in my mind.

Love isn't something you set out to achieve. It's something that happens unexpectedly.

And even more? I hate the feeling of dread that hits me because eventually, I *will* have to say goodbye to Gunner.

"That's the crazy talking," I mumble to the empty hotel room.

Chapter FIFTEEN

Chase

When I walk up to FU-Bar at nine o'clock that night, I tell myself it's to prove that I'm wrong. That Dekker's wrong.

That my want to see Gunner when I left him, and The Center, behind less than six hours ago is strictly because I crave his physicality again.

I've sat in my hotel room for the past few hours questioning everything when I don't ever question myself. I've told myself that at home, I'm normally going a million miles per hour, and therefore the desire to spend more time with someone isn't there because I'm too busy, too scheduled. And on the odd occasion that I do have downtime, I can call up my two close girlfriends and go out for drinks to let loose for a few hours.

But while I'm in Destiny Falls, everything is different. I have less work, more free time, and no friends to call that are close by.

Is that why I'm suddenly craving some company?

Or is it simply about the sex with Gunner? Our chemistry? About me being a woman with needs and Gunner being a man who very easily met and satisfied those needs?

As I take a deep breath and pull on the door, I'm well aware that all of that is a total bullshit lie.

Heads turn when I walk in, simply because I'm a lone female in a target-rich environment. Normally I'd notice and take stock of the opportunities available, but tonight there's only one man I'm looking at when I meander through the tables.

Gunner is busy, looking over to Aubrey as he finishes mixing some drinks. But when she walks away, he glances up and sees me. His smile is slow and sexy as he wipes his hand on the towel tucked in his waist before walking toward the end of the bar.

"Hi. What are you doing here?"

"I wanted a drink, some dinner, and some company and I thought to myself, I know a man who can give me all three." I slide onto a barstool that Nix has somehow procured for me at the more than packed bar.

"Oh really?" Gunner asks. "And who might be able to provide that for you?"

I smirk and tease, "*Nix*."

The crowd around me barks out laughs as Nix sits up a little straighter and dusts off his shoulders. "I knew you couldn't resist me," he says as Gunner playfully takes his beer away. "Hey!"

"You steal my girl, you lose the beer," Gunner teases.

"Don't I get a kiss?" Nix continues the charade.

"Nah, kissing is overrated," I murmur, earning a lift of one eyebrow from Gunner.

"What was that?" Gunner asks.

"I said kissing is overrated." Words I used to think were true until Gunner. Until his kisses that feel like a slow, sweet seduction, pulling you in, dragging you under, becoming a temptation like I've never known.

But I can't say that out loud.

It's hard even to admit it to myself.

So instead, I lift my chin, with a grin on my lips, and challenge Gunner.

"I'm thinking I should be offended since it's my kiss that was last on your lips," Gunner says as he comes out from behind the bar and approaches me.

There's a devious look in his eyes that makes my insides twist deliciously. I stay facing the bar and yelp when Gunner spins my chair around unexpectedly and makes a damn fine show of kissing me properly.

A cheer goes up all around us as he steps between my thighs, fists a hand in my hair, and mercilessly kisses me. For the briefest of moments, it's just him and me and this incredible kiss.

But the noise fades back in, the kiss ends, and I'm left staring at a man who has a lopsided grin and a semi-hard-on pressing between my thighs.

Glad to know he feels the same way.

He leans down to whisper in my ear. "Kissing is most definitely not overrated."

"Noted," I murmur and then smile as he steps back behind the bar.

Taking a deep breath, I turn myself back around to face the bar to find Gunner sliding a gin and tonic in front of me with the cutest smirk on his face. Almost as if he can't believe he just did that. Almost as though he's surprised that *I* made him do that.

But it's all Gunner. He watches. He listens. He acts.

And I'm one hundred percent here for it.

"It seems you left quite an impression on him," Nix says from his seat beside me.

"I'm not sure if that's a good thing or a bad thing," I say, totally aware I now have the attention of more people than I intended when I walked in here.

"It's a good thing. Definitely a good thing," he murmurs and takes a sip of his beer.

"How do you know Gunner?" I ask Nix.

"We served together."

"Here? On deployment? Where?" I ask, trying to learn as much as I can about the man who I can't seem to take my eyes off.

"Both." He meets Gunner's curious stare, and I notice a slight nod exchanged between them, almost as if Gunner is telling him it's okay to tell me more. "I know Gunner is a hero because I was there. I was one of the ones he saved that day."

"I had no idea. I don't even know what to say," I say below the noise of the bar. And I truly don't. Gunner is so quick to squash any talk about heroics that I kind of assumed the comment Nix made that first night was more a bravado thing. Him saying it so I might like his buddy more.

But when I look at his face and see the somberness there, the admiration, I realize that Nix wasn't simply being his friend's wingman. He was serious.

"Nothing to say other than I wouldn't be sitting here if it weren't for that man right there."

"Do you mind telling me what happened or is that something I should ask him?"

"You can ask all you want, but Gunner won't tell you shit. He's not that kind of guy despite the fact that the events of that day still haunt him every night when he sleeps as they do me."

"I'm sorry." I don't know what else to say.

"There's no need to be. We signed up for it." His chuckle is self-deprecating, almost resigned, before he falls quiet for a beat as we both smile when Gunner's laugh sounds out across the bar.

"But still . . ."

"But still," he repeats and snorts. "We were on routine rounds at the base of the Tora Bora mountains. We had some intel about one of the towns along the way. They were making IEDs or some shit," he says as if he doesn't remember. I know for damn sure he probably remembers every little detail. "Anyway, we went to suss out if the informant was telling the truth and walked right into an ambush. It was a firefight like we'd never seen before, coming at us from every damn direction." Nix shudders and takes another sip of his beer.

"I can't even imagine," I say, thinking how surreal it is to hear about something you see in movies and know it happened in real life to Nix and Gunner.

"We were in a bad way. Things were FUBAR," he says and tips his beer to the neon sign of the term on the other side of the room. "There were ten of us that went in and one by one we were falling. We had no cover, no help, and air support was twenty minutes out when we had only about five minutes left of ammo. It was fucking terrifying. Somehow Gunner was able to get back to one of the Humvees. It was one of the only ones we had with armor on it and the fucking guy literally starts it up and plows right through the building where some of the enemies were taking cover. He came in like a goddamn superhero."

"I can hear you, Nix," Gunner warns as he walks past to grab some more beer glasses before moving back to the other end of the bar where I think he's purposely keeping to.

"He can threaten me all he wants, but it's not going to work." Nix gives him the bird and a grin. "You need to know that he barreled through that building and back into the firefight he'd escaped from. He was like a madman, running around without us being able to lay down cover for him. We were all hit in some way or another and he did everything he could to pull us, carry us, and shove us into the Humvee so he could get us out of there to a location where we could defend ourselves until air support came. It was like he was a different person, Chase. He came in shouting orders to us left and right, trying to take out the enemy when he could, and trying to save us all at the same time. He did that three times. Three times he pulled that Humvee out and then plowed back into the village to extricate and save us. *Three fucking times* before . . ." Nix gives a shake of his head and then clears his throat as emotion I didn't expect overwhelms him.

"Thank you for telling me this much. I didn't mean to make you—"

"The Humvee, on the way out the third time . . . it hit an IED. I have no fucking clue how he didn't hit any before that considering the whole goddamn village was surrounded by them—something we found out after the fact. But he found one on the third and final way out." He shakes his head. "I remember seeing it explode. How parts, how *everything*—just blasted into the air. It was about that time that the air support arrived, so we had to take fucking cover from them hitting the town. We didn't know if Gunny or the other two guys he'd rescued were alive or dying or anything."

I reach out and squeeze Nix's hand. I don't know him other than the two times I've met him, but the emotion that swells in his voice tells me all I need to know about the man beside me. Gunner may be a hero in Nixon's eyes, but Nix was also in that firefight. He's a hero too.

They both made sacrifices. Something the men and women sitting around me possibly have too.

Silent heroes.

Unsung.

Humble.

No wonder they congregate here at a bar where others understand them. No wonder they're inseparable. No wonder I—

"He was alive. *Barely*. Shrapnel had hit him everywhere. He was a goddamn mess while the other two he had tried to bring to safety didn't make it."

"Jesus." I take a sip of my drink as I stare at Gunner laughing at the other end of the bar. I think of the scars on his chest. Of the physical damage to his body that probably has nothing on the psychological damage. And yet there he is, lighting up the whole damn room with his infectious smile and quick-witted sense of humor. "No wonder you two are like brothers."

"There's definitely a bond between us that I can't really put words to."

"Are you part owner of this place?" I ask.

His smile is slight. His eyes somber. "He opened it in their memory. The men he wasn't able to save. We all pitched in with the start-up money, but he's since paid us all back. He said he had to have a clear conscience with his debts before he started sending a percentage of the profits every month to the families of those who didn't make it."

"Wait. What?" I ask, wanting to make sure I heard him correctly. But I did. I know I did and the slight lift of his chin toward Gunner affirms it.

"Yep. You heard right. He busts his ass day in and day out and then sends money to the wives of the men he didn't save, because it eats at him that much."

"I don't even know what to say," I sputter.

"I know what you mean." He chuckles and lifts his empty beer in the direction of Gunner when he looks our way. "It's hard to believe men as good as him really exist."

"It is," I say quietly as Gunner makes his way toward us, sliding tips off the bar and putting them into a jar behind the table as he goes.

"Are you two going to cause me trouble?" he asks and grins when he reaches us.

"Always," I say and smile, wanting to stare at him, study him, a little longer than is normal.

"Then I'll stay over there." He laughs and hooks a thumb over his shoulder. "I have two burgers coming up for you guys. Is that okay?"

"Yes. Sure. Thank you. I didn't expect—"

"You said you wanted food, drinks, and company. You found the two"—he motions to Nix and Nix just smirks—"so I figured the least I could do was help your date along with the third."

"Funny," I say and roll my eyes as Nix belts out a laugh, slapping the counter.

"Dare I ask what the two of you are talking about down here?" he asks as he takes a sip of a beer himself.

"I told Nix that you were taking me on a date tomorrow and—"

"I am, am I?" he asks, tossing the towel onto his shoulder and crossing his arms as his eyes hold mine.

"Yes. You are," I state matter-of-factly. "And so, I was taking suggestions on what he thinks we should do."

"I know exactly what we *should do,*" Gunner says with a suggestive smirk.

I stand from my seat and motion for him to come closer, leaning across the counter to whisper in his ear. "While I'm all for jumping in, sometimes a little foreplay is appreciated."

Nix laughs and smacks the counter again, drawing attention back on us. "Goddamn, I like her, Gunny."

Gunner twists his lips as he stares at me. "I do too," he says. "So you were asking Nix about the best foreplay, were you?"

"Something like that," I reply.

"I've heard a lot of stories from and about Nix over the years," Gunner says, "so if you're into tipping cows for foreplay, then he's your man."

"Hey. That was low," Nix says but their grins are wide, and the pretzel on the bar that Nix throws at him is batted away with a laugh.

"So is stealing my girl," Gunner says as he flashes me a grin before heading down to where Aubrey is waiting for him with a drink order.

"Fucker," Nix says to his friend's back.

"And yet you still come here regularly to put up with his abuse." It's more of a statement rather than a question. An acknowledgment of how strong their friendship is.

"Always," he says, his voice softening as he looks down to where his thumbs are running over the label on his bottle before meeting my eyes again. "*I was there,* Chase. I was trapped in a corner, out of ammo, shot in the hip, scared to fucking death, and praying he'd be able to save me. He was my only hope. Then I was there trying to use quick clot in his wounds to save him, because the medic was worse off *than* him. I was there at his Medal of Honor ceremony. And I'll always be here for him because without him, five of us wouldn't be here right now."

I stare at this gruff-looking man with a standoffish posture and a sarcastic mouth and see true loyalty and gratitude when he looks at Gunner.

"I would say I understand, but I couldn't possibly know what you guys went through."

"Luckily, few do."

There is a raucous roar over by the pool table where it appears someone just got seriously hustled and everyone else was in on it. We watch the ribbing and laughing, and I get the weirdest sense that everyone in FU-Bar feels like they belong here. Like they all have mutually shared experiences that they can somehow relate to.

And then I wonder why I feel like I belong here when I don't.

But is it because of that man right there? The one whose dark hair has just fallen over his eyes and who is busy making some couple on the other side of the bar laugh.

"May I ask a personal question, Nix?"

"That depends."

"Why are you still in Destiny Falls? I mean, I'm sure you have a family somewhere, so why did you opt to stay here after you were discharged?"

He's quiet for a moment. The sounds of the bar filter in around us. "I think, like Gunner, it's hard to leave this place. To leave behind the families that are still suffering and to let go of the survivor's guilt we still feel."

"I never thought of it that way."

"The war stays in your heart, Chase, long after the uniform comes off." He pauses, and then sighs. "Someday, we'll both leave this town and live outside of it, but for the meantime, this provides a place to heal when we choose to let it." He pushes his beer away to make room for the food we see Aubrey coming out with. "This is my home. These guys are my home. *That man*," he says looking at Gunner, "allowed me to come home."

And there is something about that comment of Nix's that sticks with me. Long after I've eaten my food, had some more laughs over drinks, and fallen a lot more in lust watching Gunner work the bar. He laughs with some, lowers his voice and leans over to talk to others, all while keeping the bar running.

And it sits with me even after Gunner walks me to my car for a quick goodnight kiss before heading back in to work another couple of hours before they close.

These guys are my home. That man allowed me to come home.

Even as I open my hotel room and enter it.

Is that what I'm looking for?

My place?

My home?

Sure, I have my sisters and love them dearly, but haven't they all found *their* own places? Their new homes? The men who have allowed them to make and call it a home?

Is that what they long for me to find?

That person with a shared experience who gets me wholly and completely . . . *and still wants a life with me?*

Chapter SIXTEEN

Gunner

It was a great night.

Unexpectedly busy and the money in the till reflects it.

And I might just be tired enough to get a good night's sleep. That is if I can get Chase out of my head.

She showed up. She showed up and shot the shit with Nix and laughed with the regulars. She didn't freak out that my time was spent more often than not on my customers.

That's a rarity.

When the door to the bar opens, I cringe, realizing I forgot to turn the lock after Aubrey left.

"Sorry. We're closed . . . *Chase?*" I ask when I look up to find her standing in the doorway with a coy smile on her lips.

"I can leave if you're closed," she says and hooks a thumb over her shoulder.

"Don't you dare even think about it," I say as I come out from behind the bar, suddenly nowhere near as tired as I was a few seconds ago. I head straight for her, turn the key in the lock myself, before turning to look at her. "Did anyone ever tell you it isn't safe to go to bars at two in the morning?"

I itch to reach out and touch her. To see if that crackle of tension sparks when I do.

"I wasn't aware that Destiny Falls has a rampant crime problem that I need to be worried about," she says as her eyes dart down to look at my lips before meeting mine again.

"It doesn't."

"Then there's no need to be worried."

"True." I reach out and tuck a piece of hair behind her ear. The hitch of her breath tells me she's fighting the same need I am. The same craving. "What are you doing here?" *Fuck, I am so damn glad that she is.*

"I told myself that I needed to stay away from you." Her voice is barely a whisper.

"Why would you do a crazy thing like that?" I place my hands on either side of her neck so she's forced to look up at me.

"Because I can't stop thinking about you."

The pressure that had suddenly built in my chest eases. I offer a soft smile. "That makes two of us."

"What I'm trying to say is that this isn't normal for me. Coming back here after I already saw you tonight simply because I can't stop thinking about you." She gives a shake of her head as if she's frustrated. As if, even she doesn't understand why she's feeling how she feels. "I typically don't *want* people. I want the sex and pleasure they give but am not a big fan of doing more than the cursory time with the people who help provide it. Is that cold? Yes. Do I own it? Always."

"Your honesty is becoming." *And rare.* The woman is fucking incredible. Does she know that? See that? Does she have any idea that *she* is knocking me on my ass just as surprisingly too?

It's sudden and unexpected, but Christ, does it feel so fucking good that I've tried not to question or label or *anything* it. We're just in the beginning of whatever this is and she's already made it known our time is finite . . . so is it so bad to enjoy it while I can? To live in the moment as I've deemed life should be lived? To take the pleasure even though I know the loss will come at some point?

She reaches out and fists a hand in the hem of my shirt and pulls me toward her. "I didn't want to wait until tomorrow to see you, Gunner," she whispers.

"It is tomorrow," I tease, drawing a smile from her.

"Then see? I waited. Now I don't look so desperate."

"If this—*you*—are what desperation looks like, then please don't change a fucking thing."

Desire fires in her eyes as she darts her tongue out to wet her lips. "Good to know."

When she leans forward to kiss me and act on that desire, it takes everything I have to dodge it.

"I thought you said kissing was overrated," I taunt as my hand falls to the small of her back, and I pull her against me. My dick is hard and presses against the softness of her body and the feel of her, the warmth of her, adds a whole complexity to how bad I want to prove her words from earlier tonight incorrect.

Her smile is slow, stuttered, almost as if it takes her a second to see through the rejection and realize my intentions. My name a resigned sigh. "Gunner . . ."

"And that foreplay was essential," I add. I pull her hair back and lace open-mouthed kisses down the exposed line of her neck. Her gasp floats over the music still coming through the speakers of the bar. "Tell me why you're here, Chase," I say softly against her skin.

"I want you. Plain. Simple. *I want this.*" She tugs on my shirt. Her words are labored, and her flesh covered in goosebumps.

I groan at her words. At the pure simplicity and honesty in them. At needing her so fucking much but also wanting to draw it out. Craving the foreplay, the chance to make her beg, and to feel her desperation so I can show her exactly how she makes me feel.

"Turn around," I command. Her eyebrow quirks up as defiance fires in her eyes, moments before submission.

She turns around.

And Christ, it's a beautiful sight. A strong woman who knows what she wants and is trusting me to give it to her.

Her body tenses as I slip my hands beneath the hem of her shirt and slowly slide the fabric up. She lifts her arms and I pull the shirt over her head. I proceed to do the same thing with her shorts.

No words.

Just my hands relaying what I want. What my request is. And as if in perfect sync with my thoughts, she does what I want.

She steps out of her shorts so that she's standing in front of me in a black lacy bra, matching panties, and strappy sandals.

Fucking perfection.

"Gunner," she says and tries to turn around, but is met with my lips kissing right above the swell of her ass in the middle of her back. My hands grip her hips, and I use my lips and tongue and stubble to taunt and tease the line of her spine. Each open-mouthed kiss a deliberate action. Slow. Methodical. Teasing.

Torture for me on all levels.

My fingers undo the clasp of her bra as my teeth scrape over the top of her shoulder. Her back arches and her head falls to my shoulder, as my hands slide to cup her breasts. To play with her nipples as my lips find the nape of her neck, then the underside of her ear.

She speaks in moans, in gasps, in incoherent murmurs. In sounds that spur me on just as much as they turn me on.

In motions—the bow of her back, the press of her ass into me, the shifting of her feet as I tease her every sense and create every sensation.

My hands slide down her abdomen and dip beneath the waistband of her panties. They feather over her mound and then slide between the slickness awaiting me.

It's my groan this time when I find her so fucking wet as she spreads her legs for me. "Please," she moans. My dick throbs against her ass, the need to bury itself to the hilt in that heaven owning my thoughts.

Not yet.

Not fucking yet.

"Turn around." My voice is gruff, edged with the need owning me.

And I leave my one hand right where it is, fingers buried in the heat between her thighs as she turns to face me. Chase looks up at me from beneath desire-heavy lids, her lips parted, her cheeks flush, her eyes glazed.

I lean in as if I'm going to kiss her but divert to her ear. "After I'm done with you, Chase, I assure you that kissing will never seem overrated again."

My lips close over her nipples. First one and then the other. Her hands slide through my hair and tighten with each suck, each lick, each tease. We take a few steps back, my hands pushing down her panties, until the tops of her thighs are against the edge of the pool table.

I step between her legs and lift her up by the hips onto the table, shoving the balls to the other side so I can lay her down. We laugh as they ricochet back and gently hit her, but I don't worry about them.

There's only one thing I'm focused on.

Tasting her.

Pleasuring her.

I begin the same assault on the front of her that I did the line of her spine. Kisses. Licks. Scrapes of stubble. Down her abdomen, to her inner thigh, to the top of her mound.

The scent of her arousal clouds my mind, owns my actions. I put my hands on her knees and push them farther apart to give me better access.

Her moan is goddamn ecstasy as I lick my way down her slit and dip into her molten center. Her hand reaches for my hair again, and I welcome the pain as she pulls on it. Welcome, knowing what I'm doing to her as my tongue slides up and down, as I tease her clit before delving back down again.

She's heaven.

She's hell.

She's the temptation I can't resist and the torture I willingly put myself through, so I can watch her come undone before I get mine.

Her breaths grow shallow and her thighs tense against my shoulders as she comes. Her back arching, her hips writhing, her sex pulsing, my name a badge of success shouted from her lips.

I come up for air from my insatiable need to have my mouth on her and simply watch her come down from her high.

My body begs me to find mine.

But the moment is too much to rush.

She's laid out on the table, hair fanned out against the green of it, her chest heaving, her eyes hazed with lust, and fuck if I've ever seen anything more stunning.

Our eyes meet and there's a moment where we stare at each other. Even as I pull my shirt over my head, the connection remains, as if there's something we're both saying but are afraid to put words to.

She props herself up on her elbows and watches me as I undo my belt then unbutton my pants before shoving them to the floor. She keeps watching me as I jacket up and then run my hand over the length of my aching cock.

"Chase," I whisper as I lean forward.

My lips meet hers. I can't resist the need to kiss her anymore. Our kiss deepens as I take and demand. Fucking hell, the woman demands just as much in return.

And I can't hold back. With her taste on my tongue and her scent owning my thoughts, I bury myself inside her without a second thought.

Our kiss stops.

Our muscles tense.

Our bodies freeze.

Her moan owns the room as she adjusts her hips around me.

The world stops for the briefest of moments, so that the only sound is the soft hum of music from the speakers above.

Then I begin to move at a frenzied, desperate pace, unable to get enough of her. Her tongue. Her lips. Her hands. Her skin. Her pussy.

This.

Just this.

Her.

Just her.

It's all I can focus on as one of my hands holds the back of her neck and the other a cheek of her ass as we move together on the edge of the pool table.

My beginning is her end.

My exhale becomes her next inhale.

Her tightening around me is my goddamn endgame.

What the fuck is happening to me?

Chapter SEVENTEEN

Chase

Well, that definitely backfired.

It's my first thought as I wake up in my hotel room and come face to face with Gunner, sound asleep on the pillow beside me.

I went back to the bar to prove to myself that this thing with Gunner was just sex. Just physical. And now I feel more tangled in him than the sheets wrapped around our legs.

But how can I not?

And why should I even try to deny whatever this twisty, turny, fluttery feeling I have is when I wake up to find him still warming the sheets beside me?

That's not normal for me.

This is not normal.

And yet, I can't take my eyes off him nor deny the urge and desire to reach out and touch his face or the scars on his chest. To feel the bumps and ridges that mar him as I attempt to fathom the devastation he's seen, and the unspeakable trauma he's lived through.

And it just goes to show that you never really know somebody, because all I've seen from Gunner is smiles and sweet charm. And up until last night and what Nix told me, I never would've known that there was turmoil beneath the surface. That Gunner struggles in silence and private from the things he's experienced and seen.

But isn't that like most people? Everyone has things they hide from the world. The darkness that calls to them when it's quiet and lonely.

Is that why he keeps so busy? To keep the demons at bay?

Is that why *I* keep so busy? To keep my demons at bay?

I scoot closer and press a kiss to his chest, to his shoulder, and then snuggle into him. He reacts reflexively, pulling me against him with a murmured good morning before stilling when I press another kiss to his scars.

And then another.

His chest hitches as he holds his breath, but I press my hand against him so he knows I feel them—the ugly red ridges marring its surface.

"Chase," he murmurs.

"These don't scare me." Another kiss pressed against his tensed pec. "They are a part of you and they don't scare me."

I'm not sure how long we lie there like that, with him holding me close and my hands and cheek resting against the parts of him I can only imagine still remain a source of turmoil, but it's quite a while. Enough time for me to start overthinking and questioning what the hell I'm doing, lying in a bed with a man cuddling when I don't cuddle—like ever—and when I have a mile-long list of shit to do.

And it also makes me realize why I never stop, pause, *think*. Because when I do that, I see that although no one has ever seen my scars, they're there. Gunner's physical scars are fresh. And in some respects, his inner scars are too. But the loss of his dad so many years ago is an older scar that has contributed to who he is today.

As do yours. But I won't let anyone see those.

Because you live as if they don't exist.

As if they haven't contributed to who you are today.

As if they will never see the light, find the place to heal.

"You know it's ridiculous that you're staying here, right?" he finally says to break the silence bathing us, almost as if he knows I'm silently starting to freak out.

"Not this again." I laugh, thinking back to when he followed me back "home" last night to find out that my "home" was, in fact, the hotel.

"Yes, this again." He presses a kiss to the crown of my head and chuckles. "I told you I have a perfectly acceptable extra bedroom at my place that's yours if you want it."

"And I believe I told you that there is no way I'm moving in with you."

His exasperated sigh fills the hotel room, as does the scrape of his stubble when he runs his hand over his face in frustration. "You wouldn't be moving in with me. I . . . shit, I've roomed with a bunch of different characters in my time in the service. I'm looking at it as merely providing you a place to stay that's not the local hotel."

I lean back and meet his eyes. "I thank you for the offer. I do." I run a finger down the line of his chest. "But you told me you understand my independence and so—"

"Independence and practicality are two completely separate things."

"I barely even know you, Gunner. I mean—"

"You know the best parts of me though." He grins and wiggles his hips against me.

"I do believe I'm very partial to those best parts." I laugh and roll over on top of him, taking the welcome change in topic. I push myself up to a seated position and straddle him. He grows hard beneath me, and it makes it very difficult to concentrate on him and this discussion and why exactly I'm saying no.

"I'm not complaining one bit." He adjusts his hips up so his hardness grinds perfectly against my softness.

"From now on, everything I want from you, I'm going to tell you it's overrated so that you kill me slowly with it."

"Is that so?"

"Mm-hmm." I sink my teeth into my bottom lip and nod as I take him in: his dark hair against the white pillow; his tanned, sculpted skin; the deep brown of his eyes that I keep telling myself not to get lost in.

But it's impossible. I seem to be getting swallowed whole by everything he is, and I'm at a complete loss over what to do or how I feel about it.

"Are you telling me that last night I killed you slowly?" he asks with a cocky, lopsided grin, while I relive every glorious second in my mind.

"Perhaps," I tease and lean over to press a kiss to his lips.

"Hey, Chase?" Gunner asks in between kisses as his hands find my hips and grab them.

"Sex."

"Sex?" I laugh.

"It's completely overrated," he grumbles, as I lift up and he positions himself at my entrance.

"I see what you did there." I sink down onto him. Inch by glorious inch.

"What are you going to do about it?" he moans.

"I guess it's up to me to show you otherwise."

I rock my hips over him. His hands find my waist and guide me.

Our eyes hold.

Sure, we're currently having sex—have had sex—but there's intimacy to be said about this.

To it being broad daylight, where I'm sitting atop him and all his scars are on display.

And maybe, just maybe, some of my scars are trying to be seen too.

Chapter EIGHTEEN

Chase

"I DON'T NEED A TOUR GUIDE," I SAY, LOOKING AT WHERE GUNNER IS standing, shoulder resting against the doorjamb of my hotel room door.

"I know, but you told Nix we were going on a date today so the last thing I want to do is stand you up on a date I never even asked you out on."

"I didn't mean it."

A smile toys at the corner of his lips. "Yes, you did." He takes a step closer, smelling of soap and deodorant and everything desirable that is Gunner.

When he left earlier after our morning romp, the last thing I expected was for him to return for the date I joked about last night.

And now he's here, looking like *that*, and all the work I have stacked on my desk—the work I desperately *need* to do—can suddenly be dealt with later.

"I have work to do," I say.

"Ah, yes. The daunting thesis from our brilliant graduate student. New York University has a genius in their midst." He gives me a half-cocked smirk that makes me want to snuggle in against him as a means to soothe the lie. "Should I call you Dr. Kincade, then?"

"No. Please, no," I sputter, my cheeks heating and head shaking. I never realized until this moment how ridiculous the thought of me being a psych major was.

The last thing I like to do is to delve into my own mind and issues, let alone someone else's.

"Come play hooky with me."

"I have work to do," I repeat half-heartedly.

"It'll be there later." He takes a step toward me.

"You don't have anything with the boys today? The bar?"

"No, to the boys. Yes, to the bar." He shrugs. "So, see? We'll spend our day together and then we can have that space—that *Chase doesn't do people time*—tonight."

"You have this all planned out, don't you?"

"Indeed, I do." His smile is like a little boy's as he steps up to me. "Don't I get brownie points?"

"I think you've already been cashing in your brownie points."

"Brownie points are overrated," he says and then smothers my laugh with a kiss.

"I should have warned you that I'm a horrific painter," I say, looking across the table between easels at Gunner.

"That makes two of us. I mean, she's talking about fan brushes and techniques, and I'm over here just hoping that my painting will look better than a kindergartener's."

Paint a portrait of your date or something that you associate with your date.

That was our instruction when Gunner and I took seats across from each other amidst ten other couples here at *Brushes 'N' Booze*. It's a modern barn on the outskirts of town, with enormous canvases lining its walls. They are bright and colorful—animals, flowers, everyday items—and they make the place feel artsy.

Dotted around the floorspace are tables where two easels and chairs sit across from each other. The date table, as our host, Mimi, called them.

"So we'll get started in a moment," Mimi says in her way too cheerful voice and adjusts her red horn-rimmed glasses. Her funky, personal style definitely reflects in the atmosphere she's created here. "But I wanted to run over the gist of our event. It's called speed painting with a little *Brushes 'N' Booze* spin on it. You have an hour to finish your painting."

"It's timed?" Gunner laughs out incredulously, and the sound makes me feel so much more at ease knowing he's already struggling like I am.

"This was your idea." I point my paintbrush at him and smile.

"And in the theme of date night," Mimi continues, "we'll stop every five minutes for a random trivia question for you to answer about yourself to allow your date to get to know a little more about you."

Both our eyes widen at one another and we snicker. Neither of us knew about this component of the event when we decided to attend.

"Could be interesting," I say with a playful lift of my wine glass.

"Let's not hope they don't play truth or dare," he says, "or I'm in a whole lotta trouble."

"Are your truths that damning?"

He smirks and that has my insides firing awake—but it's not as if they aren't already. I mean, look at him.

"And now, ladies and gentlemen, gentlemen and gentlemen, and ladies and ladies, your timer starts . . . now."

"And the pressure is on," I stand and stare at the blank canvas in front of me, a mini panic attack starting over what to paint. It doesn't help that our easels are staggered so that every time I look at the edge of it, Gunner is in the background, his good looks distracting me.

And yet, I have to paint him or something that reminds me of him, when my painting abilities are subpar to my LEGO-building abilities.

"The first five minutes are up, so it's time for a date detail. Tell your date the one pet peeve you have. Like the one thing they could do that would annoy you."

"Ladies first," Gunner says with narrowed eyes as he studies me.

"Seriously?" I ask, suddenly hating being put on the spot.

"I'll go first next time," he says and continues to work on what he's painting of me. "We'll switch." He darts his eyes my way. "So what's yours?"

"There are so many to choose from." I laugh and realize so far Gunner hasn't done any of them. "I'll go with slurping soup or the milk when someone eats cereal. The sounds drive me absolutely batty."

"Make note to self," Gunner says, as he mock writes down a note.

"And yours? What's your pet peeve?"

His eyes meet mine and amusement sparkles in them. "I get absolutely annoyed, *furious,* when someone cooks naked with just an apron and heels on."

"What?" I laugh as I stare at his grin.

"I mean, it's so unsanitary and most times the meal never ends up getting made because . . . well, for obvious reasons."

"Obvious reasons?" I ask and am on the receiving end of a devilish smile for an answer. "And do you get annoyed with this behavior often?"

"No, but I can simply imagine how aggravating it would be to stand by and watch this happen. Bending over to put a roast in the oven distracts the meal recipient from actually focusing on the meal to be had."

I erupt in laughter and don't care that everyone turns our way. "Such a travesty, when I'm sure *he* ends up enjoying or eating a whole different type of meal entirely."

"It's a travesty that should absolutely not be done."

I laugh as we stare at each other, flirting with our eyes, before turning back to our paintings. My painting, I might add, that will confuse anyone in the room but will make Gunner laugh.

Within what feels like seconds the bell rings again, and the chatter quiets as Mimi takes her "stage" again. "Okay, next question. The first time you met the person sitting across from you, what one thing attracted you to them?"

I turn from looking at Mimi to Gunner and wish I could frame the look he's giving me forever. There's quiet intensity laced with amused adoration, and I don't think I've ever felt more seen in my life.

"That's easy," he says. "Your confidence. The sound of your laugh. The way you gave it right back to me . . . and then I got to know you, and it was all of those things and then some."

"Thank you." I'm not one hundred percent certain why tears burn my eyes, but I pretend they're not there and smile softly at him. "For me it was your kindness, your smile, your biceps"—I shrug unapologetically—" and the way you looked at me."

"How did I look at you?" he asks.

"Like I was the only woman in the room."

His smile softens as does his expression, before he gives a shy lift of his shoulders and turns back to his easel.

I stare at my canvas for a minute but swear I don't see a single brushstroke I've made. I'm too busy thinking of Gunner and how in this short amount of time he's become so important to me.

. . . and then I got to know you, and it was all of those things and then some. And part of that has to do with his ability to win me over with his kindness. *Genuineness.*

Right after that comes my typical refrain—the one that says I'm too busy for him, for whatever this is—but this time I push it away. Maybe Kelly is right. Maybe I need to step back from the stress and endless lists and simply enjoy myself for a bit.

Enjoy Gunner.

"I'm just warning you," I say from behind my canvas, "this is absolutely horrible."

"And I think you're too hard on yourself, but I'm guessing that's a normal thing for you."

"Whatever."

"I'm serious. For some reason, I can't picture you as a graduate student. Instead, I feel like you're someone who should be negotiating huge deals while wearing a sexy power suit in a high-rise somewhere in Manhattan."

I'm glad he can't see my face, because how in the world can he have me so well pegged? How can he sense the real me hidden beneath?

"Maybe someday," I murmur.

And before I can get out of my funk over the lie I'm telling him, Mimi comes back with another one of her questions. "Next up, tell your date what you wanted to be when you grew up."

"A veterinarian," I say.

"Didn't all little girls?" he asks. "Me? I wanted to be a professional baseball player."

"You did?" I ask.

"Didn't all little boys?" he counters.

"True. Speaking of which, I've been meaning to ask you if you know—"

"Oh my God. Are you serious?" echoes loudly around the barn, pulling everyone's attention to the shrill, "Yes. Of course," that follows.

When I stand to look, the couple on the opposite side of the barn from us has seemingly—by the looks of her jumping into his arms and the ring box clutched in his hand—just become engaged. The room erupts into applause and I can just make out the canvas he'd held out where he painted "Will you marry me?"

There are a few tears and kisses and then more kisses shared between the couple, followed by a picture being taken, before we all settle back at our tables.

"All the poor guys in here are probably sweating bullets that their date is hoping for the same thing now," I say, and Gunner laughs.

"That's so true. Look at the guy in the blue shirt over there." He lifts his chin to direct my eyes. "He keeps yanking on his collar and guzzling his wine."

I snort out a laugh when blue-shirt guy does just that. You can tell the guy is completely uncomfortable.

"Well, that was more than exciting, wasn't it? It was our first *Brushes 'N' Booze* engagement, and we couldn't be more thrilled. Now onto the rest of you getting to know each other so maybe you can be as lucky. Let's get to our next question. Tell the person you're lucky enough to be here with tonight the one thing that is a deal-breaker for you. It can be a trait, a situation, a something, but it's the *one thing* that is irredeemable for you in a relationship."

"You first," Gunner says, leaning back and taking a sip of wine.

I twist my lips and stare at him for a beat. "Being disrespected," I say, earning a nod and lift of his eyebrows in response. "And you?"

"Deception," he says without hesitation. "There's nothing worse than being lied to and finding out that you were."

My tongue suddenly feels thick in my mouth as I try to swallow around it and not look guilty.

Because I am guilty.

I am lying to him.

I am *deceiving* him.

And at this point I'm too wrapped up in this lie to come clean. Hell, I came up with it on the fly, while in a bar and while flirting with one *very hot* bartender.

It wasn't said as a means to deceive. My own thought contradicts itself when it comes to the definition of the word *lie*.

Have I had ample time to correct said lie? *Yes*.

But does Gunner's answer apply to me? Sure, but I didn't anticipate this—dates and laughter and looking forward to the time I'm with him while being bummed when I'm not. But is his deal-breaker only related to *relationships* and not friends who enjoy benefits too? Which is what we are, aren't we? *Temporary. Even though it*—everything—*is so good with him.*

Your justification sucks, Chase.

And yet I cling to it, because it's so much more appealing than the rock and a hard place I find myself in, considering I hate deception as well.

Simply put, I need to figure out a way to tell him. To assure him that I hadn't known we'd be more than one night when I told him the lie . . .

Luckily the next few questions are easy and more lighthearted. Gunner has me laughing as we navigate through questions about how the toilet paper should be out on the roll (he agreed with me that it should go over the top), what the best time of day is (he preferred sunset and I preferred sunrise), favorite color (I said orange and he said green), and how long do you wait until you refill your gas tank (he was when the light comes on while I said the minute it hits a quarter of a tank).

"And lastly," Mimi says, "while you use the last ten minutes of your time to finish your paintings, tell your date the one thing you fear the most they might learn about you."

"Christ," a man mutters behind me, clearly fed up with a date that now suddenly feels like a therapy session.

Gunner hears him and stifles a laugh as our gazes meet. "My turn?" he asks and I nod as concern etches the lines of his face. "I fear that you might learn I'm not as good of a person as you think I am."

"Gunner, that's the most ridiculous thing I've ever heard. I mean, look how concerned you are for poor women everywhere who cook naked. And—"

He bursts out laughing, and I'm so glad I can lighten the moment with humor, because what he just said is asinine and yet, I know he probably truly believes what he said.

Just like I do with what I'm about to say.

"And I'm afraid if you knew me in my normal life that you wouldn't like the person I am there."

Gunner stops mid stroke of his paintbrush and locks eyes with me. I've said a lot of real things to him, but I don't think I've ever been more honest than right now.

"Why would you say that?" he asks, head angling to the side, eyes searching mine as I shrug like a little kid afraid to answer.

Tell him the truth, Chase.

The phrase ghosts through my mind, but I can't find it within me to ruin the evening—to potentially damage *this*—because there is something between us.

I shrug, unable to find the words I need to use, unable to bring myself to hurt him . . . or rather too selfish to risk losing him.

"Hey," he says. He lifts from his seat so he can lean across the table and press his lips to mine. "We're all different people sometimes." Another press of his lips. "Sometimes it's easier to be who you really are when you step outside of your daily grind and everything there holding you in its normal place."

He leans back and holds my gaze as I just nod, unable to agree with him, and luckily saved by the buzzer Mimi has on her table telling us time is up.

"Ladies and gentlemen, it's now time to reveal to your date their portrait or the image you've painted that reminds you of them. Deep breath. And . . . show them!"

Chapter NINETEEN

Gunner

"You actually snorted so loud that everyone turned and looked at us," Chase says as she steps a few feet away, turning to face me as she walks backward, that coy smile on her lips.

"You painted me an apple pie." I can't even say it without laughing.

"An ooey-gooey, hot, and juicy apple pie at that." She curtsies. "You might not have been able to see those fine details, but I assure you they were there in spirit."

I all but fell out of my chair when she turned her portrait around at the studio. I definitely snorted and was more than glad I'd swallowed my drink of wine before she did, because we both burst out in laughter.

"It's the best. I'll cherish it forever," I say. "Mine is nowhere near as witty as yours is."

"Red Converse in a field of white daisies. I'm more than impressed with your painting skills," she says. "And the fact that you incorporated the rest of our date in it." She motions to the field of wild daisies that blanket both sides of the path we're on.

"I'm a much better painter than I am LEGO builder."

"I, for one, love it and know exactly where it's going to go on my shelf at home."

Home.

The word rings louder than the laughter with which she said it, because it's a stark reminder that whatever this is between us has a muddled expiration date.

Is that why I'm so free to be myself with her? To say the things I mean and want when normally I'd hold back and be more guarded? I live by the motto of live each day like you're dying and yet, I've never been this open or real with the women I've dated. I've protected myself and held them at arm's length. With Chase? Christ, with Chase, I invited her to stay at my place while she's in town. To move in with me temporarily.

The question is why?

I look around the path we're walking on. At the calm of the lake in front of us with the thunder clouds above us. The ones that litter the sky with spaces in between to showcase the pinks and oranges of the setting sun. To the bar on the opposite side of the lake that has lights strung across its patio. Its music is loud and bluesy and carries across the lake so we can hear it loud and clear.

It's gorgeous. It's captivating.

But nothing like the woman before me with a mischievous smile and curious eyes.

I tug on her hand and pull her into me, pressing a kiss to the top of her head.

"This is a good song," she says, swaying her hips, and I give in to the moment and put my hand over her head to spin her.

"That's about as much dancing as this man does," I tease and pull her back into me.

"I'm beginning to think you take me on dates to get me tipsy and take advantage of me."

She looks up at me with those big blue eyes, which do funny things to me, before she spins again and laughs.

"Yep. It's my plan. Get you tipsy so I can watch you wiggle your hips and spin like that in the sunset."

"Aha," she says and holds her finger up. "Thanks to our little trivia tonight, I now know that sunset is your favorite time of the day."

I nod, watching the streaks of sun shining fire through her hair and want her again so bad it hurts. Whether it be her smile, her laugh, her wit, or her body, I can't seem to fucking get enough of her.

"Tell me about your love life, Gunner."

"What?" I laugh, as she runs a few feet in front of me and picks up a dandelion in the field of daisies.

"You heard me. But wait, shush"—she holds out a hand at me—"I need to make my wish first." And then she proceeds to close her eyes for a beat, a slow smile crawling on her lips, before she takes a huge breath and blows the seeds of the dandelion all over the place. "Okay, now you can spill all the details."

"On one condition," I say, still positive I'll be spilling the details.

"Conditions, huh?" She lifts her eyebrows.

I nod. "What did you wish for?"

She angles her head and stares at me for a beat, her voice soft when she answers. "For more nights like this."

And even if that's not what she wished for, she has me one hundred percent sold and wanting that same exact wish too.

"Do you often self-sabotage good things? I think you asking me to tell you about my love life might be you doing just that," I warn, but my smile says otherwise.

"That bad, huh?" She shrugs. "I'm just curious. You're one of those guys that someone gets ahold of and doesn't let go so . . ."

"I'm thinking that's a compliment?" I ask.

"A huge one."

"Then thank you."

"You're very welcome." She stops walking and looks at me. "I'm more than certain you've broken many hearts over the years—"

"Says the woman I swear is the queen of breaking hearts."

"Don't you dare deflect back on me." She wags her finger at me.

"Haven't we had enough Q&A for one date?"

She throws her head back and laughs before stepping into me and kissing me absolutely senseless. Hands threaded through my hair, tongue teasing with mine, moan falling from her mouth. *The best type of kiss.*

I'm staggered how this woman is a mess of contradictions. She said she likes the sex, but not the person, and yet she's open and free and affectionate like this with me. She claims she's rigid and planned, and then she kisses me like that without any provocation or apparent care in the world.

How is it so easy, so effortless, watching her do this? Having her do this?

Making me fall for her?

That's the crazy talking and yet . . . I can't get her out of my head even when she's standing before me with those discerning, beautiful eyes and disarming smile.

Is it just because there's no pressure for more? She's leaving, and we're living by my motto: live every day like it's your last.

"Come on, Gunner, don't I deserve to know if I'm going to start getting hate mail delivered to my hotel room because I've stolen the local heartthrob?"

I snort. "Hardly."

"I'll start. I date but don't get serious. I'm not keen on getting touchy-feely, talking about myself, or about feelings at all really."

"Why's that?" I ask, curious. She's done all of those things with me.

"Because I don't have time. I have goals to achieve and accomplishments I want to reach by a set time frame, and frankly, relationships are messy and time-consuming and would distract me from doing that." Her eyes meet mine for the first time and I can tell she's almost embarrassed by her admission. "I know it sounds cold and callous and selfish—"

"Not at all."

"But if it's okay for a man to want things out of life, then why isn't it okay for a woman? And why the double standard because—"

"Hey?" I press a kiss to her hand.

"What?" She looks at me, startled.

"There is nothing you need to explain or justify about why you're ambitious. I like that about you."

"Most men say that at first and then when they want more and I tell them I can't give it to them, they become raging assholes."

Who is this woman? At the painting place an hour ago, she was worried I wouldn't like her if I knew the real her, and now she's standing before me with candor most people—*most women*—would struggle to exhibit. I like her even more because of it.

I chuckle and shake my head. "You're amazing," I finally say.

"Why do you say that?"

"Because very few people know themselves well enough to know what they want. You do. You know. And you're unapologetic about wanting it and to me, that's sexy. That's attractive. That makes me want to get to know you better so I can hear about and cheer you on as you chase every single one of those goals."

I mean it with every fiber of my being. Whether or not she'll want me on the sidelines is another story. *She might not want you past these moments.* Which I'm beginning to think is not what I want at all. *I want more.*

Her smile is hesitant, her eyes pooling with tears as she stares at me. "No one's ever said that to me before."

And before I can even respond, the first drops of rain hit. Big, fat blobs of warm water that make quarter-sized splats on the sidewalk. I look around for cover and see a gazebo a hundred feet away the city has put up for picnics.

"C'mon. This way," I say, taking a few steps toward it before looking back to make sure she's coming.

I expect a squeal. The "I don't want my hair to get messed up" or "my clothes to get ruined," but find myself stopped dead in my tracks when I see her.

Chase is standing in the rain. Her flowy skirt and tank top are plastered to her body and her hair is drenched, but her face and hands are raised to the sky, and she has the biggest smile on her lips.

I simply stare at her. I think I fall a little harder with each drop that hits her.

"Chase?"

She shouts but not in the way I expected. Instead, she twirls around with her hands out much like she did on our first date, laughing like a loon.

"Dance with me," she urges.

"Why?" I laugh.

"Because from here on out, every time it rains, you'll stop and think of me."

She's absolutely fucking right. I'll never feel a raindrop again without thinking of this moment, right now. Of her sexy smile and her wild eyes.

"You're crazy, you know that?"

"Yes." She grabs my hand and laughs. "Can you hear it?" she asks and holds her hand to her ear. When I close my eyes, I can barely hear Louis

Armstrong's "*What a Wonderful World*" from the speakers still playing at the bar. "C'mon."

And so we dance.

Body to body, as the warm summer thundershower comes down around us.

With fields of daisies on either side of us.

And something definitely growing between us.

Chapter TWENTY

Chase

THE RINGING OF MY CELL JOLTS ME AWAKE, CAUSING MY LAPTOP TO FALL off my legs and onto the bed. It takes me a second to orient myself and find my phone where it fell between the two pillows I'm currently propped up on.

I look at the screen and sigh in relief that it's not my dad or sisters. Everyone is okay and the worrywart in me can breathe a little easier.

But it is Gunner. The same Gunner who should be at work right now. *Because it's one in the morning.*

"Hey. Is everything okay?"

His masculine chuckle greets my ears and I allow myself to melt into the pillows at its sound.

"I'm good. Everything's okay. I didn't mean to startle you. Were you sleeping?"

"No. Yes. I nodded off while I was working." I have a million questions I want to ask as to why he's calling, but I do something rare for me. I sit back and wait without questioning.

"I'm at work still, so I can't talk long, but uh, I never answered you tonight, and I didn't want you to think I was hiding anything from you."

"Gunner? What are you talking about?" My mind races over all the questions at *Brushes 'N' Booze* that he answered before returning to our slow dance in the warm, summer storm.

"My love life. You asked about it and I didn't answer."

"It's okay. I haven't even thought twice about it." And I haven't, but now with those words, I wonder what is so important that he'd call me at one in the morning to tell me.

"It's not okay. You shared and I didn't." He pauses. "I don't have any skeletons in my closet when it comes to my dating life. Like you, I date, but I've rarely let anyone get close. I had a lot to deal with after everything that happened over there."

"Okay." And I'm sure that *a lot to deal with* is yet another understatement of how grueling it had to have been to recover from such horrific injuries. Mentally and physically.

"And before I start, full disclosure. I may have had a few drinks of liquid courage in order to make this call."

"Liquid courage is sometimes needed," I murmur, suddenly on edge about whatever he wants to divulge.

"As is a phone call, because to say this face to face is harder." He emits a nervous chuckle that is so damn endearing.

"Noted."

After a deep breath, he says, "After . . . *everything,* I needed to heal first. I was also still in the service and promised myself that I wouldn't ever let someone get attached to me, because what if it happened again? I couldn't put someone through that like my brothers who didn't come home did."

"Gunner, you don't have to explain this."

"I want to. Please. I've been sitting here serving drinks all night while feeling like shit that you opened yourself up to me and I didn't do the same for you. Okay?"

"Okay," I whisper.

"So it was my excuse while I was enlisted—I kept the women I dated during that time at a distance because I didn't want to hurt them. It was only after I was discharged, and couldn't use that excuse anymore, that I realized I also couldn't let anyone get close until I dealt with the trauma of it all myself. I had to come to terms with the horrific things I saw and did. While I don't think I ever will, I've learned to live with them. To cope with them. And for the longest while, I knew I had to fix myself before I'd let anyone else get close enough to see the scars on the inside that were way worse than the ones on the outside. I was afraid both sets would scare them away."

A tear slides down my cheek and I shove it away. He just freaking laid bare his soul to me, his vulnerabilities, and I'm more than stunned. Men don't do this. They don't talk like this. They don't open themselves up and explain.

Or at least I've never been with one who has. Then again, maybe I've never cared to listen.

But I care to listen to Gunner. *I want to.*

"*You are amazing*," I whisper his words from earlier back to him, a smile on my lips as another tear slides down my cheek.

"I just needed to explain that to you. To let you know that I dated but didn't get close like you, but for other reasons. You're the first person I've ever shown both sets of scars to, Chase."

"And both sets are beautiful to me."

Gunner goes to speak and his voice breaks, so he stops and clears his throat. But I swear I hear him sniff on the other end of the line, and it makes me desperately want to wrap my arms around him and hug him tight.

It makes me hope that he'll see the white lie I told at the beginning as nothing but a thoughtless, throwaway line I haven't bothered to correct. *And to beg him not to make it into a mountain.*

He knows more about me than any other person. And I don't want him to hate me. To think less of me.

Because I want more of him like this.

More of him.

Period.

"I, uh—need to get back to the bar."

"Yes. Okay," I say. Silence fills the connection, but he doesn't hang up yet. "Liquid courage or not, telephone or in-person . . . thank you for telling me."

"It was good to hear your voice. Night, Chase."

"Night, Gunner."

And when the connection breaks, I sit with my phone clutched in my hand against my chest. Isn't that the classic Gunner I've come to know? Not the man he talks about being and having to heal from, but a man who wants to make sure I don't feel more vulnerable than him. A man who called to answer a question that I haven't thought twice about since I got back to my hotel room.

Who is this man and how is he so, so good?

My dandelion wish from earlier comes back to me, and I smile as I snuggle deeper under my comforter.

For more nights like this.

I thought that true at the time and I hope it more so now.

After our dance in the rain.

After the phone call I just received.

Definitely more nights like this.

Chapter TWENTY-ONE

Gunner

Seven Years Ago

Sal yanks my arm with a force that has my body screaming. *Everywhere.* A 1965 Mustang doesn't exactly have the same safety standards that cars nowadays have—and fuck, does every muscle and bone in my body feel it right now.

It doesn't help that Sal's fists did a number on me after he found out about the accident last night.

"Thank God, no one got hurt. Thank God, you're all right." My mom's repeated words over and over did nothing to calm the situation. Not as he told her to leave the room. Not as he threatened she'd suffer the consequences if she didn't let him *teach me a lesson.* Not as her eyes met mine when he shut the door, closing her out. *Coward.*

And then, I stood there with a shit-eating grin on my face and a fuck-you lift to my chin as he showed me with his fists and insults the "lesson" he wanted me to learn.

He yanks again, and I grit my teeth as he drags me to the corner of the strip mall, where we stand a foot away from the glass storefront so no one can really see us.

"So help me God, boy," Sal sneers. "I'm going to make a man out of you one way or another."

"So what? So I can be just as pathetic as you?" I counter. "I'm not going. Not a chance in hell."

Sure, I crashed his car, but the prick had it coming to him. There's only so much a man can take, so much second-string living a person should put up with—and I, right or wrong, reached my breaking point last night.

"I don't think you're understanding the situation, *son*," he says, like it's a slur. "You drove a car drunk, *underage*, and crashed it. You then fled the scene of an accident—"

"I did not. I called you." And it took everything I had to do just that, but I was scared and hurt and Boone hightailed it out of there on foot so he wouldn't get in trouble, since he'd already had some trouble with the law. "You came to pick me up and pulled the car out of there with your Jeep."

His smile is gloating. "Really?" He feigns innocence. "Because from the way I recall it, and how I'll gladly tell the cops when I file a report, my *troubled* stepson stole my car out of spite. And despite being only twenty, he broke into my liquor cabinet, got drunk, stole money out of my safe—"

"What are you talking about?"

He yanks my arm even harder, his fingers bruising and threatening on my bicep. "And after he stole my liquor, my money, and my car, he decided to go drinking and driving where he crashed my car, injured his passenger, and then fled the scene of the crime after damaging a fence and other personal property."

"You're out of your fucking mind." I say the words, but silent panic is suddenly clawing its way up my throat.

"Am I?" He chuckles. "Officer, I know he's my stepson and I love him dearly, but I think *this time* I need to teach him a lesson. I want to press full charges for all of these infractions, because this time he got off lucky and didn't kill anyone, but next time . . . *and there will be a next time*, it might be a lot worse."

"You wouldn't dare." But the look in Sal's eyes says he would.

"I can be real convincing." Another creepy smile that makes me feel like he's been planning on getting me out of their life for some time now, and I just gave him the opportunity to put it in motion. "I already put in a call last night to my friend at the station. He said you'd be in a good three, four years." He shrugs.

"Fuck this. Fuck you." He's bluffing. He wouldn't. And yet deep down, I know he's not. He's been trying to damage my mother's view of me ever since they got married. And now that my stepbrother Marcus is getting attention for baseball, wouldn't it be easier to get rid of the one who shines brighter?

I feel sick to my stomach and not just because I'm hungover. But because he means it. He means this.

"By the look on your face, you're getting it now." He leans in closer so I can smell the stale smell of alcohol and cigarettes on his breath. "I own a piece of everything you are, Ryan."

"Go to hell."

His chuckle is low and degrading and has me clenching my fists. "What do you think your dad would say if he could see you now? At least he was an honorable man. At least he would have taken responsibility for his actions. At least—"

"You don't know shit about my father." Tears burn and rage fires inside of me. Fuck Sal. Fuck my father for never coming home and leaving me here with this asshole. And fuck my mother for letting this happen. All of it. Every damn part of it.

"What I do know, is that I'm marching you into this recruitment office and making you enlist, or I'm calling the cops and pressing charges. Fuck if I care. But you can spend four years becoming a man serving your country or four years behind bars being Billy-Bob's girlfriend. You decide, *son*."

My heart stops, *fucking dies,* at his words . . . especially when it hits me that we are literally standing ten feet from the army recruitment office's doors.

I was so preoccupied worrying and anticipating another fist, that I didn't think to notice where he parked. Where we were headed.

And now I'm frozen with dread.

"But baseball. What about baseball and—"

His chuckle cuts me off. "Baseball's dead. You have a ton of talent but you lack everything else to be successful. Everyone knows it and that's why no calls have come your way. Do you really think any coach in their right mind is going to sign an asshole law-breaker? A *kid* with no morals who steals from the hand that feeds and houses him? There are a dozen more pitchers just like you with a clean record and halo sitting atop their head. You did this to yourself, Ryan. All you. Blame yourself."

I stare at him and hate him with every fiber of my being. Tears well and it takes everything I have to fight them back.

"Jail or army. You pick."

Anything is better than being here with you.

And isn't that the fucking kicker? I was stuck here going to a junior college, playing for one because we didn't have the money—that and I feared what would happen to my mom if I left—and miraculously, only two years later, the money was *found* to send Marcus to a four-year school.

I should have left.

I shouldn't have cared about protecting my mom when it's clear she's so conditioned it doesn't matter what he does or doesn't do to her, because she'll never leave.

She'll never pick her son over her abusive spouse.

Anything is better than being here with you.

And that's what I keep saying as I stand before the recruitment officer trying not to vomit.

"You sure you're here on of own free will?" the officer asks as he eyes my black eye and the bruises on my skin.

I feel like I'm breathing through water as I stare at him, blinking, silently begging for him to see that I'm not here of my own free will. *I think he knows anyway.* That this is being forced upon me. *That I hate every fucking second of this moment.* That the sadist next to me is killing the dream I've had since I was a little boy.

That this is where dreams die.

Because of him.

Fuck you, Sal.

And I repeat those words every few seconds and after every single step of the process.

The signing on the dotted line.

The swearing in.

The fucking everything.

Fuck you, Sal.

Chapter TWENTY-TWO

Chase

"Easton Wylder? Is that you?" I say into my cell, my smile automatic.

"Sadly it isn't anyone more exciting." His deep baritone comes through the line, and I'm transported back to late-night bar trips with his team, the Austin Aces, after big wins. The man is a sweetheart and then some.

"Someone more exciting, says the man who is always the life of the party."

"Hardly." He snorts.

"How are you? How's that gorgeous wife of yours? And the twins? Tell me *all* the things." I take a seat on the bed, excited to get caught up.

"We're good. All of us. Scout is still busy running her empire. Who knew she'd have sports therapists in twenty different major league organizations? It's insane."

"Not really. That's Scout for you. She's amazing."

"You're not wrong." I love the pride I hear in his voice.

"And the kids? How are those two munchkins?" I ask of his adorable fraternal twins.

"Getting big and growing up faster than I ever thought was possible."

"Who would've thought that one day I'd be talking to Easton Wylder and listening to all the love in his voice when he talks about his wife and kids?" And I mean it. It's insane and awesome at the same time, how finding Scout changed everything about him in all the best of ways.

"Scary, huh?"

"Very."

"You're next."

"Funny. Very funny, Wylder."

"And this is where you change the topic, because you're silently freaking out on the other end of the line." I don't say a word because he's right. So damn right, and I refuse to give him the satisfaction of knowing it. Instead, he bursts out laughing. "See? I was right. You are freaking out. I've been there, Chase. If it makes you feel any better about how much life changes in a short time, it feels like just yesterday I was single and hitting on you."

"Hardly." I snort. "I was too young for you and much wiser than my years to know better than to do anything more than have a couple of shots in a bar with a professional athlete."

"Smart girl, but I think somewhere along the line your sisters missed that memo," he says. Yep, the irony that my three sisters are all attached to athletes.

"Clearly," I deadpan but grin. "And the broadcasting gig is going well? You're happy with how it's all going?"

"Yes, to the first question and yes, I'm still with that bastard of an ex-boyfriend of yours to the second question." He laughs over our inside joke in regards to Finn Sanderson. "No, I'm not transferring agencies."

"One of these days you will," I tease, only partially disappointed I've yet to pull Easton over to KSM. He's a rarity in my business. Genuine, professional, kind, and trouble free. Plus, he's highly sought after—just what I love in a client. "But that's not why I called you."

"What's up?"

I spend the next few minutes explaining about The Center and Gunner and picking his brain on the best way to find them donations or help. How to get them on an MLB team's radar for a possible sponsorship.

"Sounds like a great program. Let me look into some of the resources I use with the foundation Scout and I set up, and see if they can help narrow down the best places for you to look."

"Really? I was merely asking for advice, I didn't expect you to pull any strings or ask a favor of you."

"I know, but it's for kids and under the circumstances, all of us owe them our all given what they've sacrificed for our country."

"You're the best, Easton. Thank you."

"I'll be in touch."

I'm just about to put the phone down when it rings in my hand.

"Kelly!" I say to the empty room when I see his name on the screen, and then answer. "Hi."

"That's a very enthusiastic greeting if ever I heard one," he says through a laugh.

"It was?"

"It was." I can see him nodding. "And you have every right to be pre-emptively enthusiastic, because I found your man."

"You did?" I clap my hands together like a little kid. "Tell me everything."

"I'm sending it over in an email right now. Where to find him. All about his background—"

"You did a full PI background on him without me even asking? Thank you, Kell," I say, scrambling to get my computer and download the email despite the hotel's shitty Wi-Fi service.

"I figured you'd want every *in* on how to find him."

"You know me too well."

"Mind telling me what you plan on doing when you find him?" he asks.

"That's up for debate." I chuckle. "It's a cross between letting him know his dream wasn't baseless. If he still plays, maybe trying to get him a tryout with an MLB team so he can say for posterity's sake that he had a shot. Or it could go a whole different way and we could sponsor a veteran game to thank our heroes. Any and all of them could possibly give KSM some good publicity."

"Ha. That Finn thing is stuck in your craw, isn't it?" He chuckles.

"No. Yes. Whatever." I laugh at my own expense.

"Not sure your guy's going to bite on that if I'm being honest though."

"Why do you say that?"

"War changes a man. On paper he appears completely different now than he was then."

"Meaning?"

"I don't see anywhere that he's played since he returned. He had a small-time record before enlisting and since he was discharged, is squeaky clean. I mean, it's like the guy is a completely different person. Hell, he doesn't even go by his name anymore, just a nickname given to him by his platoon. I mean the guy's a war hero and does a shit ton for the veteran community as a whole on top of owning his own bar."

"Wait. *What did you say?*" My chest suddenly constricts, and I sit up a little straighter.

"The bar part? He owns one. I'm looking up what it's called. Give me one sec because I don't want to get it wrong—"

"FU-Bar," I whisper more to myself than to him.

"Yes. That's it. Why didn't you tell me you found him?"

"I didn't. I don't think. His nickname. What's his nickname, Kell?" At the same time, Kelly's email finishes downloading. I'm met with a picture of Gunner looking back at me. He's a little younger, dressed in desert camo, with a grin on his face and dog tags around his neck.

Jesus Christ.

I stare, blinking over and over as if doing that is going to make any sense of my current reality. As if Gunner isn't Ryan and Ryan isn't Gunner. As if everything that has happened during the past week just shifted and tilted, when it's the last thing I wanted it to do.

"Chase? You okay?"

"Yeah. Yes. Sorry. I was just reading your email." I refocus on it now, but don't really see anything. The words are a blur.

"He seems like a helluva guy. Make sure to tell him thank you for his service for me when you talk to him."

"I will." I stare at the picture again. "Thanks, Kelly."

The call ends. My phone drops to the bed beside me. And all I can do is stare at that image of a young Gunner and die a little.

How is this possible?

How have I been so busy enjoying the man I found that the possibility didn't cross my mind?

I'm mad. Furious. Because this screws everything up. *Everything*.

We both think the other person is someone else. *Correction*, I thought he was someone else, but now know he's the man I've been looking for. He still thinks I'm someone else—or that I *do* something else. What's he going to think when he not only finds out I'm a sports agent, but one who came here to let him know he was, in fact, recruitable before? The one who was coming here with thoughts of exploiting his veteran status for the benefit of my company?

Deception.

Isn't that what he said is a deal-breaker for him?

Isn't that what I've done? Deceived him?

My head spins as I walk to the other side of the room and pull the tattered envelope from my bag. I run my fingers over the handwriting and wonder who the twenty-year-old was before he became the man I know today.

Coach Bassett said he was arrogant and wild and yet the person I know is the complete opposite.

How is this possible?

How did this happen?

Dear KSM,

I just recently learned of your interest in me as an athlete and wanted to thank you. However, my dream to play in the major league is over. I've been advised to let old dreams go. To accept that life has changed forever.

-Ryan Camden

I try to make sense of everything as I walk from one side of the room to the other.

There is nothing worse than being lied to and finding out that you were.

It shouldn't matter—*he* shouldn't matter, because like we talked about last night, I have goals and achievements and everything else to do. I should just let dead dogs lie, pack up my shit, and head home. Walk away from this fling no worse for the wear other than him wondering what the hell happened.

But I can't.

I just can't, because even with all that bullshit I said the last night about not having time for a relationship, and having goals to reach etcetera, it rang hollow to my own ears. Words I've recited time and again, thoughts I've had over and over, now feel canned. Silly. I stood there and spouted the words to him while my heart ached in my chest in a way I've never felt it feel before.

And then, of course, he called me. He called me and made that ache I didn't understand burn brighter—in all the best ways.

How does someone go from not believing that something like this exists to suddenly hoping maybe it does?

This is insane.

Would you listen to yourself?

But the problem is that *I am*. I am listening and hearing and paying attention to every damn thing my body is telling me, and all it cares about is wanting more time, more moments, more laughter—*more everything*—when it comes to Gunner.

Leaving here, cutting my time short with him, isn't something I want to do.

But lying to him is even worse. *Right?*

Chapter TWENTY-THREE

Chase

With a deep breath and my heart in my throat, I walk up the sidewalk to Gunner's house. Anger owns me.

At how this happened.

At how I didn't see it.

At how I never asked him if he knew the Ryan Camden I was looking for.

At how this might all be over.

I'm just about to knock on the front door when he pulls it open and startles at the sight of me standing there.

"Hey, what are you doing—*Chase?*" he asks, immediately framing the sides of my face and bending down so we're at the same eye level. "What's wrong? You look like you've just seen a ghost."

I open my mouth to speak and then close it, because this is Gunner. Sweet, sexy, selfless Gunner who owns the bar, dances in the rain with me, and has my complete adoration.

My stomach twists in knots as I stare at him.

I can't do it.

As my anger turns to fear, and my fear turns to the understanding that the truth is going to hurt him.

I can't hurt this man in front of me. He's too good. Too selfless. Hurt enough already.

Whatever this is between us will be over.

And then I'll have to leave him.

Fuck.

"Chase? Talk to me." Concern reverberates in his voice, his breath feathering over my lips as his eyes search mine, asking for answers I don't think I'm ready to give now.

"It's nothing. No ghost." I shake my head a little to knock some sense into me and give a half-hearted chuckle to sell it. "I promise."

He didn't lie to me.

He doesn't deserve to be hurt or to know about the deception.

"I was—I was just excited."

"About?"

"Um. About. We have a family friend who announces baseball games for one of the networks. I talked to him earlier about ways we might be able to get a major league club to help sponsor The Center. New equipment, team uniforms, maybe some extra funding. He and his wife have a foundation that helps out underprivileged youth so I thought he would be the one to ask." Breathe, Chase. You're overexplaining like a little kid who's lying.

"Are you kidding me?" he asks, his eyes wide, his smile growing to megawatt proportions before he scoops me up in his arms, spins me around, and presses one of his knee-melting kisses on me. "That's incredible. Fantastic. I don't even know what to say or how to thank you or—"

"Nothing's happened yet," I caution with a laugh. This time when his lips find mine, I'm less caught by surprise. I'm so much more aware of how he makes me feel. *Of how much he has become to me in such a short space of time.*

So I deepen the kiss. Try to get lost in it, in him, to the point that I'm trying to apologize to him through a kiss without him having a clue. It's all I have. All I can manage.

"Woah," he says when the kiss ends, and he gently lowers me so my feet touch the ground. Our gazes hold, and I pray that he can't see the tears I'm fighting back. He narrows his eyes as I hold my breath. "You sure you're okay?"

Other than the fact that I'm not who you think I am? Sure. Perfectly fine.

"Of course." I clear my throat, needing a reason to explain the emotion he can clearly see. "I was just excited about it all, and happened to be driving by on my way to the coffee shop to work, and—"

"You figured you'd stop and tell me?" he finishes for me.

"Something like that," I say and then take a step back. "I'm sorry. I should have called. You're clearly on the way out the door—"

"I'm heading to FU-Bar to meet with a supplier, but don't ever apologize for stopping by with such great news or for no reason at all." He reaches out and brushes the back of his hand down the side of my cheek, his smile softening, his eyes darkening.

"What?" I murmur.

"You called in a favor to help the kids. Do you have any idea what that means to me?" I swallow over the lump in my throat and shake my head, as words are eaten by the guilt. "You're amazing. Absolutely amazing." He brushes his lips over mine one more time before saying goodbye and heading to the bar.

I'm left sitting in my car staring at his tail lights as guilt eats me whole.

Where was your normal Chase Kincade assertiveness? Where was your take-no-prisoners attitude?

Where was my honesty?

Now he thinks I'm a way better person than I actually am.

If there is one thing that has been highlighted over and over since I've been in Destiny Falls, it's this: he is selfless.

And I've just proven that I'm the direct opposite.

And I have no clue how to repair that additional lie.

Chapter TWENTY-FOUR

Chase

I DRIVE.

I'm unsettled and restless and fighting with my own thoughts while putting mile after mile on my car. The two-lane highway stretches endlessly and takes me past the base, past fields with cows, past schoolyards with kids playing. I take it all in, the normalcy of what feels like small-town America, and find myself pulling off the road when I see a baseball field to my right.

I can't figure out if it belongs to a high school or a community college, and it really doesn't matter. I welcome the sight of it. Of feeling like I'm home in the oddest sense. I'm mesmerized by the guy who's taking swings at the plate and his teammates shooting the shit in the outfield as they shag the balls and make plays with them.

This is what I know.

This is my comfort zone.

It's no wonder I sit in my car and get lost in the easy cadence and familiarity of batting practice. It's so much easier than having to face the fact that I'm a chicken.

I pick up my cell several times as I watch only to put it back down. But around the fourth or fifth time, I finally push send.

"Oh, look who's actually making time to call us and act like she cares?" Brexton teases as she greets me when she answers.

"I'm not in the mood, Brex," I say, as the kid at the plate goes deep and hits it over the centerfield wall.

"Who pissed in your Cheerios this morning?" She snorts.

"No one. Nothing." I sigh, and it pains me to even have to say the words. "I need advice."

"What?" she sputters, clearly wanting to make me suffer.

"You heard me." I lean my head back on my seat, pinch the bridge of my nose, and close my eyes.

"Wait. You're serious, aren't you?"

"Yes." The word comes out in a croak. Being the youngest of four, I've railed defiantly against asking for advice. At some point I was sick of hearing how much older and more experienced they were, so I made it a point to not ask for any advice and to pretend like I didn't hear it when it was given.

Childish? Definitely. But when you grow up without a mother, your three older sisters all try to pretend they are that to you, and the last thing I wanted was for her to be erased from my memory.

I've since learned that their advice is invaluable. I also know the bratty stigma has stuck. And they like to bring it up or throw it in my face every chance they get.

"Should I get Dekk in here?" Brexton asks, already calling her name across the office before I can answer. I was going to say yes, but the fact that she assumed just adds to my irritability.

"I'm here," Dekker says winded, but curious. "What's going on?"

"Chase needs advice," Brexton says.

"Ohhh." It's all Dekker says. I'm grateful that she's not rubbing it in. "Talk to us."

"So the bartender—"

"You mean Hot Bartender Boy, as in the one you're sleeping with bartender?" Dekker asks.

"Something like that."

"For specificity's sake, can we say yes or no so that I have a clear path to give advice with?" Dekker says, already annoying me. I'm fully aware my irritation is with myself and the situation with Gunner.

"Yes. *That* hot bartender. The one who I've known during my time here as Gunner but who earlier today, Kelly informed me is one and the same as Ryan Camden."

"Oh, shit." I'm not sure which one of them says it, but they sum up my train of thought perfectly.

"You know this doesn't count as dating two guys, right? I mean, we know you're goal-oriented and all, but this isn't what we meant," Brexton says lightheartedly, but her chuckle falls flat and dies.

"So that's my dilemma," I say, ignoring her comment entirely.

"What about it is a dilemma?" Dekker asks. "You tell him the truth, that you're Chase Kincade with KSM. That you received his letter and wanted to find out how he was, who he is, and if he's still playing. It's simple."

"And you explain that you didn't tell him who you were upfront because you didn't think anyone would give you info on *this Ryan Camden guy*. And, lo and behold it's him," Brexton continues.

I don't respond. I can't. The woman I was a few weeks ago would have clearly agreed with them. She would have said, *I know, I've already done that.*

But now I know him.

Now I like him.

Now . . . I've—

My groan is all I've got. I will not believe that I've . . . *fallen* for him. Gunner Camden is one hell of a catch. Maybe even the ultimate one, so it makes sense that I'm . . . *taken with him. Taken with him?* Jesus.

My head hurts.

No, I can't *not* like Gunner. He's one of the good guys. He's proven that over and over again. And even if I did think I'd fallen, it's just not possible. *This* isn't possible. We live hundreds of miles from each—

"Earth to Chase. You can't groan like that and then leave us hanging," Brexton says.

"She's pissed that she's not going to accomplish one of her beloved goals. She's going to tell him and he's going to tell her to go to hell and then OMG, she can't cross 'recruit Ryan Camden' off her goal list," Dekker says.

But it's more than that. So much more than that. But how do I put that in words? It shouldn't be hard with Dekk and Brex, as they know me inside out. But where are the words—

"Chase? Talk to us. You're not arguing. That means there's definitely something more going on here, right?"

"I *can't* tell him who I am, but at the same time, I *have* to tell him who I am. I'm in a no-win situation."

"Why do you say that? *Tell him.* So what if he gets mad? He'll get over it when he finds out you came to find *him,*" Brexton says. "When he knows that he wasn't forgotten. That there could be an option to play again in a PR game to support other veterans. That in itself will make up for the lie."

"I can't tell him," I whisper, despite seeing her logic.

"Why not?" Brex laughs. "You lied to him for the greater good of shock of all shocks, *finding him.*"

"It's not the same," I say.

"A little white lie has never stopped you from moving forward," she continues.

I don't respond. Can't. My head is swimming with thoughts and ideas and what-ifs.

"You're not hearing what she's not saying, Brex," Dekker says. Her voice is softer this time, more compassionate. "You like him, don't you, Chase? Like, really like him?"

"Ohhh." Brexton finally gets it. Perhaps Dekker heard it in the first phone call I had with her when I first arrived in Destiny Falls. Even though *I* didn't even understand it at that point. "That kind of changes things."

"We're enjoying each other's company. That's it," I say. Another lie.

"And that's allowed," Dekker says before we all fall silent.

"What if I don't tell him at all?" I finally say.

"And give up all your grand plans about using him as a publicity grab for KSM?" Brexton asks.

The idea feels dirty to me now. Of using a soldier and his service as a means to promote KSM's name.

"In the entire time I've been here with him, not a single second has been spent talking about baseball or pitching or that he even played in the past. In fact, the only sports we've talked about has been about what is being played by the kids at The Center." I twist my lips as they allow me to cycle through my thoughts. "So even if I tell him who I am, would it matter? It's not like he plays anymore."

"Are you telling us this or are you telling yourself this to justify perpetuating this lie?" Dekker asks in the most well-intentioned way.

"Both. Me. I don't know." I shrug with indifference when I'm anything but indifferent. "We did this trivia thing on our date the last night. I'll spare you the details, but it was a fun outside-of-the-box type of date. Anyway, one of the questions we had to answer each other was what one thing was a deal-breaker for him in a relationship. His answer was deception and being deceived." I swallow over the words. "Does that paint a clearer picture for you?"

"When has it ever mattered to you if someone thought you were something other than who you are?" Brexton asks. "You've played the femme-fatale, the ball-busting bitch, and the patient, unassuming good girl, all in the name of playing to the athlete—or man—you're wanting to get."

"Because it matters," I say.

This matters.

He matters.

"Why? I mean it's just sex, right?" Dekker says.

Brexton laughs and the sarcasm edging it grates on my nerves. "We've been there before, Chase. We've maybe even made the same excuse. Let's face it, this is more than sex."

"I said we're enjoying each other's company," I explain.

"Fine. Sure. You're simply enjoying each other's company. If that's the case, I don't get what the big deal is. You've broken many men's hearts before," Dekker says. "Unless . . ."

"No. I haven't fallen for him," I say.

"Who said anything about falling for anyone?" she asks, her tone coy and gloating.

"No one. You forget, I'm not like you two," I assert, trying to keep perspective in this conversation. The last thing I need is to give them something to gloat about.

"That's what we've all said until it was our turn," Brexton says, and of course, she's the last of us to fall prey to the whole relationship, happily-ever-after thing.

"I know I said it," Dekker chimes in.

"Look. He's a good guy. I don't want to hurt him, but is it so wrong to want to enjoy the rest of the time I have with him? He makes me laugh. He makes me feel good. I actually want to spend time with him—"

"*Whoa*. You feeling okay?" Brexton asks, and I realize how *unlike* me that comment sounds.

"Funny. I'm being serious," I say.

"Let her finish what she was saying," Dekker says.

"Is it so wrong that I simply want to enjoy the time I have left with him in whatever parameter this is—wrong or not?" I ask. "Besides, I made promises at The Center. That I'd volunteer through the end of the month. I can't let the kids down."

"And just like that, you'd walk away when it's time to come home? You actually think after all of this 'fun' you two are having that it will be that easy? *What about him?* Put yourself in his shoes. How would you feel if someone was doing the same to you?"

I'd be crushed. Pissed. Confused.

I don't answer out loud because they already know the answer. They know how much I value morals and honesty, and here I am being a total, fucking hypocrite.

"Maybe I just need to figure out why this guy, his letter, and everything about this situation has taken hold of me since day one and never let go," I murmur.

"Here's the advice I'm going to give you," Dekker says as she shifts to mom-big sister mode. "I understand what you're saying and your line of thinking, but you need to be honest with yourself. The reason you're willing to compromise your integrity and the woman we all know is because there's something more between the two of you. Is it fast? Perhaps, but sometimes when you know, you know. You need to admit to yourself that you're doing this because you *more* than like him. And you need to understand that it's not going to be as easy as you think to walk away from him in the end."

Her words make me feel like my throat is closing up on me. "That's ridic—"

"Hear me out," she says. "I'm not—*we're* not going to judge you regardless of what decision you make. But we also know you and know you feel guilty if you even think you've hurt one of our feelings. So the question you need to ask yourself is how are you going to spend all this time with him, soak him up and cram months into weeks with him, and not let the guilt eat you alive while doing so? Because if that's the case, then you're going to be so preoccupied with it, your time won't be of any quality."

"I don't know," I mumble, more to myself than to them.

"Well, you have to know," Brexton interjects. "If you're going to be there and enjoy your time, you can't be feeling guilty every damn second of it."

And she's right. I can't. "Have any advice on how to do that?"

"There's no easy answer," Dekker says.

"Maybe you have to look at it like this," Brexton adds. "If he's not yours to begin with, then he won't be that hard to lose when all is said and done."

And I'm starting to realize that that's what I'm afraid of.

Chapter TWENTY-FIVE

Chase

I'm not sure why I breathe a sigh of relief when I see Gunner's name on my cell, but I do.

Somehow, I'd concocted in my mind that he found out who I was. Whether it be by osmosis or telepathy—or that he merely googled my name—and that he no longer wanted anything to do with me.

That's what happens when guilt owns your every thought as you decide what you should do.

Or rather, when you know what the right thing to do is and you're choosing to do the opposite.

I take a deep breath and answer it. "Hey, you."

"Hi." Chills chase over my skin at the sound of his voice.

"You working?" I ask. There's the muted hum of music and talking in the background.

"Of course, I am. Just like I'm sure you are, researching your little heart out."

"Aren't we quite the pair?" I state.

"We are." He falls silent, and I hate that I wait for the other shoe to drop.

"Gunner?"

"I just wanted to make sure you were okay. You seemed upset yesterday and I hate that I had to run to work without making sure everything was good. Then I got busy with inventory issues before heading to coach the games at The Center, so I wasn't able to get back to you so . . . I don't know, I was calling to check-in."

That familiar ache is back beneath my breastbone.

"That's sweet of you. I'm fine. *I promise.*" I emit a self-deprecating chuckle and acknowledge the fact that with anyone else, I'd feel smothered by such thoughtful attention. But with Gunner, it makes me feel like someone cares for me. And I'm not sure if that's worse or better given the circumstances. "Truth be told, I felt kind of stupid that I rushed over to tell you about it when nothing had even happened yet. Add to that I'm being an overly emotional female since I'm not feeling too great."

"Are you coming down with something?" he asks, concern flooding his voice.

"That'll teach me to dance in the rain, huh?" I say, a soft smile on my lips at a memory that feels like yesterday and forever ago all at the same time.

"Seriously, you're okay?"

"I think it's just a cold. Sniffles. Headache. Nothing major," I explain.

"Can I bring you anything? Do you want to stay at my place? What do you need?"

"No. Thank you. I'm fine. I just need to sleep. Lots of sleep and I'm sure I'll be fine in the morning for the registration drive tomorrow."

"I've got the kids handled tomorrow. Stay there and rest."

"No. It's fine—"

"*It's fine* from a woman is a surefire indication that everything is not fine." His chuckle rumbles across the line. "So stop saying it, get some rest, and think of me."

"Now *that*, I can do. Goodnight, Gunner."

"Goodnight, Chase."

I close my eyes, a smile on my lips that no one can see but that I can feel.

Why does it seem as though the sound of his voice can make me feel like everything is better?

How do I do this? How do I perpetrate a lie so that I can be with him?

Because the deal-breaker is if he's in a relationship with someone. A long-term relationship. And that isn't what we have.

I don't have a choice really. He knows I'll be leaving for home at some point, so I'm going to enjoy the time I have with him, and then, fingers crossed, be able to walk away with some pride still intact.

I pull my laptop into bed with me and open up Kelly's email. Gunner is staring back at me before I begin scrolling to find a lone article about him. I skim the subtitles, but note that it covers his heroics, the bar he opened in memory of his fallen soldiers, and the incredible work he's doing at The Center. *Why couldn't I find this online when I first looked him up?*

But I can't bring myself to read it. It feels dirty. Like I'm cheating when I'm already cheating enough.

I'd rather learn this information from him. I'd rather ask him.

I'd rather get to know him with his warm smile, caring eyes, and genuine sense of humor.

I want to get to know him that way.

I close my laptop, push it away, and snuggle beneath the covers, decided.

I'm going to enjoy the time we have, soaking him in every chance I get.

Because I know that when I walk away, I'll probably never meet another man like him.

Chapter TWENTY-SIX

Gunner

"To the lost but not forgotten. To the brave and the missed. To Dickman, because he was a *dick, man*." My smile is bittersweet as cheers go up around me. "So let's raise our glass and wish Sarge a happy birthday. Sarge."

And in complete contradiction to what I say—but as is our tradition—we all tap our drinks on the bar top in front of us before saying, "Happy Birthday, *Dick*-man," and tossing back our drinks.

FU-Bar erupts in a round of applause. A Band-Aid for a celebration on what is now a lifetime of pain for his widow over his life lost.

Over a life I couldn't save.

"Gunner?"

I look toward the corner of the bar where Jenny stands. There's a smile on her lips but sadness in her eyes.

"Hey. I didn't see you slip in here. We waited for a while because I didn't want you to miss the toast but—"

"I was here. Just near the back," she says with a lift of her chin in the direction she was. "Thank you for doing this. For having this." She motions to the packed house of veterans and soldiers alike. "It's nice to know that his memory is still alive."

I nod. "I wish I could do more." I'm staring at her, but it's his cries of agony filling my ears. I'm seeing the tears swim in her eyes, but it's the desperate look in his as he grabbed my shirt and begged me for help, as he told me he didn't want to die, as I promised him I'd take care of Jenny. *That's* what I hear over and over.

"You always do too much. Feel too much." She reaches out and puts a hand on the side of my cheek. "You're too hard on yourself, Gunner."

I smile. It's what I feel I need to do, but inside I ache and rage and regret that I couldn't have done more. *That I didn't react quicker. That I didn't know the IED was there. That I wasn't able to fucking save him.* All I can do is nod. "I sent you a check last week. Did you get it?"

"Yes, but like I told you before, you really need to stop sending them."

"It's the least I can do," I mumble, catching Aubrey's eye to pull the tap and fill orders herself for a minute while I'm with Jenny.

"No, I'm serious." She reaches out and puts her hand on my arm. "I tore up the check."

It's then I see it. The shiny diamond solitaire on her ring finger. The one that's different than the silver wedding band that Dickman had given her.

"Jenny?" When I look up to meet her eyes, she's fighting tears through her smile and that's exactly how I feel. I'm happy for her but sad for Dickman, and I honestly don't know how it makes me feel. "Is that what I think it is?"

She nods and sniffs away the emotion. "I needed to tell you but was afraid as well. I don't even know what to say."

"Tell me he makes you happy. That's all I need to hear. That he treats you well and that you're happy."

"I am. I truly am when I never thought I could feel this way again, so thank you for everything, but you really need to stop sending me checks. I know it helps you cope, helps you deal with the survivor's guilt, but you don't owe anyone anything. You were the one holding their hands, trying to save them, and for all of us, that's all we need to know. That their best friend was there with them since we couldn't be."

"Yes. Okay." It's the best I can do with words, as the emotions overwhelm and battle their way through the goddamn steel walls I hide them behind. "Thanks. I need to uh"—I motion to the backroom—"get some stuff done." And with a quick hug and her lips on my cheek, I charge for its privacy. For its peace. For a place where I can let the fucking emotions overwhelm me.

One life dies.

Another life moves on.

It's the cycle, but it's so fucking hard to accept. To know that she has to move on, to be happy—hell, he'd want her to be happy—but that doesn't make it any easier to accept that three years later she's found someone. *Someone who isn't Dickman.*

I toast when the crowd toasts, sipping my water instead of the shots being shoved in front of me.

Because I can't drown this one out. I can't bury it under alcohol. It will still be there. It will still hurt.

I know from experience.

"Hey, man? You okay?"

I glance over to Nix and nod. "I think for my own sanity, I need to cut out early tonight."

"Not in the mood for celebrating?" he asks, his eyes searching mine.

"Nah. But you guys go ahead. Aubs is going to take the helm for me. She'll get better tips that way anyway, and I know she's saving up for a new car." I wipe my hands on the towel, ball it up, and toss it in the basket behind the bar.

"It's okay to say celebrating this, seeing Jenny, fucks you up. It does me too. We don't want to forget, but it sure as hell hurts to remember."

"Thanks for getting me, Nix."

"Aye." He nods and takes a sip of his beer. "Tell Grainger my apologies to his hand."

"Christ, Gunny," Grainger says as he shakes his gloved hand. "That fucking hurt."

I don't speak, just lift my gloved hand out to indicate that another fastball is coming. And then another. And another.

Grainger is wise not to speak. The catcher from the community college a few towns over always welcomes the chance to get more time in behind the plate—and luckily, he doesn't mind doing it at all hours of the night.

What he doesn't understand is that what is extra practice for him, is therapy for me.

It's how I work through the shit in my head. The hurt in my heart. The guilt that still weighs heavy in my soul.

It has been since the day I kissed the sport I loved with all my heart goodbye only to realize it provided me with so much more than I thought.

Pitching, getting lost in the motions and the mechanics, had become my therapy. I hadn't realized it at the time, but it's what I turned to when my dad came home beneath a flag-draped coffin. It's what I lost myself in when Sal was drunk and his fists were itching to fly. Staying at the field a few extra hours was so much easier than going home to deal with him.

When I was on deployment, it's how I managed the fear and boredom. The guys would take turns catching for me, guessing where I'd pitch it next. We'd make a game of it. Anything for a piece of normalcy in that godforsaken place.

And now, it's how I cope with the horrors of war, and the guilt over the ones I failed.

Fucking Dickman.

I shake my head and lob an off-speed pitch at Grainger. He falls forward on his knees as he anticipates the fastball, but is caught off guard when it's twenty miles per hour slower.

"That was wicked," he laughs out. "Tell me again why you never played in the majors."

"I wasn't good enough."

"Bullshit. If you're this good after all this time, you must have been nasty when you were my age."

I chuckle before flopping my glove to tell him another one's coming.

Because I was good.

I had the control and the speed and the size. Every damn thing the MLB scouts wanted, and yet I was sold out. Agents promised me they'd call. They told me they wanted me. And when they did call—from what I learned later—they were assured that my *lack of respect for those in authority* would only ever be a severe handicap and risk. Oh, and had they seen Marcus, my stepbrother's stats? *Asshole.*

Stepping off the mound, I roll my shoulders to clear it. I can't think about shit like that right now. I let that dream go over five years ago and made as much peace with it as I could.

"You ever thought of pitching batting practice for us?" Grainger asks.

"I have in years past," I answer, but that's all I say.

Because I'm not here to pitch batting practice or to improve my slider. I'm here to get the aggression out. The anger. The need for my life, my fucked-up head, to feel normal again when the goalposts for normal seem to be continually moved from one day to the next.

"I saw you at the Lager and LEGO thing. Who was your hot date?"

Fucking Chase.

"Fastball," I say, not wanting to talk about her.

Her, being another reason I'm here, tied up, and needing to pitch.

"Changeup." I indicate with the motion of my glove in a different way.

The woman is tying me up in knots.

"Curve." My shoulder burns with the pitch, but I don't care. I need this. To understand how I feel about her, how she made me feel when she showed up at my house with what looked like panic the other day . . . and my first thought was that she was leaving.

I stressed over it all day.

Stressed, when I'm not one to stress.

And that? That scared the fuck out of me, when we're not far enough in this relationship to be scared the fuck out of.

I've let her in.

She's the first one I have.

The dream reliving everything that happened last night.

Seeing Jenny and celebrating Dickman's birthday tonight.

Chase Kincade.

Emotions.

Fucking goddamn emotions.

That's why I'm here, in my church of sorts. In my therapist's office. The place where I always go when I need to work through memories or demons or emotions—the ones that haunt me—and the PTSD that chases me.

"You sure you're good?" Grainger asks.

Good? That's not something I think I'll ever be. I try to give back, try to give more, try to make up for not being able to save my guys that day, and yet I always feel like it's never enough. Like no matter what I do, it won't ever be enough.

And it won't.

They're gone. Just like a piece of me will always be gone with them.

Just like the hole left in the lives of their families that day.

So *good?* Never. But that's not something I'll ever say out loud, because who am I to not be *good* when I'm the one still alive?

"Yep. Just . . . just figuring shit out."

Chapter TWENTY-SEVEN

Gunner

Six Years Ago

"I'm serious, Ryan. There were calls. *Emails.* I saw them on his computer when he accidentally stayed logged into his account. *They* want you." My mom's voice, her incomprehensible pleading for me to believe her across the scratchy connection, almost feels surreal. Almost sounds like the words are a dream.

But they're not.

They can't be.

"I don't understand what you mean," I finally say.

"They emailed Sal, sweetie. Agents. Four of them. They were interested in representing you. In getting you signed into the major leagues."

The hope in her voice is like a dagger to my heart.

"And you're just finding this out now?" I look at the sparse walls of my barracks and hear the night patrol watchman's radio faintly in the distance.

"Yes. I had to help him with something on his phone and saw them," she explains. No one is allowed to go near Sal's computer when he's logged in. *No one.* So the fact that she saw the emails, that he left them sitting open on the computer screen so she could read them, tells me it was all part of his plan to manipulate her. To show her who is in control. "It was an accident. This all was a misunderstanding." But the catch in her voice confirms she knows she's lying. "He thought they were calling for Marcus. He gave them Marcus's information by accident, and it was all just a silly mix-up that I'm sure we can get straightened out."

My snort of derision is loud.

"Are you listening to yourself, Mom? Are you really hearing yourself make excuses for him? You've somehow been able to watch him lay into *your son* time after time for years. You justify why he hits you. That's on you. But now you're justifying why he fucking screwed me over, and you bet your ass I'm going to call you out on it."

"He promises it was an accident."

"Yeah. A perfectly calculated accident to get me out of your lives while pushing his own son's success."

"He can undo what he did. I promise. All he has to do is call them and explain it. Explain the confusion that he had two sons—"

"Do not ever call me his son again," I grit out through clenched teeth.

"All he has to do is explain that he thought they were calling for Marcus," she repeats, never missing a beat. "That he—"

"I'm not sure what I'm finding harder to comprehend. The fact that you're buying this BS or the notion that you think this can be undone."

"It can. I know it can."

"Mom? Are you listening to yourself? I'm in fucking Afghanistan. Do you think the US Army will let me out because some agent showed interest in me before I signed my life away—before your husband threatened me and made me sign my next four years away? *They don't fucking care.*"

"But they want you." Her voice sounds less certain now. "They know how good you are."

"*Wanted,* Mom. Past tense."

"We don't know that."

I've never hated her more than right now. A wishy-washy woman who is defending her asshole husband. Sure, life has dealt her a shit hand, but that doesn't mean she has to be weak. That doesn't mean she has to kowtow to a man. She's worth more than that, but I'm so sick and fucking tired of being the only one fighting for her to see it.

The anger that courses through my veins is like a drug. I don't know how to dampen it, and at the same time don't think I want to. I need to feel it. Need to own it. Need to hold on to it, because it's the only thing that's keeping me sane at the moment.

"What are you going to do about it?" I ask her, needing to hear her answer. Needing to hear her say she's leaving him because of what he's done to her son—her own flesh and blood. Needing to know she's choosing *me* over *him*.

"I don't know what you mean," she stammers. My heart sinks. Just once I wanted her to fight harder for me than she's fought to keep someone around to support her.

"I mean, your husband screwed over your son. *Me*. He threatened me. He gave me the ultimatum of jail or enlisting. He took away a chance to make *our* life something other than paycheck to paycheck. He took away *my dream*. HE DID THAT," I scream into the phone, not fucking caring who's around or what they think. "So you tell me, *Mom*, what are you going to do about it?"

"Ryan," she mumbles in that soothing voice she used to use after my dad died. When I cried myself to sleep and she didn't know how to comfort me, she used that voice. That tone.

She doesn't know what to say or how to comfort me.

"You're talented. I'm sure you'll still be good when you come home. When you're discharged."

Does she not understand in order to be that good you have to play every day? Practice on a schedule. Get coaching. Face competition.

But how could she know that when she never went to my games? The stands were always empty. At first, it was because she was working to supplement the death benefits we received for my father, and then it was because Sal didn't let her.

There was always an excuse as to why.

And then there was simply silence.

"It's always been about him, Mom. *Always*. And now, maybe you'll see it. Maybe you'll stop making excuses. Maybe you'll see what he's done to us and—"

"That's not true," she screeches, so used to defending him.

I hang my head and pinch the bridge of my nose. Nothing's going to change. I could talk till I'm blue in the face and she won't hear me. She's so conditioned to believing his lies. Why bother trying to change it? *Her* choice. *Her* life.

"They loved you, sweetheart. They want to represent you."

Do you really think any coach in their right mind is going to sign some asshole, law-breaker? A kid with no morals who steals from the hand that feeds and houses him?

They might have loved me and wanted to represent me, but my fucking mother doesn't do either.

"Don't worry about me. You keep going on with your life while I'm out here being made into a real man."

"Ryan. Honey. Please don't—"

"It's okay, Mom. Don't sweat it. It never would have worked. I'm a screwup, remember? I've got to go," I lie. "Bye."

Fuck that shit.

And when I end the call on the sat phone, I hand it to the next guy waiting in line to call home. Once on my bunk, I try to hide the tears I'm holding back, which burn like a motherfucker.

They loved you, sweetheart. They want to represent you.

Those fucking words repeat over and over in my head. They taunt and torture and haunt me.

I was good.

They wanted me.

The tears that slide down my cheeks as I shove my pillow over my face are hot and angry, and each one feels like it slices me open. Each one a painful reminder of what I gave up and will never get back.

Dickman was right.

The life I knew before coming here is one hundred percent done and over.

Fucking gone.

The letter I wrote, which is shoved under my mattress, I might as well send.

Goodbye baseball.

Goodbye dream.

Goodbye, Ryan Camden.

I'm Gunner now.

A soldier without a family other than the guys around me.

A man without the dream that's guided his whole life.

Simply Gunner.

Simply another soldier who might die in the line of duty.

But a soldier who won't be missed by anyone *back home*.

Chapter TWENTY-EIGHT

Chase

"THANK YOU. WE CAN'T WAIT TO HAVE YOU ON THE TEAM AND TO PLAY with us," I say to an adorable, freckle-faced little boy with glasses.

"But I've never played before." He worries his bottom lip between his teeth and looks over at the court where kids are shooting hoops. "What if—"

"You've never played before?" Gunner asks, as he walks into the front office of The Center, smile big. The little guy shakes his head. "That is the best news ever."

"It is?" he asks, eyes growing wide.

"Yep. I'm Gunner." Gunner holds his hand out.

"I'm Robbie," he says as they shake hands.

"Can I tell you how excited I am to coach you and teach you how to play basketball and baseball?"

"You are?"

Gunner nods. "I talked to your mom on the phone the other day and she was telling me how much you've wanted to try this."

Robbie nods and then swallows loudly. "I was waiting for my dad to teach me, but . . ." His bottom lip trembles and my heart lurches into my throat.

"But he's busy getting better at Walter Reed, isn't he?" Gunner says without flinching.

"Uh-huh."

"I heard he was busy being a superhero and ended up getting hurt." Robbie's bottom lip quivers. "It's okay. I've been there too and look at me. The doctors there patched me up good as new."

"They did?"

"Yep. Good as new."

The lump in my throat grows as I sit back and become a bystander to their conversation. A kid who has to grow up way too soon and a grown man who can relate to him more than I've ever seen before.

I notice Robbie's mom in the periphery, watching from where she's filling out forms. She dabs the corner of her eye with a tissue as she watches just like I do.

"And that means that I am more than excited to coach you and teach you until your daddy can come back and take over for me. Sound like a deal?" Gunner asks and offers his fist to be bumped.

Robbie's timid smile grows wide as he bumps Gunner's fists. "Deal."

Gunner gives me a glance and a soft smile, before he's pulled away to another kid, to the start of a practice, to being just the incredible guy that he is.

It's not until I'm sorting through the new registrants and putting the last ones in the computer system when I see him again.

"You're still not feeling good, are you?" He rests his butt on the desk in front of me, putting his hand on my forehead to check my temperature.

"I'm fine. I told you, it's just a little cold."

"A *little cold* while you're staying in a hotel, living out of a tiny refrigerator and having to go down to the lobby to put something in the microwave if you want warm food." He tucks a piece of hair behind my ear and meets my eyes. "You're staying at my place."

"Gunner—"

"Argue all you want but I'm going to win in the end." He presses a kiss to my forehead. "I'm not beneath throwing a tantrum to get what I want."

"Good to know," I say as he pulls me against him. I revel in the feel of his arms around me.

Truth be told, all of his points are valid. I'm sick of reheated takeout food and grab-and-go snacks. I'd kill to have decent Wi-Fi and to not wonder how many germs still live on the comforter I sleep under.

Or if there are any bed bugs lurking, despite checking before I lie down and after I get up.

And a selling point he's not even privy to? I *want* to soak up more time with him. As much as I can get, if I'm honest. I know how bleak life will be as soon as I cross the border out of Destiny Falls on the way back home.

I don't like that it means deliberately hiding anything KSM from him, which might make it difficult to take phone calls, but I can make it work.

I know I can.

I don't want him to be hurt, thinking I was only here to deceive him. This kindhearted man does not deserve that. So, I'll hide anything I can to avoid that.

And besides, who in their right mind would turn down an incredibly sexy man telling them that he wants to take care of them when they're sick?

Not this girl.

Chapter TWENTY-NINE

Chase

"Are you sure I can't get you anything else?" Gunner asks. He tucks me under his arm and adjusts our position so I can rest my head on his chest.

"Let's see. You've made me homemade chicken noodle soup—something I don't even know how to make myself—set me up in your spare bedroom so I have my own space, and then built a fire because I said how much I miss real fires in fireplaces." I snuggle in harder against him. "Oh, and now you're snuggling with me and rubbing my back simultaneously. I think you pretty much nailed every damn thing, Gunner, so much so that you're going to have a hard time getting rid of me."

"No complaints with that here," he says into the crown of my head. We're on his couch in front of a whitewashed brick fireplace. Flames crackle and snap. I can't believe he built me a fire simply because I said I missed having one in my New York apartment. "Are you tired? Do you want to sleep or catch a movie or—"

"I want to know more about you," I say.

"Me?" He laughs the word out.

"Yep. Tell me about your childhood. Where you grew up. Were you a pain in the ass who caused your parents headaches or were you a perfect angel?" He snorts and I laugh. "Did you always want to enter the service or was that a decision made later in life?" I ask leading questions, because I genuinely want to know. *And I refuse to rely on Kelly's information as my source.*

"Why all the focus on me? Don't I get to know more about you?"

"You're the mysterious one," I counter. "I don't even know your last name."

"Camden," he says without hesitation. I don't know why I expected him not to. It's not like he was hiding it on purpose or even knew that I was looking for him. But it just feels weird to have him offer it up so easily.

"*Camden*," I murmur, getting used to the feel of it rolling off my tongue.

"Ryan Camden to be precise, but ever since my first tour in Afghanistan, I've gone by Gunner."

"I'm sure there's a story there. But see? I told you that you were mysterious."

"Says the sexy grad student who lives in New York and is researching a topic I've lived, but who I don't know much else about."

"Yes, you do. You know I have three sisters and that my mom died. You know I have an affinity for Converse, dancing in the rain, putting things in order, and can't paint for shit."

"Any dislikes?"

"Beside bed bugs, men whose biceps are bigger than my thighs, and Neapolitan ice cream? No, none that I can think of."

Gunner barks out a laugh. "You're something else, you know that?"

"Who me?" I look up at him and bat my lashes, once again struck by just how damn handsome he is. And the more I get to know him, my attraction seems to grow stronger. "I'm known for being the picky one."

"Apparently not too picky seeing as you're here with me."

I desperately want to kiss him but don't want to get him sick, so I do the next best thing and press my lips to the underside of his jaw, close my eyes, and savor him. The scent of his soap. The strong rhythm of his heart beneath my hand. The warmth of his hand as it runs up and down the length of my back.

I'm uncertain how long we sit like this, simply drinking each other in with the warmth of the fire in front of us and the quiet presence of each other.

"I was a good kid growing up," Gunner says and breaks the comfortable silence. "Then I wasn't." His chuckle is self-deprecating. "My dad left for deployment when I was ten. I remember giving him hugs outside the depot, him making me promise to take care of my mom while he was gone, and then . . . then the car pulling up to our driveway. The knock on the door. My mom's shrieks as she fell to the floor."

"Gunner." His name is a mixture of apology and understanding. I squeeze him tighter but don't say anything else.

"I was ten without a dad and around kids who picked on me. I turned to baseball and who knew? I was really good at it. At that age, it was easier to be at the field than at home watching my mom grieve. That and it was the place where kids started to respect me instead of tease me."

"You found your coping mechanism. Your thing," I say gently, earning a look from him as if he's not used to someone understanding that concept.

"Yes. Little did I know how important that would be to me later in life."

I want to ask what he means but just nod and snuggle back into him, ready to hear his story.

"My mom remarried twice. None of them were nice to her, and the promise I made to my father to take care of her always weighed heavy on me. No matter how many times I tried to get her to see it as abuse, she refused to. And then Sal came along," he says with a foreboding sigh that has me closing my eyes and picturing a younger version of him trying unsuccessfully to be the man of the house. "He was stepdad number two, lover of alcohol, keen on control, and prone to use his fists to make sure his stepson knew his place in the pecking order."

Oh God. It's one thing to lose your dad, but to be hit by a man who should care for you? Why didn't his mom do more? How could she?

"I'm afraid to even hear more."

He shrugs with an indifference only someone who has been through something like this can. "Baseball was my escape. I spent more and more time on the mound—"

"You were a pitcher?" I ask, feeling like a hypocrite.

"Mm-hmm. A decent one or so I was told, but that only comes from the fact that I basically lived at the field." He reaches over and takes a sip of his water, as I try to fathom the notion of not wanting to be at home or that home isn't a safe space. "Sal had a son. He played baseball too. He was mediocre in talent but Sal wasn't having any part of that, especially when I was getting attention from four-year colleges and MLB scouts."

"You must have been good."

"I was decent," he says and sighs. The agent in me wants to shake him senseless and tell him for MLB scouts to be looking at him, for my dad to be interested in representing him, he was more than decent.

A one-hundred-mile-per-hour arm that has command of five pitches is not decent.

It's utterly, freaking phenomenal.

But I can't say a word, and I think, of all of this charade, that's the toughest part. I want to tell him he was incredible. I want to tell him that a team would have taken him and signed him for a one-year contract just to see if he could hack it. I want to tell him that regardless of what was his perceived lack of control, teams would have still been interested. That they overlook things like that when you have a one-hundred-mile-per-hour arm.

But that's where part of my dilemma comes in. The part where I can't be honest with him and tell him that even though Sal was a raging asshole who discredited him out of jealousy, Gunner really was quite incredible.

I try in the most muted sense possible.

"If major league teams were looking at you, I'm pretty sure you were more than decent."

He shrugs. "It's all relative. I truly loved the game and the escape it provided me from the toxicity of my house. I stayed home longer than I should have because I was trying to fulfill that promise to my dad to take care of my mom. I was trying to do what was right and make sure she was okay. I don't know . . . Shit got bad. I didn't care that I was acting out—hell, maybe I was acting out hoping she'd notice and pick me over him. Whatever it was, I thought I could help get her out of the situation with my stepfather, but I learned you can't change people or make them see things differently. That realization came at a brutal cost to myself."

"What do you mean, if you don't mind me asking?"

Gunner explains about Coach Bassett believing in him and sending letters and videos out to agents and scouts. About stealing his stepfather's car and crashing it. The brutal ultimatum given to him the next day between service or jail. Then the hard truth he found out months later that agents had called, had wanted him, and that Sal had supposedly ignored or misdirected them to his son instead of letting Gunner know.

That part got to me. Why didn't agents persist? Why did they contact Sal when Gunner wasn't a minor and they should have contacted him directly? *Why did they give up on him?*

But I know the reasons. Too many athletes, not enough time for the one who doesn't call you back or shows zero interest. Difficult people—in this case, Sal—to deal with, so it's just not worth the effort unless you see a star in the making.

No one saw the star. No one looked close enough to see his ability to shine.

And my heart breaks for him because of it.

But it seems that no one looked close enough at his situation for a long time.

He continues on to his time in boot camp, deployment, and how he realized life how he'd known it had changed.

"And then Dickman, our sarge, said we should write letters to those who mattered. To say goodbye to our dreams because life as we knew it was over. Even if we returned, we wouldn't be the same men. And he was right. Not just because of what we experienced, who we lost, what we endured. But well, it was too late for me."

"How do you know—"

"Because life had rolled on regardless of the darkness we saw every day, Chase."

"Oh." He should be angry. Or maybe he's already grieved. Had his moments of anger. He shrugs again, and I lean in deeper to his hold.

"Anyway, we wrote our letters. I wrote to the agencies my mom mentioned had contacted Sal—don't even remember who they were now—and thanked them for their interest."

My dad. He'd written and thanked my dad. Even that made him a good man to say thank you.

"So that was your goodbye to a game you loved."

He nods. "Something like that. But the funny thing is, I still use it as my therapy. I still go out at all kinds of hours when I'm off work and throw the ball with one of the catchers from the junior college."

"You do?" I ask, thinking of the clerk at the hotel and wondering if it was, in fact, Gunner she saw.

"Yep. When things get too much—emotions, memories, stress—I go throw the ball for a bit. It helps me work through it all."

"Memories? Of what happened over there?"

His sigh is heavy. "Fucking Nix."

"The guy loves you with all his heart. He meant well by telling me."

He pulls me closer to him. "How about we stop talking about me? I assure you there are much more interesting conversations we could be having."

"Like?" I ask. But I totally disagree with him.

The man is fascinating. I thought it before and now I definitely know it.

"Like what's your deal with bed bugs?" he asks and I laugh.

"Do I detect this topic of conversation as being over?"

"You do. The one thing I hate more than hearing myself talk is talking about myself."

"Now that? I can agree with you on." And I've been so lost in the conversation, in listening to him tell his story, that I never noticed it grew dark outside. I bolt up, startling both of us. "Oh my God. The bar. Your work. You forgot to—"

He offers me a shy smile and tugs me back down to where I was snuggling against him. "Don't worry about it. I called in sick."

"You what? Why?"

"Because I have a feeling it isn't very often that you let someone take care of you. I figured I'd take advantage of the opportunity."

He presses a kiss to the crown of my head and my insides melt.

"Thank you," I say and press a kiss to just above his heart. If I was smart, I'd walk away right now. This man is too good. Too kind. Too genuine. Too thoughtful. Too . . . everything. *I. Don't. Deserve. Him.* But I'm not smart.

I already know that my heart is going to hurt when I leave, and that's totally my fault. I own it.

I'm selfish, I'm sick, and he's right. It's been too long since I've let anyone take care of me. So, I take the extremely lame approach and ask, "Is there any chance you'd like to watch a chick flick like *Die Hard 4.0* with me?" He laughs. And I'm sure it's *at* me, which I don't care about in the least.

"You mean *Live Free or Die Hard?*"

"Exactly. *Die Hard 4.0.*"

"Gotta say. That's the first time anyone has referred to one of my favorite movies as a chick flick."

"What? There's romance in it. There's a kiss in there somewhere."

"Okay then. *Die Hard 4.0* it is. Your request is my command."

I chuckle, which makes me start coughing again. And even though I feel both heartsick and physically sick, there's no other place I'd rather be right now.

Chapter THIRTY

Gunner

I've never had a woman live with me.

Not even for a few days.

Simply put, I haven't found someone I like enough.

But there's definitely something intriguing about having Chase here. Little things I notice here and there. How the bathroom towels on the rack are squared and fussed over when they're usually crooked. How the dishwasher is loaded with all like silverware in each section of the tray. How I smell faint traces of her perfume at the oddest times. Almost as if it's slowly weaving its way through every molecule of air so that when she leaves, traces of her will be everywhere.

"You getting any sleep, Romeo? I'm sure it's more than taxing to ignore your new houseguest?" Ellie asks, fighting her knowing smile.

"It's not like that." She levels me with a look, and I laugh. "Okay. It is like that . . . but she's been sick, so it's been pretty chill."

"Pretty chill as in she rides you reverse cowgirl so as not to breathe germs in your face—"

"Jesus, Ell," I sputter. "I can't believe you just said that."

"Why? Sometimes you have needs even when you're sick." Her shrug is followed by a laugh that tells me she's enjoying making me uncomfortable way more than I am.

"Is this the part where I put my hands over my ears and pretend I can't hear you so the visual isn't scarred into my brain?"

"Well, every time the two of you look at each other, I'm well aware of what your eyes are saying you want to do when you get back home. Bow chicka wow wow."

"You are—"

"Awesome. Indispensable. The one you can't live without?" She gives me a Cheshire Cat grin and all I can do is laugh.

"Exactly. Those were exactly the words that came to mind." I wave to Robbie, who runs out onto the turf area where some of the friends he's made are hanging out. It's that limbo period between the school bus dropping them off and practice actually starting.

"He's doing well," Ellie says, catching my line of sight.

"He is. I think his dad has a tough row to hoe, so I'm sure he'll have his ups and downs. Luckily he's here and the other kids understand what it's like."

"Thanks to you and what you created."

I glance over to her. Praise is rare from Ellie, kind words about me even more so, so I just stare at her and narrow my eyes. "You feeling okay?"

"Yes. No. I just thought you ought to know you've done good here with this place."

"Ellie, don't tell me you're leaving me," I say as panic fills me.

She laughs and swats at my arm. "Don't be silly. Although I may leave you for Chase if she comes through with that sponsorship she's talked about," she teases.

"No shit," I say with a shake of my head. "It's pretty incredible. I wouldn't even know how to go about finding opportunities like that."

"Apparently she does," Ellie says and walks to the mini-fridge in the corner of the office and grabs a water. "Lucky for us."

I nod. "Definitely."

"So what are you going to do when she leaves?" Ellie asks.

"What do you mean?"

"I mean, let's address the elephant in the room. She's made no secret that her time here is short-lived, so, head-over-heels boy, what are you going to do then?"

"Head-over-heels boy?" I laugh.

"Well . . ." She lifts her eyebrows.

"That's implying more than I'd like to admit at this point in time."

"That's such bullshit and you know it. You've fallen for her—and I can see why. She's gorgeous and intelligent and has a great sense of humor. What's not to love? But she's leaving, Gunner. She never had any intention of staying and has been upfront about that. So what does that mean for you? How does that affect you?"

I stare out the window and twist my lips, knowing she's right. "Isn't that fucking life, though? Nothing is ever perfect. You have to take what you can get, enjoy it while you can, and just be fucking grateful that you even get the chance to experience it." I step back and look at Ellie. "Will it sting like a bitch? Yes. Undoubtedly. But at the same time, is that sting enough of a deterrent to push away the good while I have the chance at it? No. I've lost a lot of people, and the one thing I've learned is to enjoy them while you can. Love them while you can. That way you can't say you regretted not laying it all out on the table while you could."

"No regrets."

"Exactly. No regrets. So . . . I'm going to cram as much as I can in these next few weeks. Fun dates and slow kisses and great sex and laughter. All of it. And then when Chase leaves, I'll be sad, but I'll know I left it all on the table."

"You wouldn't try to make a go of the long-distance thing?" she asks.

"I don't know. I see it through the skewed lens of deployment and how it rarely works."

"Um . . . it works." She raises her hand. "We were able to manage. Lots of people do. There just has to be trust and honesty between the two of you."

"Chase is the most brutally honest person I know, so at least we have that going for us." For some reason I think of her bed bug story, the expletives that flew from her mouth during it, and chuckle. "I don't know, Ell. It's not something we've talked about. I think we're both just trying to enjoy each other as much as we can, while we can, and figure we'll worry about that when the time comes."

"Avoidance at all costs. I like that in a plan."

We both laugh and finish closing The Center for the evening, but there's something that sticks with me as I do it, as well as on the drive home. I just openly admitted that I've fallen for Chase Kincade.

It's one thing to admit it to myself, it's another to acknowledge out loud to someone else who can make my life miserable by teasing me every time they see me.

Or just knowing about it in general.

But when I pull up to my house and see the lights on inside, I can't help but feel content. Happy. Anticipatory.

It's weird and wonderful and new to have someone to come home to. A warm greeting when you walk in the door. A soft hum of the TV in the background acknowledging someone is there. The subtle scent of her perfume tickling your nose.

But she's leaving, Gunner. So what does that mean for you?

As I open the front door, I shove away Ellie's comments. I'm here, getting to experience this when guys like Dickman and Shotgun aren't.

I'll take the hurt in order to experience the bliss.

No regrets.

"There you are," Chase says as she slides her hands around my waist and presses her lips to mine.

It's only been a few days since we last kissed because she's been sick, but I didn't realize how long it felt like until now. Until her tongue has slipped between my lips and since the heat of her body has pressed up against me and warmed mine.

It's heaven and hell, and I want to dive into her in a way like never before. Absence may make the heart grow fonder, but seeing the woman you want day in and day out, showing restraint because she's sick, is plain fucking torture.

"I see you're feeling better," I note against her lips, my hands on the sides of her face then cupping her ass . . . then just everywhere I can at once.

"Mm-hmm," she says as she kisses her way down the hollow of my neck, my dick already hard and begging to sink into her. "I have a surprise for you."

That knocks me out of the moment and I lean back to look at her. "A surprise?"

It's only then that I take in the fact that Chase is standing there in a coat—my coat—with a pair of heels on.

"Oh." It's all I manage to say as she steps back and shimmies the coat off her shoulders, proceeding to drop it to the ground.

But I'm not looking at where it falls.

Nope. My eyes are fixated on her and how she's standing before me in heels, a red and white gingham apron, and the biggest, sexiest smile I've ever had the pleasure of being on the receiving end of.

"Now that's a welcome home if I've ever gotten one."

"You like?" she asks and does a curtsy. Her breasts jiggle out the sides of the ruffled section, which partially covers her chest and ties around her neck.

"I like all right."

She does a little twirl, the tied bow resting above her bare ass, and my mouth waters and fingers itch to touch her.

"I made you an apple pie," she says over her shoulder as she turns and heads toward the kitchen. "It's ooey and gooey and warm and waiting for you to blissfully sink right into it."

I stand there and watch. Take in the view of her hips swaying and ass moving, and I groan.

But hell, if she wants to tempt and tease and play coy, then I'm definitely game.

"An apple pie? I didn't know you baked," I say as I follow behind her, my eyes glued to every goddamn curve of hers.

"That's all you have to say?"

"Oh, I have a hell of a lot to say but right now I'm just enjoying the view."

"Does this give you a better one?" she asks and then proceeds to pull the oven door open and bend over to take the pie out.

Holy fucking shit.

And it's only seconds—but it's too damn long between the time she shuts the oven, puts the pie on top of the stove—and I have her whirled around with my mouth on hers.

She still has the oven mitts on, but I don't care.

All I can think about is her.

Right now.

"No regrets," I say between kisses as I lift her up and sit her ass on the island. She yelps from the chill of the granite, all while heating up every part of me.

Our kisses are hot and hungry and laced with desperation. The kind that feels like it is going to eat you alive if you don't have more. Take more. Give more.

We're both frenzied. Her hands pulling my shirt over my head while mine are on her ass pulling her to the edge of the counter. My fingers pushing my shorts down, as hers thread through my hair at the back of my neck.

The only time we slowdown is when I jacket up and push into her. Our kisses swallow each other's gasps as she tightens around me—a desirous torture in and of itself—as I bury all that I can within her slick, merciless heat.

There is no thought of anything but driving to the endgame. Of fucking her into oblivion.

I try to hold still.

I try to go slow.

But Chase writhes against me, her teeth nipping my bottom lip, her heels digging into my ass, as she begs me to take her there.

"Fuck me, Gunner," is the whisper in my ear, and it's all I need to hear.

Nothing else matters except for her and me, and the way she looks as she lies back on the slab on her elbows, her tits bouncing with each thrust, her pussy growing wetter with each pull back out. *She is so fucking hot.*

Even sexier is when she slides her perfectly painted red fingernails between her thighs and starts working her clit from the outside, while I work her from the inside.

It takes everything I have to hold out, to not come, because Jesus fucking Christ. Does she have any clue how goddamn hot she is in that apron with the red of her nails against the pink of her pussy, and her eyes glazing over with pleasure? Does she have any idea how she feels wrapped around me?

There is no sweet seduction this time around.

No soothing words or gentle requests. It's her and me and want that's turned to greed and greed that's given way to need.

The orgasm slams into her, robbing her of breath and tightening every damn thing in her body.

I'm not complaining, because that tightening, that writhing, that pulsing around me yanks me by the balls and pulls me over the edge.

"Chase," I groan, losing all sense of everything other than the shockwaves slowly reverberating through my every nerve.

I rest my head against hers as our breathing evens out and our pulses decelerate.

"No regrets?" she asks. When I straighten up to leave her still propped on her elbows, she has a coy smile on her lips and one of her brows is lifted.

I chuckle. "Sorry. I had a conversation with Ellie today. We discussed basically how you only live once and have to do it with no regrets. I thought it seemed fitting."

"I agree." She pushes herself up and kisses me. It's long and slow and void of the promise for sex, which I never knew could be just as much of a turn-on as when it did.

It means she wants me.

It means this is *more* for her too.

"Did you really bake me an apple pie?" I ask, glancing over my shoulder at where it rests on the top of the stove.

She laughs. "No. I bought one and stuck it in the oven to play the part. It was either sexy Chase or domestic Chase, and I chose the former for you."

"Good choice. Sexy Chase was definitely a good choice." I kiss her again.

"No regrets."

Chapter THIRTY-ONE

Chase

Days pass in laughter.

Nights crawl slowly as we make love.

Regardless of what we're doing, we can never get enough of each other.

I can never get enough of him.

And even now, staring at Gunner as he looks over his shoulder and parallel parks his truck, I'm not sure if I ever will.

He's so different than my norm, but maybe that's the problem. Maybe I needed to think outside the box. Maybe what I thought I needed wasn't it.

But is Gunner it?

I shake loose the thought, which is more and more frequent after spending so much time together. You can learn a lot about a person in a short amount of time when you're sharing space with them.

Like how clean someone is, how they like to spend their downtime, what their pet peeves are, and how they act when they're tired or hangry. The funny thing is Gunner is like me in all of those aspects other than he never puts things back where they belong. And I'm not talking in places I think they belong, but rather in the places he had them to begin with.

We've had banter over it. And tiffs.

Regardless, in the end, we've laughed and then snuggled on the couch . . . or more often than not, kissed each other until the kissing turned to snuggling in other ways.

But it's nice waking up in someone's arms. I'm not sure why I never knew that. I'm a person who always wants her space and time to decompress or sit in silence. The fact that I can do all those things without feeling smothered is new and insanely unexpected.

When Gunner looks back to the front of the truck, he catches my eye and smiles. "What?"

"Dare I ask where you've taken me?" I look around at the nondescript strip mall where we're parked. It's in the downtown area of a town about thirty miles east of Destiny Falls. There's a decent-sized sports bar across the street, a park in the distance, with huge swaying trees and a busy playground. The parking lot houses a nail salon on one end, a dog groomer on the other, and in the center is a large shop with blacked-out windows and a huge sign above the door—in font that looks like it's blurry—that reads RAGE.

"We're going there." Gunner points.

"The haunted house-looking place?" I ask, referring to the place called Rage. "Should I worry that you're trying to off me in some creepy ritual?"

"Don't be ridiculous," he says. He leans forward to press a chaste kiss to my lips before getting out of the truck, leaving me staring at him with curiosity.

When he opens my door, I simply lift an eyebrow at him, asking for more information.

"It's a rage room."

"What the hell is a rage room?" I ask as I climb out of the truck.

"After you told me about your mom the other night, about losing her at such a young age like I did my dad, about how sudden it was, and how you're not one hundred percent certain you ever really dealt with it, I figured this is exactly where you need to be."

I stare, blinking at his handsome face and kind eyes as I try to figure out what I did to deserve him. To deserve a man who actually listens to the things I say and tries to make them better.

"Gunner—"

"You mentioned in passing—maybe you didn't even mean to let it slip—that this week was the anniversary of her death. And while I don't want to pry, ask how it makes you feel, or any of that other psychobabble shit that would only serve to piss you off or make things awkward, I thought this might be a place where you can let it all out. Even for just a little bit. A place where there will be no judgment for however you choose to express yourself."

I stare at him—at this man who doesn't just listen, but really *hears* me—and am more than touched that he thought to bring me here. That he caught my slip the other night about my mom, didn't choose to call me on it, but rather opted to give me an avenue to express the mixture of grief, discord, and anger, which has been hitting me haphazardly at random times throughout this week.

Just further proof that he gets me in a way I'm not one hundred percent certain I even get myself some days.

"Look, I've been there. I've tried to shove death away, reason why it happened, you name it—and all that succeeded in doing was make me angrier. So I understand where you are, I get you, and I hate for your sake that I do." He takes my hand and points our linked fingers at the entry to Rage. "But today, we're going to take a small step towards healing the tiny cuts inside of you that break open every now and again."

"Thank you. I don't even—" I tug on his hand for him to stop, so I can lean up and press a kiss to his lips.

"You can keep thanking me if you want," he murmurs against my lips.

"I will once you explain to me what the hell we're about to do."

"Let me show you."

Over the next few minutes, I'm signed in, waivered up, and put in plastic hazmat-looking plastic coveralls.

Gunner is grinning ear to ear.

A rage room. A place where you're given time in a room to break shit. Whether it be for fun or to relieve stress or to get your anger out.

"How in the world did you ever find this place?" I ask Gunner, as he adjusts his very sexy (not) goggles over his eyes.

"Someone mentioned it in the bar a while back. Some of the guys and I came here to check it out. I thought it might be a good way to let some of that bottled-up emotion out."

Normally I'd be pissed if someone said that to me, as if they were judging me or telling me what to do, but Gunner's words don't elicit that reaction.

He's lost his father.

He's lost his friends.

He understands.

And maybe, just maybe, I want him to understand me better. In fact, I like the fact that he understands me.

"To make the most of your experience, change your weapon every few minutes," the employee tells us as he stands at the door to the rage room. "There are bats, hammers, clubs—you name it. Also, music helps. You can change that as often as you want as well or pick a theme song and stick with it. Loud is good. Blaring is better." His grin is infectious and implies he's had some fun in here before. "Oh, and make sure to scream and yell and get whatever it is you're here for, all out."

I look around the padded square room where a row of weapons of sorts hang on one side of the wall and a table sits in the middle. The table has electronics on it, glass vases. There are metal—what looks like kegs—in another area right below the row of shelves of stacked dishes.

"Some people even prefer to write what they're angry about in Sharpie on the plates so when they smash them, they can feel like they're breaking it." He steps toward the door. "I'm going to give you five minutes to get ready, and then I'll start the music and timer for you."

Gunner and I both nod in agreement and then the minute the door shuts, we both start laughing. "This is crazy," I say.

"Just wait till you see how good you feel after." He walks toward the plates. "Now I, for one, am going to write some things on the plates so I can enjoy smashing them."

"Like what?"

"Sal is pretty much one of my go-tos." And the way he says it, as if he's completely okay with letting me into the struggles he still has over his asshole stepfather, makes him even more endearing to me.

"Let's do two for him," I say and he laughs.

But then I find myself looking at plates with a Sharpie in hand and too many things I want to write and let go of. I take the first plate and write Mom. She's the one thing I'm most angry at. Not her, of course, but that she was taken away from me and missed out on so much of the important things in life. Then I write Finn. He is my ex—the man I first let in, who cheated on me—a man who strangely hurt me deeply. And then when the siren warns that we only have a minute left to prepare to rage, I write on two more plates. The first is "time," because my time here with Gunner is running out when I don't want it to be.

And for the last one, I write my name. *Chase.* Because I hate myself for deceiving Gunner . . . and for knowing that when I leave Destiny Falls it has to be like I was never here. Like I never existed. It's not like I can give him my address and tell him to come and visit me. It's not like he can ever know who I really am.

So I write my name down because I hate myself for deceiving him, and I hate myself even more for not allowing this to be anything more than it is.

"You good?" Gunner asks as he glances over at my stack of plates and probably mistakes the tears welling in my eyes to be over the loss of my mother. They're equally for knowing I'm going to lose him too.

I nod and force a smile, still thinking this is a little silly. "I'm ready."

The siren sounds and Gunner picks up his first plate and throws it against the wall as hard as he can. It shatters into a million fragments, the sound of it breaking just above the fray of Jagger singing about how he can't get any satisfaction.

I take my first plate in my hand and follow suit. There's something to be said about the crunch of glass and the exertion you've given to make that happen.

It's satisfying. Cathartic. And with each item thrown, each smash of the hammer against the computer monitor, every swing of the bat against the metal barrels, I feel parts of myself unwind.

Is this going to fix the brain aneurysm that took my mom from me, the fact that she's gone, and how she missed all the milestones in my life? No, but it feels damn good to be thinking about it and angry over it while I'm swinging the bat as hard as I can.

I lose myself in the task. In the smashing and aggression, so much so that when the buzzer rings telling us our time is up, besides being out of breath, I am completely unaware that there are tears staining both of my cheeks.

Gunner notices but only nods. In fact, he doesn't say a word to me while we're removing our protective equipment and gathering our personal belongings.

And I'm glad he doesn't, because I'm a mess.

His hand on my lower back ushering me out of the place—*and* his absolute silence—shows me he understands the tumult of emotion I'm going through. *He's giving me time to sort through it.*

And it's only when we clear the building and we're about to get in his truck that the tidal wave of feelings hits me and drags me under its hold. Gunner wraps his arms around me while I sob.

I'm angry that she's gone. I hate that I haven't had a mom for more than half of my life. I hate that my dad lost the love of his life. I loathe that I let Finn's infidelity affect me. I'm furious that Gunner's mom and stepdad hurt him so remorselessly. I'm crushed that I've met this amazing, wonderful man, and I can't have him in my life after I leave.

And I'm angry at myself.

Because I might be another person to cause him pain.

The pain and hurt surges in a whirl of sorrow. I've never felt this before. Never known I was capable of feeling this . . . distress. And if you asked me a month ago, I would have said I was a pretty happy person. In this moment, I can see why I'm so driven. Why I keep pushing forward. Why I stick to lists and spreadsheets.

They can't hurt you.

And through this mess, Gunner holds me. He continues to silently comfort me. When the sobs subside, he grabs my hand and says, "Some fresh air and a walk might do some good."

So we walk.

Toward the park and on its meandering path. Around games of hopscotch and between kids riding their bikes.

He allows me to sort out my feelings without asking, and there's something so powerful in that to me. That he knew me well enough, understands this well enough, knowing what I needed when I didn't even know.

"I can admit that I'm mortified I just had a major meltdown, but it's not going to do anything to take it back," I say as we circle around the small lake that edges the park.

"Why be mortified? Death is permanent while coping with it is a living, breathing emotion that you have to adapt to on the daily," he says, his words making more sense than most people's. "I just hope it helped. It's bizarre, because at first, you think it's a weird idea. And then you get the spiel from the guy and figure you'll just go along with it. Then before you know it, you're smashing shit and getting caught up in the emotions that only you know and understand, but it feels so damn good to let it all out."

"How do you know exactly what to say and how to say it so that I hear you?" I ask, prompting him to stop and stare at me.

His hands come up to frame my face and his eyes hold mine. "Because we're two peas in a pod, Chase. We may have gotten in that pod by different routes, but somehow, we fit there. Somehow, we understand each other. Somehow, we know it works." He presses a tender kiss against my lips. "Who are we to question it?"

Chapter THIRTY-TWO

Chase

"Are you not calling me on purpose or should I just assume you're super busy and not feel hurt over it?" my dad asks as a greeting when I answer his call.

"Funny. Very funny." I glance to the backyard where Gunner is mowing the grass. He's deliciously shirtless—his every muscle glistening with a mist of sweat. And as much as I'd like to admire him, I'll take this time while he's outside to discuss work things with my dad. That's been the hardest thing about this whole setup with living at Gunner's.

I can do work just fine on my computer without him thinking I'm doing anything other than my thesis, but it's the phone calls that pose problems.

And me being on the phone is an essential element of my job.

"I could also think that you're avoiding me, but I'll assume you'll refute that handily, so do you want to tell me what exactly you're doing?"

"Brexton and Dekker haven't told you?" Shock filters through me. My sisters are always first to run and tattle about what little Chase is doing. I love and I hate it—depending on the day—because as annoying as it is, it also shows me that even with their busy lives, they care.

"They told me about the pitcher—Gunner or is it Ryan—but I was hoping you'd at least call and fill me in."

"I only know him as Gunner. So that's what I call him, but I found him, Dad. I found him and he's nothing like I expected." *And like everything I never knew I wanted.*

"But you're not telling him about the letter because he doesn't know who you are, right?"

"Something like that," I say quietly, waiting for his lecture about honesty and being upfront.

But it doesn't come.

That, in and of itself, has me pursing my lips and wondering what he's not saying.

"Okay," he says. "So you found the pitcher who's no longer a pitcher. You're volunteering at the place he volunteers and trying to do good things there. Then at nighttime, you're getting to know him better. Then, what? You're just coming back home in the near future?"

"I guess Dekk and Brex didn't tell you the whole of it," I say in regards to the getting to know him better part.

"Oh, they told me all right. I know you're dating him. Doing things with him." He clears his throat, clearly uncomfortable with that aspect, and I fight my grin.

"Oh. Okay."

"Did you expect me to say something else?" he asks.

"You're not going to tell me to get my ass back to New York because I'm slacking in getting shit done?"

"I'm not going to tell you anything. I could tell you that you have contracts piling up and requests coming in that need your attention. That regardless of your absence, I'm impressed with the progress you've made with marketing and social media and excited to see how this will help KSM move forward. I could sit here and badger you with questions, and tell you that it's ridiculous to play out this charade, one that I hope won't hurt you in the end. But I won't. When you left here, you told me you'd be home on a set date, and I'm going to trust that you will be since you haven't told me otherwise."

I watch Gunner doing normal, weekend things and wonder how it's going to feel to miss this when I do go home. The ease. The comfort. The having someone who gets me.

"Honey?" my dad says.

"Hmm?" I don't trust myself to talk, because I think my voice would betray the nonchalance I'm attempting about leaving here.

To leaving Gunner.

"Remember this. The best relationships are the ones you never saw coming."

"Who said anything about a relationship?"

His chuckle is low and comforting and a tad mocking. "Because I know you, and if my Chase wasn't going to get the prize, she would have had her shit packed and be headed home as soon as possible. My Chase doesn't like failing at anything and so—"

"I didn't fail," I say and then realize it only serves to prove his point.

"No, but you didn't come home." I can hear the smile in his voice. "That tells me all I need to know."

"Dad." The lone word is an exasperated sigh.

"Don't apologize, Chase. Enjoy your time. Paint the town red. Sometimes life just happens and you have to jump on the merry-go-round till it's time to get off."

I don't know why tears come to my eyes but they do, and I blink them away. "How do you know when it's time?" My voice is barely a whisper when I ask.

"Sometimes it's never time. Sometimes you have to get used to that incredible dizzy feeling. It forces you to readjust the way you look at the world, because you realize you can't live without it like you once did."

I clear my throat and try to find the words to respond. "I don't have that option, Dad."

But his words stay with me all day.

As Gunner and I laughed and had an impromptu dance party while we barbequed burgers. As we had a mini make-out session on the couch—simply kissing, and nothing else. I can't remember the last time in my adult life a man simply wanted to kiss me, to enjoy the act, without using it as a precursor to sex.

It was refreshing.

It was sexually frustrating.

And there was something special about it that simply owned my heart.

Yet, my dad's talk about merry-go-rounds and being dizzy spun in my mind and now I can't sleep. So I wander through the house. I look at pictures on a bookshelf. One of him and a woman who looks so much like him, I assume she's his mom. One of four soldiers in addition to Gunner and wonder if this is the group he talks about often. The one he celebrates the birthdays of even though they're no longer here.

I walk past Gunner where he has fallen asleep on the couch. Sleep comes so hard for him, even after a long day and closing down the bar, I've noticed he's usually fitful in sleep. So much so that many nights I wake up to find the bed beside me cold and when I get up to look, he's typically sitting on the couch or at his desk in the alcove off the kitchen. Anything to exhaust him to the point of no return so as he says, "the nightmares don't come."

But tonight, he fell asleep on the couch when he got home after closing FU-Bar. I laid a blanket on top of him and went to bed alone, not wanting to disturb him, but his sleep isn't peaceful.

It was his struggling with someone in his sleep that woke me even from where I was asleep in the bedroom. I contemplated waking him up to pull him from the dream but by the time I got to the family room, he was settled.

But the nightmare is still there, still troubling him, and I wish I could do something to soothe him or make him feel better. I know I can't. I know soft words from a girlfriend aren't going to erase the horrors of war that his mind relives, and that's hard for me to accept.

"Stay with me. Shotgun. *Come on*. Don't you fucking die on me." He groans and kicks his feet around. Normally he settles down after an outburst, but this time he continues to be agitated. A tear slides down his cheek. He gurgles, like he's drowning. He thrashes his head from side to side.

I watch him for what feels like an eternity and can't take it any longer. I do the only thing I know to do. I squeeze my ass onto the couch beside him and gently rub my hands up and down his chest so as not to startle him.

It's something that first my mom and then Dekker used to do to me when I was a little girl and struggling with a nightmare.

Gunner startles awake, disoriented with wide eyes and his chest heaving, ready to fight against me as if I were the enemy.

"Are you okay?" he asks me when he catches his breath and orients himself.

"Mm-hmm," I say quietly, as I stay where I'm seated but lay my chest on top of his so I can slide my arms around him. It takes him a second before he accepts the silent comfort and compassion and wraps his arms around me in turn.

We lie like this for some time. With his chin on the crown of my head and my head on his chest, with the strong staccato of his heart against my ear.

"I don't sleep well most nights," he murmurs after a bit, finally breaking the silence.

"Understandably."

"I have to work myself to the point of utter exhaustion before I crash or else the nightmares come."

I'm the furthest thing from a psychologist, but the one thing I can imagine is that most nights Gunner feels completely out of control against his memories. It's an assumption—maybe it's even something I read in the Military Life magazine in my hotel room—but it's enough to make me want him to feel in control of this conversation at least.

It's not much but it's the best I can do.

"I'm here if you want to talk about the nightmare. I'm here if you don't want to talk about it." I press a kiss to his chest. "I'm just here, is all."

Gunner runs his hand up and down the length of my back and blows out a sigh. "I led the guys into the village that day. I'm the one who trusted our interpreter and thought he was trustworthy. I was pissed about everything back home and didn't care what trouble we got ourselves into. I was the selfish one because while I felt that way, they all had families at home and people who loved them."

"As did you," I whisper.

"No. I had nothing anymore. As I explained, I'd said goodbye to everything that had mattered to me before in the letters Dickman suggested I write. One went to my mom where I told her I loved her, but that I could no longer live in her world full of excuses and misgivings. A few went to sports agencies telling them thanks, but no thanks. Another to the girl I had been dating at the time. I had nothing and no one who I felt missed me, so I was the reckless one, leading my men, *my brothers*, into danger."

His words cut through me like a knife, and I struggle how to comfort, how to acknowledge, how to relate when there's no possible way I ever could. "I don't even know what to say."

"There's nothing you can say. It was what I had to do to survive the situation I was in. But it also made me dangerous to those around me, because I didn't care what happened to me since I'd already said goodbye to everything I'd loved."

"Jesus, Gunner."

"Yeah, I know better now. I know how precious life is and all that I would have missed out on . . . but that day, I didn't care. I didn't care, and so I pushed our team to go into that village and get the intel I was told was there. I harassed Dickman when he said no. I got the guys rallied up over it. I was the one who caused it."

"You're not at fault for what happened."

"Men died, Chase. My friends, *my brothers*, died. And I'm the one who has to bear that burden my whole life." His sigh is heavy, his chest shuddering right after. "I told you I wasn't as good as you've made me out to be in your head."

His chuckle is self-deprecating at best and the sound of it holds so much grief and guilt that I can't not argue with him. I sit up so that he's forced to meet my eyes.

"You weren't the commanding officer. Dickman could have said no. He could have told you to go to hell. You are not—"

"I pushed for it though." His eyes glisten with tears that destroy me. "I was so desperate to feel again that maybe I craved the thrill of a fight. Maybe I needed to make sure I wasn't dead . . . and in the course, killed four of my friends."

I frame his face, my soft hands against his rough stubble, and wish I could take away his pain, but know I can't. "I can tell you till I'm blue in the face that you're not to blame, but I know you won't hear or accept it. So I'm going to tell you this, Gunner Camden, and I hope you hear it. You are an incredible human being who not only saved lives that day with your heroics—"

"Chase—"

"No. *You listen to me.* You saved lives that day, and in the process, almost got yourself killed. Since then, you've dedicated your free time to kids who don't have parents and created a successful business where you give a part of the earnings from your hard work to widows of your fallen soldiers." I lean forward and press a kiss to his lips. "*You* make a difference, Gunner. You've devoted your life to trying to ease the survivor's guilt you have, while you make so many more lives better. You make a difference."

He doesn't say anything, but his Adam's apple bobs as he swallows, and he blinks away the tears welling in his eyes.

And I'm okay with the fact that instead of words, he pulls me back down to his chest and just holds on tight.

His chest hitches and each time it does, my heart breaks a little more and fills with love at the same time.

And it makes me coming to terms with what I've done and what I'm going to have to do that much harder.

While I thought it would be okay to walk away from him not sharing my truths, I know I can't do that now. Given his complete honesty, his honor, his heart, he deserves my utmost respect. I don't want him to believe that I set out to delude him, but he does need to know that in withholding the truth from him, for lying to him, he has the right to feel deceived.

Shit. I hate this.

Tears form in my eyes. Apart from my family, it's never mattered so much that someone not think badly of me. Knowing Gunner may hate me for dodging the truth is tearing me apart.

I love him. Simple as that. But I know I won't know his love in return. I'll have to leave before I can feel that. *And that is the worst type of pain.*

I'll hurt, but as I've thought before, he doesn't deserve to be hurt anymore.

Chapter THIRTY-THREE

Chase

"I'll get that contract over to you ASAP. I'm sorry it's late, I'm just a little buried right now," I say as I look out the open reception window into the gymnasium area where Joey and Robbie are practicing their free throws.

"Buried? Since when do you get buried? You're a badass, Kincade," Darius Tomlinson, three-time Pro-Bowler and one of my long-standing clients, says with a laugh.

"I get buried. Now get your ass back on the field and prove to me you're worth every penny I just negotiated for you."

"Yes, ma'am."

I end the call and drop my cell on the desk.

"Get your ass back on the field?" a voice from behind me says, causing me to nearly jump out of my shoes. "Negotiations?"

"Ellie. My God." I whirl around. "You just scared the shit out of me."

How much did you hear?

My heart is in my throat as I stare at her and wonder what she heard.

"Sorry. I was just coming to hand over some checks that a few parents gave me when they dropped their kids off. I didn't mean to interrupt your negotiations," she says. I hate the feeling that she's asking me to explain without asking me.

"Negotiations." I chuckle, thinking on the fly. "That was my cousin. He's in college. I negotiated with his mom to buy him a new pair of cleats if he wins his upcoming game."

The lie rolls easily off my tongue and I hate that it does. That this is what I've resorted to, but it's necessary to keep this ruse up.

"Oh, and here I was selfishly and now embarrassingly hoping it was about the gear for The Center." Her cheeks flush.

"That's coming too. I promise. I heard back from my friend and he's gotten the baseball team, the Austin Aces, to contribute new gear and uniforms for the kids. We also have a new sports court coming courtesy of the NHL team the Lumberjacks, as well as some new turf as a donation from the New York Raptors."

Her eyes widen and her surprise makes me feel good about doing this. About helping The Center out. About helping to make a difference in some small capacity.

"That's amazing," she says. "Gunner didn't tell me all of that."

"I think he's holding his breath to see it happen first, and I totally understand that, but I'm going to make it happen." But when I glance back toward the gym area, I'm immediately drawn to the doorway when I see Joey pointing to Gunner's neck.

"What are those?" Joey asks, his voice loud and innocent.

"What are what?" Gunner asks, half distracted with showing Robbie how to roll the basketball off his fingertips.

"Those red marks on your neck," Joey continues. "Nick said they're from where you were abducted by aliens, but I think you were hurt."

Gunner stops what he's doing and turns to give his full attention to Joey. "Nick is wrong and you were right," he says, his voice softening as he lowers himself to the floor and sits cross-legged so he's eye level with Joey. "Would you like to see them?"

Joey nods slowly, earnest and cautious eyes staring at Gunner as if he's not sure if he should be embarrassed that he asked.

"Sure," Gunner says and proceeds to pull his shirt over his head. I'm used to what they look like so I don't flinch at the sight of the angry, red scars. But there is something about seeing him there, shirtless and vulnerable, being stared at by eight little boys that makes them seem so devastating.

The reactions of the boys are a mixture of gasps and whoas, but Gunner just sits there as if it's not a big deal to be sitting there and stared at.

"Do you have questions?" he asks softly.

"Do they hurt?"

"How did it happen?"

"Did you almost die?"

Questions are asked unabashedly as only kids can do, and Gunner spends time explaining to them. "They don't really hurt anymore but they did when they happened and a long time afterward. I had to be in the hospital with lots of doctors to try and make sure I was going to heal properly."

"How did it happen?" Robbie repeats his question.

"I was in an accident," Gunner says. "There was an explosion on the side of the road and it hit my Humvee."

"IED?" Gregory asks. It kills me that these boys use these terms so nonchalantly. It's something they should never be so familiar with and yet . . . they are.

Gunner nods and meets his eyes. "Yes. An IED."

There are more questions. Will they ever go away? Does he have metal plates under his skin? Is he embarrassed by them?

But it's the last question spoken so very quietly that has both Ellie and me holding our breaths.

"Were you scared?" Joey asks in the softest of voices that has all of the kids turning to look at him—as if that's the one unspoken question they all wondered about. And before Gunner can answer, Joey continues. "I bet my daddy was scared."

My breath hitches at the question and at seeing Gunner motion for Joey to come closer. When he does, Gunner sits him on his knee and says so everyone can hear. "Yes, I was scared, but I knew your daddy, Joey. And I know he wasn't scared. He was too busy thinking about you and your mommy and how much he loved you guys and how proud he was of you."

Joey's chin quivers and mine does right along with his. I watch Joey reach out and run his hand over the top part of Gunner's shoulder to feel his scars. "Do you think he hurt?" Joey asks.

Gunner works a swallow down his throat and shakes his head. "No. I don't. I think you guys loved him so much that all that love protected him from the hurt."

"You sure?" Joey asks as a single tear slides down his cheek.

"I'm sure," Gunner says, his voice breaking. "Any other questions?"

"Can we play basketball now?" Carl asks and everyone jumps up, but not before I notice Gunner whisper something in Joey's ear that has him nodding. They sit there for a moment, staring at each other, before getting up and joining the group like that was as normal as normal can be.

But not me.

The whole scene has shaken me to the core in a way I never could have expected. I knew Gunner was a good man, but he gets these kids in a way most can't. *Even though it sounds like no one was there for him. No one held him. No one reassured him.* That exchange with Joey right there might save him years of worry and stress over his dad's final moments. But because he trusts Gunner, he'll now believe what he said. He'll now maybe have some peace.

"He makes it impossible, you know," Ellie says beside me, as she wipes smudged mascara from under her eyes.

"Who makes what impossible?" I ask.

"Gunner. He makes it impossible to not fall in love with him."

"I'm not—I can't—"

"Sure. Justify it any way you want, but you are."

She states it so matter-of-factly that I don't even disagree. And maybe by not agreeing, I'm trying to pretend it isn't true. "I have a life to get back to. A job. A family. My thesis."

Her eyes hold mine for the longest time. They reflect compassion and understanding but also a fierce protection for her friend. "It's funny how sometimes the things you left behind feel different when you return to them after new experiences. It's like what was important suddenly shifts and a whole new set of things replace them."

Chapter THIRTY-FOUR

Gunner

My chest hurts.

It's the first time in as long as I can remember that throwing the baseball as hard as I could didn't help things.

It's the second time in as long as I can remember that I called in sick to work and had someone cover my shift when I wasn't really sick.

Fucking Joey. And his innocent and heartbreaking questions and my downright lies. I can't shake the look on his face when he asked me if his dad was scared. What was I supposed to tell him? That I'm sure he was as terrified as I was as pain owned my body and the metallic scent of blood and explosives was all I could smell. That like me, his every instinct was to get up and run, to fight, but that he couldn't. I couldn't think, couldn't comprehend anything other than sheer terror. I may have said goodbye to everything I loved, but I still wanted to live.

I didn't have a wife. Or a sweet little son. All I had was a sport and an opportunity missed.

When I woke up in that hospital bed, all I could think about was making sure the second chance I was given was earned.

Yet the question often rattles around in my head—*why am I here and he's not?* Especially on days like today when I'm faced with a pair of innocent blue eyes asking me questions I don't have answers to.

I take the turn down my street. My legs ache and my chest burns, as my feet pound the pavement, step after step. My head's still a fucking mess, but all of those things assure me I'm alive. They tell me . . . no regrets.

My pace quickens when I see the house.

When I see the light on and know there's someone there waiting for me. Wanting me.

Is it a waste to have this life, this second chance, *this woman* I want to come home to, and not live it to the fullest? To not fight for more with her? To not wonder what it'd be like to have a little Joey of our own to watch grow up?

Slow the fuck down, Gunner.

You can't want that with her.

Hell, you've never even wanted that yourself until now. Until her.

She's not staying.

And yet when I see her shadow pass in front of the window, I wonder what it would be like.

I question what it would take to change the situation.

I force myself to wonder just how hard I'm willing to fight.

But I don't know the answer. I don't have one, because this whole situation has taken me by utter fucking surprise.

Don't think, Gunner. Just feel.

Don't question. Just enjoy.

Chase.

I feel broken but know there's only one way to fix me. One place to go. One person to wrap her arms around me and make the pain lessen. To make me feel that much better.

And I'm not certain how I'm going to let her go in the coming weeks but then again, no regrets.

It's all I can rationalize as I jog up the walk, needing her more than I've ever needed someone before.

No fucking regrets.

Chapter THIRTY-FIVE

Chase

"CHASE?" GUNNER'S VOICE AND THE SLAM OF THE DOOR THAT follows takes me by total surprise.

He's supposed to be at the bar. He's not supposed to be home until two in the morning.

In an act of desperation, I take all my work—notepads and endorsement contracts and . . . freaking everything I have on the desk in front of me—and shove it into my oversized bag so he doesn't see it.

"In here," I stutter and snap my laptop shut before tripping over my bag—which in turn regurgitates some of its contents back out. With haste, I shove it back in and practically jog to find out why he's home.

"Gunner? Is everything okay?" I ask as I clear the family room to find him standing there. His T-shirt has a small sweat-darkened V around his neck and his chest is heaving, but it's the look on his face that owns me. Confusion. Melancholy. *Need.* "Gunner?"

He crosses the room towards me and without a single word, wraps his arms around me, pressing my back to the wall, and kisses me.

There's desperation to the kiss. Urgency. An underlying emotion I can't place.

"I just need you right now, Chase," he says when he comes up for air. "I just fucking need you."

Our eyes meet, and I know in that moment anything he asks for is his. After the emotion with Joey today and the look in his eyes now, it's clear he's struggling and needs connection.

I don't know what I can offer besides getting lost in us, but I'm here. *I'm his.*

He doesn't say another word. Instead he kisses me again, the pace a little slower, the emotion in it almost palpable.

"Chase," he whispers as he pulls my shirt over my head and closes his lips over my bra-clad breast. "I just need you."

"I'm here," I whisper as I pull his shirt off too.

There's no forethought to our actions. No planning to move to a bed or make sure we've given each other equal foreplay. There's just him and me and this swell of unexpected pain that's drowning us whole.

My hands run over the lines of his body. Sculpted edges marred with raised scar tissue. My lips express words I don't speak. My body pressed tightly against his, showing him that I'm here for him however he wants or needs.

Words are irrelevant as we move toward the bedroom. The only break in kissing is when clothes are discarded. The only breath of air is the other's exhale.

I kiss my way down his body as we stand at the foot of the bed. Over scars he hisses at when my lips connect. Over abs that tense beneath my mouth. Over the length of his cock, hard and ready for me.

His moaned exhale is the only sound in the room as I take him in my mouth. His hard crest. His full length. The salty taste of him on my tongue. The feel of his hands bunching in the back of my hair and tightening as I slowly work him in and out of my mouth.

His breathing grows harsh, his thighs grow tense, and with a feral growl, he drops to his knees in front of me, brandishing his lips to mine once again.

"I—just—you—Chase." His words make no sense, incomplete thoughts as he tries to process this, *us*.

"I'm right here." My lips meet his again when he leans back against the bed and I straddle myself over him.

"Look at me," he moans. "Look at me."

And when I do, when our eyes lock, he guides my hips to slowly sink down onto him. It's ecstasy. It's torture in the most pleasurable of ways. It's everything to watch his eyes grow cloudy and his mouth grow lax as he groans with the same pleasure that's assaulting every nerve in my body. My name ghosts over his lips and for some reason, I know the sound—how he says it—will stay with me forever.

It's as if he has everything he's ever needed in this moment.

Tears spring to my eyes in complete contradiction to the bliss I know is coming. And when one slips over and slides down my cheek, he presses a kiss to it.

"I know," he says quietly against my skin. "I know."

My breath catches then, because he begins to move. It's slow but not timid, desperate but not urgent.

As two bodies connect and become one.

As we begin the slow process of subconsciously saying goodbye.

And afterward, when I'm in the bathroom trying to scrub the tear stains off my cheeks, I know walking away from Gunner Camden is going to be the hardest thing I'll ever do.

"Hey," he says from the doorway and startles me.

I look up from the sink and stare at him through the mirror. He's dressed and his keys are in his hand, but his eyes are still heavy with a wariness I can't pinpoint.

"Are you leaving?"

He stares at me for a bit longer before finally speaking. "This is crazy, and I don't understand it whatsoever, but I've fallen for you, Chase. Fallen, when I've told myself it's not possible to because I know you're leaving and this will be over. But I promised myself after everything I went through, that I'd never leave anything on the table again, and so yeah . . . There you go." He chuckles nervously, while I just stare at him through the mirror, trying to process words and feelings I don't know what to do with either. He gives a shake of his head. "I'll see you later."

"Wait. What?" I ask as I spin around to face him. He can't drop a bombshell like that on me and then leave. "Where are you going?"

"Out."

"Out? Why?" My voice cracks.

"Because this," he says motioning to the two of us, "isn't *you*. I know it and you've made sure to let me know it numerous times . . . so I'm going out to give you some time to come to grips with what I just said. I either just screwed up and you're going to be gone when I come home, or you'll be here and we'll at least spend the rest of our time knowing where we stand."

He strides forward with a purpose that was absent earlier and presses a chaste kiss to my lips. Without saying another word, he walks out of the house with a slam of the front door, leaving me behind, staring at where he just was.

And then I freak.

I can't get to the door fast enough. His truck's not there and I panic that he's already left, but then I realize that he ran home so he has to walk back to wherever he left his truck.

"Gunner!" I yell when I spot him halfway down the block.

My feet move toward him as he stops. At first in a fast walk and then at a jog until I reach him and jump, wrapping my legs around his waist.

He laughs and staggers back a few feet from the impact as my mouth finds his again.

"This isn't normal for me. I don't do this," I say in between kisses.

"Kissing someone on the sidewalk? Neither do I." He laughs and then kisses me back.

"The person you've fallen for isn't the normal me. Normally I'm Big City Chase in high heels and a million things to do and a stress level through the roof. This—being here—is a different version of her. You might not even like her for all I know."

His laugh is muffled against my lips. "It sounds like you're trying to talk me out of liking you, Kincade."

I lean back and look at him, my look so intense that when I try to drop my legs to the ground, he lets me.

"Chase?" he asks as the words clog in my throat.

"I've fallen for you too, Gunner. I'm scared to say it. To admit it. Because I don't know how to deal with this feeling. All I know is when you walk into the room, I sit up a little taller, wanting you to notice me. When you leave the room, I can't wait for you to come back. When I wake up at night, I feel safer knowing you're close to me. And when I look across the breakfast table, I smile when I see you there."

"That says a lot considering I'm a scary sight when I wake up."

I shake my head and laugh, suddenly feeling more than shy as we stand on the sidewalk for the world to see. Although, it feels like it's just the two of us.

"So what do we do now?" I ask.

"I get it. This isn't you. This town. The single movie theater. The Center. You have your sights set on stadiums and neon lights. I admire that about you. You go after what you want and you have goals. A ton of goals that I'd have killed for when I was younger. If I had, maybe things might have ended up differently . . . but it didn't, and I love my life, Chase. I can't ask you to be who you're not. I can't ask you to stay when you have a whole goddamn world to conquer."

I stare at him, at this incredible man, and wonder how my whole world just narrowed in such a short time and became solely about him. My world used to have no beginning or ending point but now when I look at him, he's both of those to me.

But he's right. Completely and utterly right. I have things to accomplish. The world to conquer, and I can't do that sitting here in some small town in the middle of nowhere-ville.

But I don't put words to my thoughts, to my concerns. I simply press my lips to his while figuratively burying my head in the sand.

"We'll figure it out," he says. "I've fallen in love with you, Chase." He reaches out and touches the sides of my face, that shy smile of his owning his lips and my heart. "I've never said that to anyone before."

He doesn't wait for me to say it back. Maybe he already knows that I'm struggling with accepting the truth of it and kisses me.

And late at night when we're lying in bed and I'm staring at the shadows dancing on the ceiling, I realize I made a huge mistake.

In the midst of the euphoria of feeling the power of love for the first time, I forgot that this can't be real.

That this *can't happen.*

And I realize I just did something worse than leaving him when this is over.

I gave Gunner hope that there could be more.

Chapter THIRTY-SIX

Gunner

"Yeah. Let me get it. I think I brought it home with me," I say to Ellie as I stumble through the house, half asleep but on a high from trying to process last night.

The low of Joey.

My confused feelings.

Then coming home to Chase.

I love her. Fucking love her. It feels like a weight off my chest to be able to say it out loud all while knowing she feels the same.

"I saw it under your arm when you left," Ellie adds, having no clue I'm over here in a love fest of my own. "But that was like three or four days ago."

"Shit," I mutter as I stub my toe.

"That good of a morning, huh?" She chuckles.

"Yes. I'm just tired. You know better than to call me this early." I shuffle through the papers I set on the console when I walk in the front door. "Not there," I mutter to myself and run a hand through my hair as I yawn. Then I head to the kitchen counter to see the pile I set down when I came in the house last night, but the rosters aren't there either.

"Where was Chase?" she asks.

"What do you mean where was Chase?"

"I mean, I'm sure that's where you set the folder down, because no doubt you walked inside and went straight to her since you two lovebirds can't keep your hands off each other."

I roll my eyes but she does have a good point, so I head into the second bedroom to the desk Chase works at. I start shuffling through the small stack of my stuff on the corner, accidentally knocking over her bag.

"Shit." The contents come spilling out. "One sec, Ell. I knocked something over."

"Figures," she teases as I set the phone down.

I'm halfway through putting the disarray of folders back into her bag when something catches my eye.

It's an orange envelope on the floor next to my foot. I freeze as memories collide with the sudden confusion roiling around inside of me.

There's no way.

It can't be.

It's a common envelope.

It's merely a coincidence.

Yet when I pick it up, when I see my handwriting on the front of it and my name in the upper left-hand corner, my whole world lifts off its axis and crashes back down in a completely different location.

All the air is sucked out of the room as a suffocating, confusing feeling dizzies my head.

I can't breathe.

My pulse pounds in my ears.

I can't think.

To make the memories and the pain of that night, of writing this letter, go away.

I can't fucking process.

To make the sudden gut punch of seeing this—in my house—ease.

This was in Chase's bag. Why would she have this? Why would . . . but when I look closer at the faded sports agency it's addressed to, it's like a lead weight drops through me.

KSM.

How did I ever forget what that stood for? How did I not make the goddamn connection?

Kincade Sports Management.

Chase *Kincade.*

My stomach churns as I stumble to the spare bed and sit, trying to comprehend what I'm seeing. What I'm assuming.

"Gunner? *Gun?*" I barely hear through my cell I set down.

I grab it. "I have to call you back," I say, but don't wait for her to respond before I lower my phone.

Chase knew who I was.

She knew all along.

My hands are shaking as the past—a past I'd long ago walked away from—collides with the future. A future I thought I was possibly walking into.

"Gunner? Are you here—" Chase's words stop about the same time the padding of her feet on the floor do.

It's going to kill me to look at her. It's going to gut me to look at this woman who's wearing my T-shirt and whose hair is messy from sleeping in my bed—*a woman I love*—and know she deceived me all along.

Chapter THIRTY-SEVEN

Chase

My stomach drops to my feet when I see Gunner sitting on the spare bed. My bag is on its side, the contents partially fallen out from his surprise return home last night, but it's the letter he's holding in his hands that devastates me.

My head shakes back and forth as panic ricochets through me.

No. No. No.

"It's not what you think." They're my first words and an absolutely shitty first defense, but it's all I've got.

Gunner stares at the envelope in his hand as if I've sliced him completely open, allowing every memory and every vulnerability to be laid bare. But it's when his eyes finally lift to meet mine that I realize an iota of the devastation I might have caused with this charade.

The deep brown of his eyes beg and question and despise me all at the same time. I struggle with what else to say or what to even do. I want to look away. I want to hide from the hurt I've caused but know that I can't do either.

I owe him that much at least.

"Where did you get this?" he finally whispers.

"It was delivered to my office a couple of months ago." My voice is timid. I'm so afraid to do or say the wrong thing when I've already done so much wrong to begin with.

"To *your office? Kincade* Sports Management is your office?" His voice escalates in pitch with each word. "I thought you were a grad student working on her thesis. I thought you were learning about military life, deployment, and Jesus Christ," he says and runs a hand through his hair. "Kincade Sports Management. I remember it now. The dad and the daughters working for him. You're one of his daughters. YOU are part of it. You're a sports agent."

"Gunner." His name is a plea to forgive me, to let me explain, to anything.

"Now it all makes perfect sense to me. Fucking perfect sense—*don't you take another step toward me*," he thunders, causing tears to spring to my eyes and stopping me in my tracks.

"It's not what you think. This is all a mistake. A white lie that tumbled out of control before I could fix it, and by then it was too late. By then I was falling for you and knew deception was something that was a deal-breaker for you—"

"You're goddamn right it is. Have you not listened to me? About the deceit that cost me the life I had? The dreams I once had?" He shoves up off the bed and paces back and forth in the small space, the orange envelope gripped in his hand. "I thought you were . . . everything I thought about you . . . *you're not you*." His voice is barely audible. The disbelief edged with hurt in it is like a knife to my heart.

"*I am me*. I promise. I just got—"

"You warned me. Fucking told me I wouldn't like the real you and I . . . I argued with you about it. Fought you on it and"—his eyes are defeated but sparked with anger as he shakes his head—"*you were right*."

"No. Don't say that. I am me. I am the same person. I just—"

"What about the boys?" he asks, switching gears as if he can't focus on one thing at a time. My surefooted Gunner is anything but that right now. "*You made promises to little kids*. And for what? To win me over. To use them to get to me—"

"Those promises are real," I shout with an exasperated desperation. "You have to believe me. The boys have nothing to do with this. I never would—"

"Believe you?" He laughs, arms out to the side, looking at me like I'm crazy.

"Gunner, you have to believe me—"

"*You played me*." He pounds his fist on the desk beside him and then storms past me out of the close confines of the room. I scurry behind him, desperate in a way I've never been before. "And for what?"

"I thought . . . I thought I'd find you and maybe, I don't know. Get you an audience in front of a major league scout." He snorts, and I hold up my hands in front of me. "I know *now* you don't play anymore, but I thought it would be cool to realize your dream. To tell your grandkids someday that you did it."

"All this off a letter, huh?" The muscle in his jaw pulses as his eyes bore into me.

"I just . . . I thought we could make a whole thing of it. KSM would host a veterans' game type of thing. Raise some money for a good cause—"

"What cause would that be?" he snaps.

"I don't know. The Center? Wounded Warrior . . . you tell me."

"You didn't know The Center existed until you got out here. Until you met me. Until you pretended to be someone you weren't." His voice escalates in pitch with each and every word. "So what's the real story, Chase? What is it exactly that you wanted from me because from my experience, agents only want you if it's good for them. Screw your talent so long as you can make them money or give them notoriety or—oh my God." His face falls as he stares at me with wide eyes full of disbelief. "You saw me as a publicity stunt, didn't you? That has to be it. You saw the attention that one agent got a few months back and figured you'd get yourself some of that attention too. You thought you'd get me an audience with an MLB scout or hold a charity game, all while having KSM strategically placed everywhere so the world would know who was doing all of these selfless, good deeds." Sarcasm drips off his last words as I swallow over the lump in my throat.

"That's a lot of supposition." My voice cracks, and for some reason the sound feels like it's an admission. "I wasn't—"

"Anything to make a profit, right? I can see it now. The great benevolent agent goes searching for a wounded vet whose letter was lost in the mail. She'd swoop in, put him on display. A dog and pony show of sorts so you could claim you were doing good, but it would only benefit yourself." There are tears in his eyes when he looks at me. He blinks them away but the sight of them will be forever burned in my memory. Betrayal and hurt. Disbelief and disappointment. "*You were going to use me.*"

Each word cuts.

Not just because they hurt him, but because they are true.

Because I was that callous, that selfish. I was so fixated on a goddamn goal that I never once stopped to consider how the faceless Ryan Camden I'd yet to meet would feel about it.

How Gunner would feel about it.

"That's not fair."

"You don't sound so sure of yourself." His eyes narrow as he stares at me. "I thought Big City Chase always sounded sure of herself."

"That was never my intention."

"The dog and pony show part or the you lying about who you were part?" he yells.

"I was warned that military protected their own. That if I asked about you, people would close ranks and—"

"Warned, huh? Because we're such a crazy group of people."

"No, because my questions would be frowned upon since I was an outsider."

"So you thought it would be better to lie?"

"No. I didn't know you and Ryan were one and the same until after"—a sob hiccups out of me—"until after we danced in the rain, and then it was too late to tell you the truth."

"But you lied about everything else. About school and your thesis and . . ." He grabs a pillow off the couch and squeezes it so hard with a feral growl. "Was everything you said to me last night a lie too?"

The tears in his eyes are unmistakable now. He doesn't blink them away, doesn't hide them. This time the pain and betrayal are much more evident.

"That wasn't a lie," I whisper as my own tears course down my cheeks. "Please let me explain. I *need* to explain."

"There's nothing to explain." He looks down to his hands, to his cell phone in it, and sighs. When he looks back up, the hard glint in his eyes scares the shit out of me. "I'm going to leave now. I have to get the fuck out of here and away from you." He sniffs. "And when I come back, I want you gone. I want it to be like you were never here in the first place."

"Gunner. *No.*"

But the last look he gives me before he grabs his keys and walks out of the house tells me everything I need to know.

No amount of pleading will fix this.

Nothing will.

I did this to myself.

I did this to us.

I stumble backward and slump onto the couch. Agony swallows me whole.

I stare at the front door hoping he'll come back in. Wishing he could see through his anger. Desperately begging for him to give me a minute to explain how this spiraled out of control.

To look past his devastation and see mine too.

To know that with every step he runs from me, my heart is also breaking like thousands of shards of glass. Like the plate I shattered with my name on it in the rage room.

But he doesn't come back.

And that's what I deserve.

He's not coming back.

"I have to get the fuck out of here and away from you. And when I come back, I want you gone. I want it to be like you were never here in the first place."

That's when I completely understand what misery feels like. Because my heart will never recover.

And I will never, ever forgive myself for the utter despair and anger I put on Gunner's face and in Gunner's heart. I will never forgive myself for breaking a man who never deserved anything but good.

Chapter THIRTY-EIGHT

Gunner

I DRIVE.

My route is aimless and it does absolutely nothing to clear the noise in my head and hurt in my heart.

She wasn't a grad student collecting info on military life.

Does it matter? Yes. *God yes, it does.* Not because she wasn't a grad student but because she didn't tell me who she was.

Because she lied to me.

Because she *deceived* me.

I end up at the national cemetery several towns over. I sit in the truck and watch the American flags wave in the breeze on the headstones. They're a sober reminder that I'm alive and this is a blip in the game of life . . . but why does it hurt so fucking much?

In my head I can hear Dickman's voice telling me to suck it up. That she's only hard to lose if I let her be. That life sucks, but you've got to move on.

After the cemetery, I end up sitting beyond the outfield fence watching a high school baseball game. The innings wear on but nothing becomes clearer in my head. Instead, the hurt becomes more, the reality of it all settles less, and I'm left to wonder how I could have been duped. How I could have fallen for Chase Kincade so effortlessly when normally I'm so guarded?

I drive some more.

Through wooded neighborhoods and farmland, but nothing eases the ache beneath my breastbone. Nothing calms the doubt I feel toward my own judgment. And nothing is going to make any of this any goddamn easier.

I've never wanted to talk to my mom again more than I do now. She received one of those orange envelopes too. She chose Sal over me, and I had to move on for my own sanity. For the first time since I sent it, I wish I could call her up for no other reason than to ask her how she can love someone and hate them simultaneously.

I know that's how she felt about Sal.

And it's currently how I feel about Chase.

When street signs become blurred and night calls to the sky, I finally go home.

The house is like a ghost town. Deserted when she had been everywhere. Quiet when it had been so full of life.

I want it to be like you were never here in the first place.

But who am I to lie? Chase is fucking everywhere. Her hint of perfume still lingers in the air. The blanket she folded in that triangle is still on the couch. The goddamn kitchen island we made love on sits there as a reminder.

No regrets feels like it has a whole new meaning now.

Chapter THIRTY-NINE

Chase

"Are we going to talk about how you're sitting at your desk—here in *our office*—and no one knew you were coming home?" Brexton's voice asks from the doorway of my office.

"Just trying to catch up on work," I say without lifting my head up.

Truth be told, I've been back in town for four days but this is the first day where my eyes don't look like I've been crying.

"You couldn't even peek your head out and say hi to us? We wouldn't even have known you were here if Letty hadn't told us," she says, referring to our receptionist.

"I got in early." I steel myself before looking up to meet her eyes to make sure I won't cry when I do. And if I don't look at her, she'll know something is wrong. "Did you see the stack of shit on my desk to do?" I meet her eyes and give a quick, tight smile. "It would have been nice if you guys helped out a little. Christ."

I've given her enough of a look and a semi-bitchy comment, so when I avert my eyes, I assume she'll walk away.

Instead she sits down in front of my desk.

"I don't have time for this right now. Maybe we can catch up after work?" I offer, full well knowing I'll bolt out and say I have to deal with a client and dodge her.

"No. We can catch up now."

Silence settles through the room and even though I keep typing away, not really having any clue what I am, in fact, typing, the weight of her stare grows heavier and heavier.

"You've been gone for seven weeks. You cut off communication with us except for the obligatory emoji response to our texts after you asked Dekk and me for advice. And now, out of the freaking blue, you just show up to work without warning? All that and you don't think I'm going to plop my ass down in your chair and demand to know what in the hell is going on?"

My fingers are flying over the keys as the tears threaten. All I can do is keep my head down, staring at my monitor. "Everything is fine. I promise."

But I never should have added those last two words because when I do, my voice breaks. It breaks in front of my sister—who gets me way too well and knows exactly what that sound means.

"Chase. Look at me." Her tone softens. Where it was previously annoyed, now, it's soft and compassionate. Of all my sisters, she's the one most used to the heartbreak that comes with love. Now of course she has Drew, but before him, there were many men who made her cry.

Of all my sisters, she'll understand me right now.

I bite my bottom lip and shake my head as my eyes blur with tears. "I can't," I all but whisper. "I just can't."

"Okay. I'm going to leave you alone and tell the rest of the staff you're on some calls negotiating and not to bother you." I nod but keep my eyes on my screen. "And I'm going to tell you that I know it's not something you want to hear right now, but know this—heartbreak sucks. It hurts and it feels like you're broken. But when the smoke clears, you'll be able to take something from it that will make you a better and stronger person somehow. And even simpler than that is the notion that every heartbreak brings you one step closer to the one who was meant for you."

"I can't do this right now," I repeat, my voice hoarse, my heart aching.

"I know." The chair squeaks as she gets up from it. "I love you, and you know I'm here for you if you need me."

"Thanks."

When the door clicks behind her, I let out a shuddered breath as the first tear slips over.

But I only allow myself one.

I can't do this.

I won't do this.

I repeat the same thing I've said to myself ever since I left Destiny Falls and Gunner behind.

My heartbreak was inevitable.

Regardless if he knew the real me or not, I was still leaving. There was still no future when it came to us.

And still, a piece of me was holding on to the possibility. A possibility that I could have told Gunner every detail *before* he found out the way he did. That if I had been able to do that, I'd have had the chance to tell him how falling in love with him completely crushed me—*because of* my lies between us. I'd give anything to have not hurt Gunner. To have not sent him running from me.

A bigger piece of me was hoping that love could conquer all. Because sadly, my sister was wrong.

When the smoke clears, there's nothing I'll be able to take from this pain. *Gunner* is the one who made me a better and stronger person. And now he's gone.

Chapter FORTY

Gunner

"Just call her."

I look over at Ellie and sigh. She's leaning back in the office chair with her feet up on the desk and her eyes on me.

"Why should I even give her a chance to explain herself?"

"Why should you not?" she counters.

"What is it with you?" I'm irritated and hate that for the last week all she's done is grill me on this. "Aren't you supposed to be on my side? Aren't you supposed to be telling me what she did was shitty and shady and that you understand how I feel?"

"She was shady and shitty and I do understand how you feel, but man . . . what I saw between the two of you was real. It was clear as day."

Her words punch me in the gut because I felt the same way. I thought what we had was real too.

Ellie has no idea how many sleepless nights I've had since Chase left. How many nights I've picked apart our every interaction, looking for any evidence from our time together that proves that what we had wasn't real.

I couldn't though, other than the obvious.

And that makes the knife cut that much deeper.

"But real isn't built on lies. Real is built on honesty and trust and being straightforward."

She nods and twists her lips. "It is."

"She came here looking for the *old me* to use."

"Maybe you're right. Maybe she was going to exploit war hero Ryan for her own good. Maybe she wasn't. The problem is you don't know if she was or wasn't because you never gave her a chance to explain why she was searching for you in the first place. And you sure as shit haven't done anything more than delete her texts or messages."

I close my eyes and lean my head back on my chair. "I'm so sick of thinking about this. Of second-guessing myself. Of missing her and hating her at the same time."

"As one does with heartbreak."

"It never would have worked anyway. She's from New York, and I'm from here. She has her big-city life and I have the bar and this town, The Center—"

"And you keep on talking yourself out of every coherent reason why it might be feasible." My loud exhale is the only response I give. "People change, Gun. And to use your words, she came looking for the *old* you. What if the woman who showed up here originally was the old her? A different version of herself from before she met you that she's not one hundred percent proud of anymore? What if meeting you made her look through a different lens? A lens that changed how she viewed things. Viewed Ryan Camden?"

I hate that I want to hold on to Ellie's words and take them as truth, but more than anything, I want to stop talking about this. About her.

As it is, Chase owns my thoughts more than I want her to.

"Yeah. Sure. Perhaps," I say and head out the door toward the parking lot where a big moving truck has just blocked the entrance to the gym area.

"Hey!" I say, waving my hands to catch the attention of the driver. "I can't have you parking here. If you have a delivery, go to the main office on the other side." I point.

The burly-looking guy looks at the top page on his clipboard. "I'm looking for Gunner Camden or uh, a Chase Kincade with The Center. You one of them?"

Jesus. Can I not talk to anyone without the mention of her name?

"Uh—yeah. I wasn't expecting any deliveries though."

"Well, I have a big one for you."

Have I been so distracted with everything with Chase that I missed something?

"It says here the delivery is from Major League Baseball care of Easton Wylder."

"Easton Wylder?" I ask, the name of the former MLB catcher and now sports announcer taking me by surprise.

But it shouldn't now that I know who Chase is. Now that I know athletes like him are just a phone call away for her.

"I think you have that wrong."

I war with indecision. With accepting something from the woman who currently crushed me and thinking this is something for The Center and the kids here.

Me or them.

"Here. The list is too long to read." I shove my pride aside as he hands the clipboard to me. My own hurt doesn't matter in the moment. Only the kids. Only fixing their hurt.

The two delivery guys start rolling up the back door of the truck while I look at the contents list. My jaw drops. There's a detailed inventory of new uniforms, cleats, bats, gloves, baseballs, practice equipment like tees and fungo bats—more than I could ever imagine. And the quantities and the sizes provided are so vast that we'll be able to outfit kids and those without for years and years.

I open my mouth to speak and then close it, overwhelmed by it all.

"See? I told you it was a lot of shit." The driver points to the clipboard again. "Pages two and three have even more."

"Pages two and three?"

When I lift the top sheet, I'm greeted with specifics on more ridiculous quantities of sports equipment—and not just baseball gear. There's basketball and soccer equipment, cones and goal nets, field hockey sticks . . . and the list goes on and on.

"What in the—" Ellie asks as she walks outside. When she sees the first pallet of gear being offloaded from the truck on a pallet jack, her smile is slow and steady. "She wasn't lying about this, now was she?"

My sigh is heavy. "No. No, she wasn't."

"Uh-uh. Don't you get that look on your face, Gunner. Don't you start wondering if she did all of this to get back in your good graces." She grabs the clipboard from me and starts searching for something. "Aha.

Right there." She points. "This has been in shipment since last week. There is no way she could have coordinated all of this just to win you back."

"I never thought that." *But I did.*

And now I feel like shit for it.

It's so freaking confusing to want someone and hate someone at the same time. Even worse is almost wanting my theory to be right so there's justification for hating her.

"You know you have to call her and thank her, right?"

I pinch the bridge of my nose, knowing it's going to kill me to hear her voice. That's why I've deleted all of her voicemails. Her voice was sunshine.

But she took that away when she left.

Hell, I couldn't even welcome the gloomy skies and sprinkles that hit this morning, because she changed how I look at rain too.

So I deleted her voicemails because hearing them, listening to them, is a reminder that life will once again go on without her. It will go on, but will be lacking something crucial.

Joy.

Her.

The better man she made me become even in such a short time.

But despite her deceit, this incredible truckload of generosity—of thoughtfulness—needs to be acknowledged.

Despite my agony, Chase's *goodness* needs to be thanked.

Shit.

Chapter FORTY-ONE

Chase

"No. That's not an acceptable counteroffer. I won't even bring it to Jorge. He's worth more than that. I know it. You know it. And he most definitely knows it," I say to the GM of the Pittsburgh Steelers. His shirt is stretched tight over his belly, the buttons straining against it, his mouth pulled just as tight.

"I don't have any wiggle room, Chase."

"Sure you do, Larry." I take a step back from his desk and shrug. "A lot of other teams would love to have a former Heisman Winner and last year's NFC Player of the Year on their roster. He's yours to lose."

"You love to just grab on tight and not let go, don't you?" He laughs.

"It's one of the perks of the job. If you're lucky I'll twist them while I'm at it." I give a sharp smile and stride out of the room.

He'll call.

I give him twenty-four hours, and he'll call me with a salary figure more suitable for Jorge.

I walk outside the Steelers' front office and take a deep breath. It feels good to be back negotiating. To feel normal. To try and control something when my emotions still feel raw and out of control.

But I haven't cried today. That's a step.

"Fancy meeting you here."

My entire body freezes at the sound of my ex's voice. My cheating ex's voice I should say. "Finn. I would say it's a pleasure meeting you here . . . *but it's not.*" The smile I offer is bright enough to rival the sun.

"I thought we'd be over this hostility by now," he teases in that smooth, charming way he has. The same smooth, charming way that won me over—until I found out that monogamy wasn't something Finn thought was important.

"Women never forget a man, what he's done to her—good or bad—and especially if he's an asshole. Plus you know me well enough to know I hold grudges well."

"Obviously." He laughs, completely unfazed by my comments.

Finn Sanderson stands before me, handsome as ever with a devilish smirk on his face that still gets to me even after he stomped all over my heart without so much as an apology.

"Can't we call a truce? Is that in your heart?" he asks.

I'm about to tell him that there's not a chance in hell when something else strikes me. "You know what?"

"What?"

"*Thank you.*"

"For what?" His expression reads confused, as it should from my one-eighty turnaround.

But Brexton's words run through my mind, and for the first time, I realize she's right.

"I always thought I wanted a guy like you. Driven. Professional. Structured in business and in your personal life. I was wrong. Thank you for breaking my heart. Thank you for hardening it so that it took the right one to break down the walls that needed to be broken down again."

Finn nods but his eyes narrow as he studies me. "You okay?" The concern in his voice is unexpected and hits me harder than it should.

I bite my bottom lip and nod. "I will be."

I turn to walk away when he calls my name. "Chase?"

"Hmm?" I look over my shoulder at him.

"Whoever he is, I hope he treats you well. You deserve that and so much more."

Our eyes hold for a beat, before Finn gives a brief nod and then walks toward the office door.

I stare after him for a moment, curious over his about-face. His words shouldn't faze me. I shouldn't even think twice about them after everything we've been through and yet, I stand in the sunshine staring after him.

Was that regret in his voice? Apology?

And why do I suddenly care if it was?

Because we all make mistakes. Isn't that the one thing I've learned over the past few months? That sometimes what starts out with the best intentions can turn into a disaster of epic proportions? That what you thought was going to happen morphs into something completely different?

I'm not justifying that as an excuse for what Finn did to me, but at the same time . . . didn't I just screw someone over just as badly? Didn't I hurt Gunner like Finn hurt me? It's not like you can rank lies and deceit on a scale, but didn't that happen in both instances?

Who am I to ask Gunner for forgiveness if I can't look at Finn and give a little as well?

My sigh is loud.

Christ. Maybe Gunner *has* changed me. Made me into a better human.

I take my first step toward my car when my cell phone ringing startles me out of my thoughts.

But when I look at the screen, I can't move fast enough to answer it.

"Gunner." My heart leaps into my throat, and I don't give a shit that I sound desperate and breathless when I say his name—because I'm both. "Hi."

There's silence, and I'm almost afraid to breathe for fear of ruining it.

"I wanted to call to say thank you," he finally says, his voice raspy, timid, but freaking music to my ears. I blink back the tears and, before I can find my voice to speak, he continues. "A huge shipment of donations arrived at The Center today. It was unexpected and incredibly generous, so yeah, I wanted to thank you for arranging that."

"The kids deserve it. It's an incredible program you've created and run." I take in a fortifying breath. "How are you?"

"They'll be excited when they see it later."

His voice is stoic. No emotion. And not even when I first met Gunner did he sound so . . . empty. Passionless.

I did that to him.

My hope crashes.

This is the only reason he's calling.

Not to talk about things between us.

Not to let me explain.

But purely because he has good manners and it's the right thing to do.

"Gunner?"

"I've got to go, but I wanted to thank you."

"Okay." My voice squeaks. I try not to start crying as I walk through the parking lot to my car.

But rather than him ending the call like I expected, there's another long silence that stretches between us.

"You know the one thing I can't wrap my head around?" he asks and my feet stop. "Was it all a lie, Chase? Did you look at me and see a sucker who could be manipulated, or did we ever really have a chance? Because when you love someone, you don't go into it knowing you're going to hurt them at some point. And that's what you did. You loved me, you let me love you, knowing you were going to hurt me . . . and that's something I can't bring myself to get over."

When the call ends, I'm left with a hand to my lips, tears spilling over. The hope I had in seeing his name on the screen crashes down all around me, shatters and mingles with the little pieces of my heart I've yet to even attempt to pick up.

Chapter FORTY-TWO

Gunner

"If you're going to keep being a miserable fuck, can you at least allow me to get drunk so I can tolerate you being an asshole better?" Nix asks from his perch in the bar.

"Leave me alone," I mutter and muster a smile at the customer in front of me as I slide her drink over to her.

"If you're done with Chase, tell her," he continues. "At least face it so you can stop moping around here, making all of us want to drink more to put up with you."

"It's good for business."

"Running all your customers out by snapping at them isn't though."

"Fuck." I sigh and hang my head before looking back up at him. "I did tell her. I kicked her out. I haven't returned her calls. How much more can I tell her?" I ask, exasperated.

"You told her, yes. But have you told *you* that though?"

"Nix. I'm going to kick your ass out if you keep this shit up."

"Dude, I'm only trying to help." He lifts his hands in surrender. "In case you forgot, I'm the one who's been here every night if you want to talk."

"You're here every night regardless," I counter.

"Yeah, but I never want to hear you talk. This time around, I'm telling you I'm willing to put up with it and shit."

A smile tugs onto my lips. He's right. He's trying to be a good friend and I know it, but it doesn't make anything better.

It feels like nothing will.

"Thanks." I tap the neck of my beer against his. "Truly. I appreciate it. This is just something I need to get over on my own."

"So you're going to get over her then?"

"What choice do I have?"

"From the way I see it, you have lots of choices, but you seem pretty set on letting her go. But if that's what you're going to do, then fucking do it so you can move on. I liked you before. I liked you with her. But I don't like this guy"—he motions at me—"and frankly, I'm worried about him."

"You don't need to be worried about me," I say and pull the tap to pour a beer.

My eyes wander to the orange envelope I've pinned to the wall behind the bar. A reminder to myself why I'm here, what I gave up, and that Chase lied to me.

I hate the idea that comes to mind but think it might just be what I need to do.

It worked once before.

It's time to pull the Band-Aid off.

It's the only thing I know how to do right it seems.

Chapter FORTY-THREE

Chase

My pulse races as I stare at the envelope on my desk.

It's not orange this time, nor is it faded and tattered at the edges, but it's the same penmanship addressed to Kincade Sports Management.

The only difference is under KSM, it says "Attn: Chase Kincade."

My hands shake as I pull the letter out and read it.

Dear Ms. Chase Kincade,

Thank you for your time. I just recently learned of your interest in me. Maybe if you had been honest from the start, we could have made this work. At this time, it's best if we both move on as if we never met. To let dreams we might have had go. To accept that life has changed forever.

-Gunner Camden

I reread the letter over and over till my tears blur so much that I can't see the words.

And then Dickman, our sarge, said we should write letters to those who mattered. To say goodbye to our dreams because life as we knew it was over.

He wrote me an "If I Die" letter.

He wrote me out of his life just like he did the sport he loved and the life he lived.

If I thought there was any hope of us figuring things out, this just basically annihilated it. *Every single ounce of it.*

"Chase? Honey?"

I startle at the knock on my door and my father's voice. I don't know how long I've been sitting here staring out at the world beyond our high-rise with the letter clutched in my hand.

"Yeah?" I croak.

"Do you want to talk about it?" he asks, moving into my office.

I shake my head. "There's nothing to talk about."

"Okay." He sighs with a helplessness I feel deep in my bones. "I'm sorry you're hurting. If there's one thing a parent hates more than anything in the world, it's seeing their child hurting. Part of being a dad is trying to protect your kids from the hurt. Kissing a scraped knee. Defending you from monsters under the bed. Stealing some of Finn's business for cheating on you. But I know I can't fix this. I know a broken heart is way stronger than the tools I have in my arsenal, but God, how I wish I did."

"It's okay. I deserve this. I lied. I'm paying the consequences. There's no one to blame but me." I meet his eyes for the first time and force myself to give him a smile.

"I admire that about you. Your responsibility. But at the same time, maybe things will change. Maybe time will heal the hurt. Maybe the two of you had to fall apart in order to realize how much you need to fall back together."

"I think we more like exploded apart rather than fell. There was nothing graceful about it," I mutter.

He chuckles. "You're making jokes, that's a good sign."

"Jokes are all I have." I shrug and avert my eyes from his, because the sympathy in them might just be my undoing.

"Chase?"

"Hmm?" I look out the window at the skyline beyond.

"Look at me."

The room falls silent as the weight of his stare hits me. When I finally look up, there is a soft smile on his lips. *He too understands.*

"Why does it hurt so much?" I finally admit. "Just when I think I'm over that hump, I get sucked right back down into the despair again."

"Only the ones who are worth it hurt that much."

"That doesn't help," I say and rub the heel of my hand to my chest.

"I hurt your mom once."

"You were married. Of course, you did. It's not normal to be with someone that long and not have a fight," I say. Although, I really don't remember there being much fighting in our house.

"No, it was before the marriage part." He picks up the small frame I have on my desk of her and smiles bittersweetly at the image of her, young and smiling. "Your mom and I had a falling out. And being a guy, the first thing I did was go out with the guys to get drunk. To pretend I wasn't at fault and to bury the pain I saw in her eyes."

"What did you do?"

"*What didn't I do?*" He laughs. "It's taken many years and a lot of her love to make me the refined man you see today."

"Oh please," I say but smile, loving how he still talks about her all these years later like she's still here, still a part of our lives.

"I kissed another woman."

I stare at my dad as if he'd grown two heads. "You what?" I shriek, shocked.

"I never claimed I was smart, Chase." He chuckles. "We had been dating for a few months when we had a fight. It was over her father thinking I wasn't good enough to be with her, and I believe she told me I needed to step up to the plate and be that man then."

I smile through the tears. "That sounds like Mom."

"It sounds like *you*," he murmurs and holds my gaze.

"Anyway, I went to the bar and got drunk because, screw your grandpa. No one was ever good enough for his daughter type of thing. Anyway, the alcohol wasn't an excuse by any means, but there was a woman there who was hitting on me, and I was feeling sorry for myself. When she leaned in for a kiss, I didn't say no."

Is it ridiculous that despite all the years that have passed, I gasp when he says that?

"It was just a peck, but when I looked up, your mom was there with fire in her posture and hurt in her eyes. It was that moment with her chin trembling that I knew I'd move heaven and earth to figure out how to be the man her dad thought she deserved. The man she deserved."

"I don't understand why you're telling me this, Dad."

"Because if Gunner's worth it, then fight. Fight for what you have. For the relationship. The friendship. For the stolen moments that make you miss him the most right now." He puts the picture frame down in front of me so that I am forced to look at the image of my mom. "If I hadn't fought to apologize, to redeem myself, to win her back after my stupid mistake, none of this would ever have been."

"It's not the same. It's—"

"Isn't it, though? You live in a black and white world, sweetie. It's okay to fight for the one who adds color to it."

"I can't fight for someone who doesn't want to be fought for."

He smiles and nods. "It's hard asking someone with a broken heart to fall in love again. Especially when you're the one who broke it in the first place . . . but if the person means that much to you, you'll fight like hell to salvage what you have."

Chapter FORTY-FOUR

Gunner

"WHAT CAN I GET FOR YOU?" I ASK THE CUTE LITTLE BRUNETTE, WHO sidled up to the bar while I was in the back getting more ice.

"Water, please." She laughs and turns to rub her pregnant belly.

"Sorry. I didn't see there were two of you," I say, wondering why a pregnant woman came into a bar by herself. "One water it is."

I pour her a cup of iced water and then slide it across the bar to her.

"Thanks."

"Waiting for someone else tonight or just need to get off your feet for a bit?" I ask, making conversation since the bar is slow tonight, something I'm more than fine with.

"I was heading into work—at the hotel—and I thought I'd stop in to see how Chase was."

Her words startle me. "Chase?"

"Yes." She smiles sweetly. "I know she came in here often while she was staying at the hotel, so forgive me for assuming you might know where she is and if she found *him*."

My tongue feels heavy in my mouth. "Found who?"

"The baseball guy," she says. Her naivete's in her favor as my stomach twists in knots.

"What baseball guy?"

"The one who wrote the letter she had."

I swear the rest of the noise in the bar fades away, as I stare at this unexpected guest like she's the only one in the place.

"Why?"

Her smile is sheepish and her cheeks heat. "Because I thought it had the makings to be the most romantic story I'd ever heard."

Now she definitely has my interest.

"What do you mean?"

"A letter lost in the mail for five years from a soldier in a faraway land. A message never intended for her and yet when she held it in her hand, she said she felt a connection to the soldier, to the man. Indescribable. That was the only way she could describe him. I didn't get to talk to her much about it, but I really liked that because of this bond she felt, she couldn't rest until she found, met him, and knew he was okay. So she came here. I think someone had told her not to ask too many questions, as well. You know how it is. We're protective of our own. But can you imagine being in the town with this long-lost soldier, and trying to hold your tongue?" She takes a sip of water and I stare at her, my pulse racing and my heart pounding in my ears. "It's like a Nicholas Sparks novel."

"Who?"

"Romance." She smiles. "I read a lot while I work the night shift," she explains. "I wanted to see how her story ended. Did Chase find him and was the connection real? Did they fall in love and run away together and live happily ever after?" She shrugs and sighs in a way that makes me want to believe she's right.

But I know she's right.

I lived it.

And even though I lived it and know the pain, even though I wrote the letter to try and get over her, the dull ache in my chest won't go away.

At first, I thought it was heartache. Heartbreak.

But now I'm beginning to think it's my heart waiting to beat again.

It's my heart reminding me it's waiting for her.

Because despite everything, I miss her. I still love her.

"So do you know what happened? Did she find him?"

I look at her and smile. "She found him and after a few hiccups, a breakup where he pushed her away and then was miserable for longer than he ever thought possible, he decided it was time to chase after her."

"So did they end up with their happily ever after?" Her eyes are expressive and her smile is wide.

"I don't know yet, but I plan on giving it a damn good try."

Chapter FORTY-FIVE

Chase

"I HAVE NO PROBLEM GOING TO LUNCH WITH YOU, DEKKER, BUT IF YOU order some off-the-wall pregnancy craving again, I'm walking out."

"What's wrong with liking French fries with sweet and sour sauce?" she asks, as I do a mock gagging motion in my mouth.

"For that alone, I'm picking where we're going," I say and stop in the middle of our office building's lobby to search on my phone for somewhere to go.

"Who the hell is that hot hunk of a man?" Dekker mumbles and nudges me with her elbow.

"You're married and pregnant. Shouldn't you be satisfied with your own husband?"

"I'm not talking about me. I'm talking about for you. Perfect rebound material at that."

"I'm not interested."

"But he's walking this way."

"Great. Good for him. He can keep on walking for all I care," I finish, just as his shoes come into view. I keep my eyes focused on my phone and Dekker sucks in a breath. "Thanks, but I don't want any," I say without ever looking his way.

"Not even a dance in the rain?"

My breath hitches at the sound of his voice.

"Gunner." My voice is a whisper as I look up to meet his eyes. God, I missed those eyes. The deep brown of them and the compassion and spark in them. "You're here."

He nods and his Adam's apple bobs. "I don't know what is up or down anymore since you picked up my world and tilted it off its axis. All I know is it's not the same without you in it."

A shuddered sense of hope begins to flutter.

"I've spent days, weeks, trying to understand what you did and how you did it. I don't think I'll ever understand the why behind it, but last night I came to realize *the why* doesn't matter as much as I thought it did. The why is what brought you into my life. The why made me feel in ways I'd never felt before. *You* made me feel in ways I've never felt before."

"I feel the same way," I whisper. My heart beats so hard I feel like it's going to fall out of my chest. "But before you say anything else, I have to tell you that you were right. I was there for the things you said—the dog and pony show and all that. For that, I'm ashamed and sorry because I never saw the other side of it. I never thought about how you'd see it. So you were right and I'm sorry. I'm not that person anymore—"

"Hey." He steps into me and frames my face with his hands, and it takes everything I have not to sag into his touch. Words escape me as that fluttering hope morphs into full-blown anticipation. *Please still love me.*

"Gunner."

He presses his lips to mine and kisses me with the same longing I've felt.

Things I never thought were possible—emotions, feelings, love—surge inside of me from the simple touch of his lips.

"Neither of us are the same. We changed each other." He wipes a tear off my cheek with his thumb.

"But how do we do this? You live in Destiny—"

"We figure it out, because the only thing that matters is this. *Us.* We're the only ones who can write our own story. Chase, the only person I want to write my happily ever after with is you." He presses his lips to mine again, and then whispers, "You broke my heart. You shattered it into a million tiny pieces, but you know what? When you left, when I was left in a world without you, I realized that was never your intention. I believe you. I believe that you would never have deliberately tried to hurt me. And you're one of the few people in my life who I can say that about."

"It's true. I didn't mean to—"

"I still love you, Chase Kincade. I can't let you go. I won't let you go. No regrets?"

Tears spring to my eyes as Gunner wraps his arms around me and pulls me in against him.

"No regrets."

And standing in the middle of the lobby with business people walking all around us, oblivious to how life-changing this moment is for us, I've never felt more complete.

More loved.

More at home.

Epilogue

Chase

Eighteen Months Later

The night air tickles my hair against my cheeks, as I lean against the railing with what I'm sure is a ridiculously goofy grin on my lips.

Sure, I've had a few or maybe a lot of glasses of wine tonight to aid in the goofiness of that grin, but it's not just the alcohol that's bolstered it.

It's this.

All of this.

The twinkly lights overhead as Brexton and her new husband, Drew, dance the night away. I'm surprised her wedding dress even touches the ground with how high her head is in the clouds tonight. Then there's Drew and the look in his eyes—complete and utter adoration—every time he looks at her.

Laughter to the left of the dance floor draws my eyes to where my eldest sister, Dekker, is swaying to the beat of the music. Her husband, Hunter, stands behind her, his arms around her, and his chin on her shoulder as they watch my one-year-old nephew attempt to dance with his aunt Lennox.

But instead of dancing, he keeps getting distracted by Lennox's pregnant belly, his hands reaching up to touch it and hopefully feel my soon-to-be niece kick. Because in pure Lennox fashion, she's wearing a devastatingly snug and sexy dress, despite her eight-months-pregnant swollen belly.

And then there is her husband, Rush, sitting at the table beside where Lennox is dancing. He has a ghost of a smile on his handsome face, his eyes rarely move from her. It's quite a sight to see the bad boy head over heels with the woman who never took love seriously.

And if that's not the pot calling the kettle black, I don't know what is as my eyes skim to the seat across from Rush, to see Gunner sitting there, enjoying taking it all in.

My Gunner.

The man I never expected, *the man I never wanted,* but the one who looks at me every damn time with that same reverence, *that same love.*

How has it been over a year since I found him? It feels like yesterday and forever all at the same time. How did I not know how incomplete I felt until *him?*

Sure, we've struggled at times as we settled into our new normal with my traveling to and from New York every other week to take care of my work, but I know there is nothing—*nothing*—that would ever change the irrevocable love I have for him.

"How's my girl?" my dad asks, sliding an arm around my shoulder.

"Your girl is just having a sappy moment to herself," I say and rest my head on his shoulder.

"I didn't think my Chase had sappy moments in her." He presses a kiss to my head, the teasing tone of his voice making me smile.

"I found them somewhere. There are times I wish I hadn't."

"Ah, but those sappy moments are what makes life, kiddo. They make it beautiful and tragic and meaningful and unforgettable. All those moments stacked on top of each other are what make you feel and love and live."

He pauses, as I take in his words and know they're right, because how could they not be? When I look at Gunner, I know I want to keep stacking those moments, one upon another, until we have a life carved out for ourselves.

"She would have loved this, you know?" he continues, his voice soft, reminiscent, and so full of love. "She would have loved watching her girls grow and love and become mothers themselves. I'm so sorry she didn't get a chance to see it, but I have a feeling she's had a strong hand in guiding it."

I sniff away the tears that are blurring my eyes. "Now look who's being sappy," I tease, knowing how very right he is.

She would have loved every minute of this. The tiny details in planning Brex's wedding. The traveling to the UK to visit Lennox and have one-on-one time with her. The spoiling of her first grandson and passing on motherly advice to Dekker. The knowing when she looked in my eyes how truly happy Gunner makes me.

"Yeah, she would have loved it, Dad. Every crazy minute of it. But you're right, she helped plan all this in some way, whether through what she instilled in us in the short time we had with her or in some other magical way . . . because I feel her more now than I ever have."

And I do.

Between that thought and the sight of my family happy and healthy in front of me, my heart has never been fuller.

So full it's almost bursting.

"I know. I know," he says.

Gunner looks across the distance and his eyes meet mine. His soft smile is all I need in this world. *Just that and him.*

"I love you," he mouths to me, and I pat over my heart in response.

The DJ interrupts the moment and announces it's time for the bouquet toss. "That's you," my dad says, as he puts a hand on my back to guide me to the dance floor.

"I'll let some other woman catch the damn flowers." I laugh as we step onto the dance floor.

"You'll do no such thing," he states emphatically. "It's called tradition, Chase. Just suck it up, stand there, and take part in it."

"Save me," I mouth to Gunner, who's having a good laugh watching my dad practically hold me in place.

The DJ goes through the instructions of where to line up and what to do. I stand in the crowd as Brexton turns her back to us and the DJ does a countdown.

Three.

Two.

One.

But instead of throwing the bouquet, my sister turns and walks toward the lot of us. We all turn to look around, confused and thinking something has happened. Especially when she puts the bouquet directly into my hands.

"What? *No*. That's not how this works. You don't get to pick who gets these. You don't get to choose—"

"But he does," she says with tears welling in her eyes and a smile on her lips that has chills chasing down my spine.

"What—Who—Brex—"

When she looks over my shoulder and gives an even softer smile to the person behind me, I turn, confused.

And the rest of my thoughts are knocked out of my head just like the breath that's lost at the sight before me.

The crowd of ladies has separated, and Gunner Camden is on one knee before me. His eyes are swimming with a love that's uniquely ours, and his smile says I'm all he sees. All he knows. All he wants.

"Gunner . . ."

"You're a hard one to corral, Chase Kincade. From the moment I met you, you told me that love wasn't your thing. That kisses are overrated. That being with someone wasn't on your oh-so-busy agenda." He chuckles with the slightest shake of his head. "But somehow I proved you otherwise. Somehow, I was able to break through that very motivated brain of yours and show you that you can still be *you* with your aspirations and ambition while loving *me*."

"Gunner," I whisper through tears I'm not remotely trying to fight.

"So when I asked your dad and your sisters for your hand in marriage, I told them this might be a hard one for you to accept. Tying you to me for life is a big step for a woman who didn't have time for love to begin with. But they agreed with me. They told me that somehow, we—*you and I*—were better together. That somehow, our two broken and jagged halves made one *incredible* whole."

I glance up to the body of Kincades behind him. My dad. Dekker. Brexton. Lennox. And the honorary Kincades, the men in their lives, who have completed my sisters and our family in ways we all never expected. All of them have smiles on their faces and hope in their eyes.

I've never felt more loved.

I've never felt less alone.

"And I tend to agree with them. There's no one else I'd rather go through life with, Chase. There's no one I want to fight and make up with, to love and laugh with, to sit and hold their hand in silence with. It's always been you. Maybe that's why that letter found its way to you all those years later. Maybe not. But something greater than us has worked in our favor since the get-go, so who am I to question it?"

"I love you," I whisper.

"When it was suggested I ask you here, at their wedding, I told Brexton and Drew that I didn't want to upstage their day in any way. They told me I was being ridiculous. That it wasn't a true Kincade family function without their littlest sister getting special treatment." A chuckle ripples through the crowd of friends and family, because that might be true. "So here we are, Chase. One orange envelope, one mistaken identity, and one dance in the rain later, and there's nowhere else I'd rather be or person I'd rather be with. Will you marry me, Chase Kincade?"

I don't wait for him to stand as he lifts the ring up to me. The ring is just a symbol, but it's the man that I love. So instead, I drop to my knees and take his face in my hands so he can see my eyes when I tell him the truth.

When I tell him he's my forever.

"There's no one else for me, Gunner. No one." I press my lips to his as the crowd erupts around us. "Yes. Yes. Yes."

Epilogue

Gunner

Six months later

"Where are we going?" Chase laughs as I hold my hands over her eyes. We walk awkwardly down the busy Manhattan street, with her in front of me.

The streets are oddly empty for this hour—maybe it's the intermittent rain that's been hitting the city—maybe it's simply perfect timing on my part. Whatever it is, I'll gladly take it.

"Just a few more steps," I say and skirt her around a puddle on the sidewalk before walking up to the storefront. The door is open and I direct her inside. "Take a step up," I say and then move us inside.

"You know I don't like it when I'm not in control," she mutters.

I laugh. "Tell me something I don't know."

Meeting the eyes of Monique standing across the empty interior space, I nod as she lifts up her camera to start taking pictures.

I allow myself to consider this moment with Chase. The woman she is. How she's changed my life. How she's made me a better man.

How did I ever deserve this?

I press a kiss to her shoulder, remove my hands, and step away. "Surprise."

Chase whirls around, confusion etched in those gorgeous lines of her face, and I smile.

The soft clicking of Monique's camera draws her attention amid the confusion, so she looks from the photographer then back at me. "What—"

"We're always on the go, always needing to be somewhere on a timeline, and I wanted to give you those engagement photos you wanted."

"Gunner." My name comes out in a whooshed breath of surprise and appreciation.

"I know we cancelled ours because baby McKenzie decided to make an early appearance," I say of Rush and Lennox's baby girl, "so I thought I'd make them up to you."

She eyes me, almost as if she's wondering what else I have up my sleeve.

Can't get anything by my girl, but I'm damn well going to try.

"I know it's not the park or wherever you wanted to do them, but I thought this old place might tell our story."

She looks around at the old bar. It's been neglected for years. Old chairs and tables gathering dust. A bar top with dim and dilapidated lights overhead, a mirror behind it, and half-empty bottles in front of it.

"Our story?" she asks as she takes a step toward the bar top and its worn, green leather stools.

"Mm-hmm." I step beside her and link my fingers with hers. "In case you've forgotten, we met in a bar. I do believe I was worn down much like this place is and you stepped inside and lit up the room." I press a kiss to her hand.

"You're being ridiculous."

"I know. And you love me for it." I tug her toward the bar top. "Humor me?" I ask. "Take these with me and we can do another round somewhere of your liking, but I saw this place and couldn't resist doing some photos here. A setting that defines me in a city that characterizes you."

"Okay." She draws the word out as she eyes me. "This is so unlike you."

"I know, but I wanted to do this for you."

"I'm Monique," the photographer says, stepping forward to shake Chase's hand. She tells her what her thoughts are for background and pictures.

Their laughter soon fills the space as they talk about staging while I open the garage door-style windows that roll up and open the restaurant area out to the street.

"Should we get started?" Monique asks.

We spend the next forty minutes posing in different locations inside the bar. The laughter flows as freely as I imagined the alcohol once did in this place.

"It's raining," Chase whispers as the puddles outside begin to ripple with its drops.

"It is."

"It's perfect." She stares as the cadence of the rain picks up.

"You're serious," I say as she tugs on my hand and leads me outside, the little clicks of the camera following closely behind us.

"Dance in the rain with me, Gunner." Chase twirls out onto the sidewalk, her face held up to the sky, her smile contagious. And when she looks at me again, I see my whole fucking world.

And so we dance.

In the rain.

The beating of our hearts and the drops of the rain the only music we need.

My lips meet hers as my hands come to the sides of her face. Water streams down our cheeks as our tongues touch and express how we feel without words.

"Could you have planned this any better?" she whispers against my lips, as our foreheads rest against each other's. Busy New Yorkers scurry past us, umbrellas in every color in their hands, but we don't see a thing.

We only see each other.

But then again, haven't we always?

"I didn't plan a thing, but somehow with you, Chase, things always fall into place."

Another kiss. Another reminder why she's my whole world.

"Can you look this way?" Monique asks from the chair she's perched on, taking pictures.

I wonder how long it will take before Chase sees it. Before it all computes.

"Gunner?"

Bingo.

"I'm smiling. I can't talk," I tease. But with her hand in mine, she takes a step closer to the front of the building and stares at the sign.

At the first and only thing I've bought so far for my new venture.

"Jackpot?" she asks before looking at me.

"Yep. It's a term our Rangers used to use for a mission that went perfect."

"So the opposite of FU-Bar?"

"Polar opposite," I say and grin.

"What am I missing?" She looks around, at the street signs to get her bearings, and at the building before her. "I've walked past this place before and that"—she points to the sign—"wasn't there before."

"You're right. It wasn't. The new owner put it up last week."

"New owner?"

I nod. "You've been killing yourself for most of the past two years going to and from the city so I don't have to adjust my life. But being together, sharing a life with one another, is about compromise. It's about taking turns. It's about trying to give more than you get." I reach out and tuck a piece of hair behind her ear. "Here's my compromise. My taking of turns. My giving you more than I'm getting."

"This is yours?" she asks, eyes wide.

I nod. "It needs some love to shine bright, much like I once did and you gave me. How you helped turn my life from FU-Bar to Jackpot. We've applied for all the right licenses and permits. Once those come through, we'll start renovating it and making it a sister establishment to FU-Bar."

"How—what about FU-Bar—I mean—"

"It's Nix's turn to heal," I say. "He offered to run the place, become a partner with me there, and take care of my baby for me."

And there's no one I'd rather turn it over to.

"What about The Center? The boys? I mean—"

"I'm a military brat, Chase. You know that. I'm used to moving, to hurting, to having to forge ahead."

"I refuse to make you choose—"

"You're not making me choose. I'm choosing. It's time I build that life I was given a second chance at. Besides, I trust Ellie there. I'll visit for events, but I can't stay there forever. I can't live in the guilt anymore." I shrug, as if coming to that realization didn't take the hours and hours of soul searching it did. "Besides, there are plenty of kids here in the city I'm sure I can help."

I missed out on having a dad around. I missed out on learning from a good role model for a father. I've had plenty of practice with other people's kids.

I want to apply that to my own family.

To the one I can't wait to make with Chase.

"Chase, I don't do anything half-heartedly, so why would I start our life together that way? You've been the one making the sacrifice, traveling at will, to make this work. I appreciate it. But now? Now, it's my turn. Now, I need you to know that you are my number-one priority."

"I've never felt like I wasn't," she murmurs, but the tears in her eyes show she understands what I'm saying. That I'll move heaven and fucking earth for her.

"Jackpot." She rolls the name around on her tongue and looks at me with tears in her eyes.

"That's you. You're mine." I shrug.

"Seems to me like you have it all figured out."

"I'm sure I've forgotten a few things." I laugh.

"Like kissing me."

"Now that? That I can do."

And so I kiss Chase.

On the sidewalk.

In the rain.

Talk about getting a second chance.

At having a family.

At making a difference.

At life.

Baseball was once my shelter. My therapist's office. My first love. One that somehow brought the two of us together.

But now, my only love is the woman standing beside me.

The woman I can't wait to make new memories with.

Share new hopes with.

Fulfill my dreams with.

Coming Soon

You fell in love with Hunter and Dekker in *Hard to Handle.*

Then Rush swept you off your feet in his and Dekker's story in *Hard to Hold.*

Not to be overshadowed was Drew and Brexton in *Hard to Score.*

And you just finished Chase and Gunner's story in *Hard to Lose.*

I thought I would be done with this world when I typed THE END on Hard to Lose, but there is **one more character** nagging for me to write him: ***Finn Sanderson.***

Stay tuned for Finn's story in **Hard to Love**—coming this summer. You can preorder the book HERE: www.kbromberg.com/books/play-hard-series/hard-to-love

About the Author

New York Times Bestselling author K. Bromberg writes contemporary romance novels that contain a mixture of sweet, emotional, a whole lot of sexy, and a little bit of real. She likes to write strong heroines and damaged heroes who we love to hate but can't help to love.

A mom of three, she plots her novels in between school runs and soccer practices, more often than not with her laptop in tow and her mind scattered in too many different directions.

Since publishing her first book on a whim in 2013, Kristy has sold over one and a half million copies of her books across twenty different countries and has landed on the *New York Times, USA Today*, and *Wall Street Journal* Bestsellers lists over thirty times. Her Driven trilogy (*Driven, Fueled*, and *Crashed*) is currently being adapted for film by the streaming platform, Passionflix.

With her imagination always in overdrive, she is currently scheming, plotting, and swooning over her latest hero. You can find out more about him or chat with Kristy on any of her social media accounts. The easiest way to stay up to date on new releases and upcoming novels is to sign up for her newsletter or follow her on Bookbub.

www.ingramcontent.com/pod-product-compliance
Lightning Source LLC
Chambersburg PA
CBHW061525250926
52052CB00010B/2801